COVER UP

COVER UP

Patricia Hall

This first world edition published 2017
in Great Britain and the USA by
SEVERN HOUSE PUBLISHERS LTD of
19 Cedar Road, Sutton, Surrey, England, SM2 5DA.
Trade paperback edition first published
in Great Britain and the USA 2017 by
SEVERN HOUSE PUBLISHERS LTD

British Library Cataloguing in Publication Data
A CIP catalogue record for this title is available from the British Library.

ISBN-13: 978-0-7278-8695-8 (cased)
ISBN-13: 978-1-84751-803-3 (trade paper)
ISBN-13: 978-1-78010-867-4 (e-book)

All Severn House titles are printed on acid-free paper.

Severn House Publishers support the Forest Stewardship Council™ [FSC™],
the leading international forest certification organisation.
All our titles that are printed on FSC certified paper carry the FSC logo.

MIX
Paper from
responsible sources
FSC
www.fsc.org   FSC® C013056

Typeset by Palimpsest Book Production Ltd.,
Falkirk, Stirlingshire, Scotland.
Printed and bound in Great Britain by
TJ International, Padstow, Cornwall.

ONE

Detective Sergeant Harry Barnard could have kicked himself for a fool for bothering to call in at the nick, after he and Kate O'Donnell had strolled across the West End at peace with the world after seeing the new Elvis film, *Viva Las Vegas*. Barnard slightly regretted persuading Kate to go in the first place. He had been blown away by Elvis when he burst upon the world in the fifties with classics like *Jailhouse Rock* and his gyrating version of *Hound Dog* which had scandalized Middle America, but he could see that his Beatles-obsessed girlfriend, born and brought up with the Merseybeat, had never been hooked by the King. And to judge by this latest offering, he had to concede that Elvis's crown was looking tarnished. His own reaction was not as cool as Kate's, but the magic, he admitted to himself, if not to her, had gone.

The summer evening was hot and sticky, with a hint of thunder in the air, and Barnard had decided on a whim to call in at the nick, where he had parked his car, to pick up a jacket that he had left in the CID office before meeting Kate for a meal after work. She reluctantly took a seat in the front office, where the desk sergeant surveyed her with hot eyes after Barnard went upstairs. As soon as he opened the office door Barnard realized that his decision was a serious mistake. DC Peter Stansfield, the department's latest recruit, who had in no way impressed his colleagues during the short time he'd been there, spun towards Barnard with a look on his face that was not far off panic. A pale, skinny young man at the best of times, he was ashen-faced as his colleague walked in.

'Harry, mate,' he said. 'Am I pleased to see you! We've got a problem and I can't get hold of the DCI. He's at some Masonic do, apparently, and uniform are saying that someone's just dumped a body in Soho Square. What the hell am I supposed to do about that?'

Barnard scowled at Stansfield, wanting nothing more than to turn on his heel, pick Kate up and take her home, where he'd hoped to round off a pleasant evening with an even more pleasant night between the sheets. But he could see from the younger officer's incipient disintegration that that was not going to be an option, at least not immediately. Not for the first time, the thought crossed his mind that DC Stansfield must have used some sort of back-door method to land his job in CID, though he couldn't imagine what that was. Stansfield might be a Mason, he supposed, but he was a bit young to wield much influence there.

'Who've you spoken to?' he snapped irritably. Stansfield should not be minding the shop on a busy Friday night when the West End was choked with revellers looking for a good time. But he knew that if it got back to the DCI that he had been in and not helped Stansfield out his already problematic relationship with his boss would plummet even further. 'So who told you about this?' he asked more evenly. Maybe there was a bit of credit to be gained by helping Stansfield out.

'Just the patrol car that called in,' Stansfield said. 'They asked uniform to try to locate Jackson, and when that didn't work they called me here in CID.'

'I guess they didn't reckon it was natural causes?' Barnard asked.

'They think it's murder,' Stansfield said, looking miserable. 'The blokes in the patrol car are dancing around with excitement down there, with the naked body of a woman – or half-naked, anyway – laid out on the grass.'

'I bet they are,' Barnard conceded. 'Anyway, I'll help you set the wheels in motion at least. We'll take a look and see if it's as suspicious as it sounds. Wherever the DCI is, we'll have to dig him out if it looks like murder. You won't get any brownie points if you leave it any longer. Come on. We'll tell uniform we're on our way for a recce, and once we've had a look let them know what's really going on. We'll go in my car, but first I've got some explaining to do to my girlfriend. She won't be best pleased. This was supposed to be a pleasant night out on the town.'

Stansfield followed Barnard down the stairs to the front

office, where Kate was still sitting trying to avoid the appreciative glances of the desk sergeant, who flushed and ducked his head into his paperwork as soon as he saw Barnard approach. Kate stood up, obviously anxious to move out of the door as fast as she could, but her quick smile was overcome by disbelief when Barnard explained to her what had happened and what he felt he had to do about it. Her smile disappeared soon enough to warn him that there might be repercussions later.

'This is Pete Stansfield,' he said, waving at his obviously embarrassed colleague. 'I need to go with him to check it out, as the patrolmen say she's certainly dead. It shouldn't take long.'

'So what do you want me to do?' she asked, conscious of the desk sergeant's ears almost visibly flapping as he strained to hear what was being said.

'Can you get yourself home on the Tube?' Barnard asked quietly. 'You could pick up a cab at Archway if you don't want to walk up the hill.'

'I suppose,' Kate said without enthusiasm. He reached for his wallet and handed her a fiver.

'That should cover it,' he said. 'I'm really sorry, Katie, but I don't have much choice. Someone has to take a look and the only other option for you is to sit in the car and wait for me. If the worst comes to the worst, it could be a long night. But believe me, I'll get home as soon as I can.'

Kate nodded resignedly, trying to mask her disappointment. This, she thought, must be what it was like to be married to a copper and she wondered if it was really what she wanted. She knew that divorce rates were high among the police, and suddenly she could see exactly why.

'Have you got your keys?' Barnard asked.

'Yes, of course,' she said sharply. 'I'll be fine. It's not very late.'

'I'll get away as soon as I can, but if it's as serious as they say I'll have to locate the DCI. I'll ring you in an hour to make sure you're back home safely.'

'I'll be fine,' she said again. 'Highgate's a far cry from Scotland Road, la. You don't need to worry about me. I know how to deal with scallies.'

Barnard nodded, knowing she was probably right. The attractive girl from Liverpool was a lot tougher than she looked.

'I'll drop you off at Tottenham Court Road underground,' he said. 'Don't wait up.'

When Barnard pulled into Soho Square – with Stansfield in the passenger seat, still with the smirk on his face that he'd adopted when Barnard gave Kate a fleeting kiss on the cheek as she got out of the car – the only sign of a problem was a patrol car with its blue lights flashing, pulled across one of the gates to the dimly lit central gardens, and a couple of uniformed officers lounging against the bonnet. Barnard parked next to them and got out, with DC Stansfield close behind him.

'You took your time,' one of the PCs said. 'We've closed off the gardens, like the nick told us, but without CID we thought it best to leave well alone.'

'There's no doubt she's dead?' Barnard asked, wondering whether the two officers, who looked as if their main ambition was to star in *Z Cars*, should have called an ambulance.

'No doubt about it, stone dead,' they said almost as one.

'I felt for a pulse but there wasn't one and she was stone cold,' the older officer said. 'After that we didn't touch her, just shut off the gate, called it in, and waited for you lot to turn up.'

'She's a nice-looking bit of stuff,' the other added. 'Not a dolly bird exactly, but not bad if you go for the more mature type.'

'Right, we'll take a look,' Barnard said. 'I'm not actually on duty, as it goes, but I happened to call into the nick and there was no one else around except DC Stansfield here so I thought I'd best come over too. Soho's my manor, after all.'

'Vice, isn't it?' one of the uniformed officers asked. 'A cushy number, then?'

And when Barnard scowled, his partner butted in.

'This way,' he said, opening the gate and leading the two plain clothes officers across the grass to a secluded area of low bushes beneath the overhanging plane trees. 'Looks like one for the Vice Squad, I'd say. You'll be the right man for the job.'

'Did someone see what happened?' Barnard asked. 'Do we have an eyewitness?'

'In theory,' the PC said. 'Some beggar called in from that phone box over there.' He pointed to where the phone kiosk stood on the far corner of the square. 'Told us what he'd seen and then hung up, so we've no idea who he was. Stupid beggar.'

Barnard shrugged.

'Someone who didn't want his nearest and dearest to know he was hanging around in Soho looking for a good time, I guess,' he said. 'This isn't suburbia, where upright citizens rush to help the police. There are hundreds of reasons for staying anonymous, most of them female and wearing not much more than this one. Did you talk to anyone else who might have seen what happened?'

'Kev here did a trawl round but he didn't find anyone else who'd even noticed anything unusual. The punter on the phone was quite close to this gate, but if you were walking on the other side of the gardens or behind the parked cars you wouldn't see much, if anything. And people move on quite fast round here, as you must know, all heading somewhere they probably shouldn't be seen at or on their way home.'

Even in the dim light from the streetlamps, which barely penetrated the trees, Barnard could see that the body sprawled in front of them was almost naked.

'Have you got a flashlight?' he asked. The two uniformed officers directed the beams of their powerful torches at the spot beneath the bushes, and Barnard and Stansfield both drew breath sharply. Scantily clad in bra and pants, the female body sprawled on the dry grass was covered in dark bruises and there were marks of strangulation discernible around her throat. Barnard could just make out where, buried in her plump folds of flesh, a ligament of some sort had been pulled viciously tight. There could be no doubt that the woman was dead, and there was no way anything that had been done to her could have been self-inflicted. In the case of a suspicious death there was every reason why none of them should attempt to move the body, but ignoring his colleagues Barnard reached towards her distorted face and brushed his fingers across her cheek while Stansfield turned away with a heavy exhalation of breath, which Barnard knew was to keep nausea under control.

'Stone cold, as you said,' Barnard commented quietly. 'I'd be very surprised if she died here. She would have been noticed long before she got as cold as this. She's been dead some time.'

'Is she someone you know, Flash? One of the local girls on the game?' one of the uniformed officers asked with a sly grin. Working for Vice was not always taken very seriously by other branches of the Met, as Barnard knew only too well. But that was an idea he knew he'd better jump on hard before the brass arrived.

'I've never seen her in my life before,' he snapped. He took one of the flashlights and ran it up and down the woman's body.

'Silk underwear and a bloody great diamond on her finger. She's a cut and a half above the working girls round here, even if she did let someone do this to her.'

'The phone caller said she was dumped from a car,' one of the PCs reminded him. 'Two men pulled up over there . . .' He indicated the low fence that separated the garden in the centre of the square from the narrow pavement, which was lined with parked cars. 'Lifted her over the fence, dropped her, and then drove off at speed.'

'No registration number?'

'Big dark car. No number.'

'Right,' Barnard said. 'We'd better get the wheels in motion. We need the doctor and the DCI for a start. It looks like being a long night.' It took Barnard some time to report back to the nick on the patrol car's radio and persuade the uniformed night staff that the hunt for the DCI, and also for the police surgeon, had now become a top priority. After the best part of an hour's waiting, DCI Keith Jackson and the police surgeon eventually arrived in a black cab and full evening dress. Neither of them looked best pleased at being called away from whatever social occasion they seemed to have been at together.

In the meantime, Barnard had phoned his flat and was relieved to hear that Kate had arrived home safely. She sounded no happier than when Barnard dropped her at the Tube.

'I'm stuck here for a bit,' he said. 'I'm sorry, Kate, but the dead woman has been strangled. I'll have to wait for the DCI. I can't leave Stansfield here on his own. He's already looking an ominous shade of green.'

'Should he even be a copper then, la, if he's such a fragile flower?' Kate asked tartly.

'Probably not,' Barnard said. 'But there's not a lot I can do about that.'

'I'll go to bed then,' she replied levelly, though he could hear the growing disappointment in her voice and his heart sank.

'I'll come in quietly,' he said. 'I'll try not to wake you.' If the worst came to the worst, he thought, he would be sleeping on the sofa tonight. He walked slowly back from the phone box wondering, not for the first time, how long Kate would put up with being let down like this. He was jolted out of his introspection by the sight of another police car pulling into the square.

'What are you doing here, Barnard?' Jackson asked, his eyes full of suspicion, as soon as he spotted the sergeant's approach.

'I called into the nick to pick up a jacket I'd left in the office, guv. Young Stansfield had just been alerted to all this and I thought he might need some back-up as he hadn't been able to contact you at that stage. We came straight over.'

'And what have we got?'

'A dead woman,' Barnard said. 'She's been pretty viciously attacked, and strangled by the look of it.'

'You haven't touched the body?' the police surgeon snapped. Barnard guessed that the contempt with which he felt like treating this question was best kept under wraps and bit his tongue.

'Of course not,' he said.

'Is she a tom?' Jackson asked. 'Do you know her? Professionally, I mean?'

'No,' Barnard said quietly. 'I've never seen her before in my life, and there's not many women in Soho I can say that about. Her face is badly bruised, but she's definitely a stranger to me. And judging by the size of the diamond ring she's wearing, she's a bloody sight more prosperous than the working girls round here. If she's a whore, she's a high-class whore and maybe her sugar daddy turned nasty on her. Or maybe she's not a whore at all.'

The doctor offered nothing more than a grim harrumph as he crouched down to take a close look at the woman's remains.

'She's been dead some time,' he said almost immediately. 'And, as is very obvious, she's been beaten and strangled and sexually assaulted. You'll get more detail at the post-mortem of course. There's not much to be said here, with this poor light. I'll arrange for her to be taken to the morgue. Then you can organize your searches and so on and get on with the forensics.'

'We'll cordon the area off until daylight,' Jackson said. From his tone of voice, Barnard could tell that whoever the woman was his boss had already written her off. In Jackson's puritanical view of the world, women who allowed themselves to be sexually assaulted and then killed had generally been the agents of their own destruction.

Jackson turned to the two uniformed officers.

'Have a trawl around the square again to make sure no one apart from the phone caller saw anything,' he said. 'Barnard, you can get off duty now. Stansfield can cover anything that needs to be covered overnight. You can take over in the morning.'

'Guv,' Barnard said, relieved that he would be able to get home to Kate so easily. She had made it clear enough that she was not be best pleased that their evening out had ended so abruptly. But when he pulled into the parking space outside his block of flats in Highgate, his heart lurched uncomfortably. All the windows were unlit. For a moment panic threatened to overwhelm him. Perhaps she had decided to go out again for some reason, he thought, although he knew the idea was irrational.

He hurried to the front door, and when he turned the hall light on was relieved to see that the coat Kate had been wearing in town was flung carelessly across the chair in the hall. He went quietly into the living room and poured himself a generous measure of Scotch before sitting in his favourite revolving chair. He took a deep draught and contemplated his shaking hands. This, he thought, not for the first time recently, was getting serious. Ever since he had been forced to stand impotently by while others more expert than him were trying to locate Kate in pitch darkness on a lethal marsh, he had known she had a hold over him that few women had gained in his life before. What was driving him to distraction was the life-changing decision about what to do about it. And after what had happened this evening, he guessed that Kate might be as unsure about the future as he was.

He finished his drink, put his glass in the kitchen sink, and gently opened the bedroom door. He could hear Kate's even breathing in the darkness. For a moment he hesitated in the doorway, then located his pyjamas, retreated to the bathroom to undress, and made himself as comfortable as he could on the sofa in the living room. Whatever remained to be picked over between the two of them about the night's unexpected events would be better discussed after they had both had a decent night's sleep, he concluded ruefully.

Barnard was the first up the following morning, feeling muzzy after a fitful sleep tossing and turning among the cushions on the sofa which made a humid night even more uncomfortable than it would have been between cool sheets. Once or twice he had been wakened by rumbles of thunder and the sound of heavy rain outside, but evidently Kate had not been disturbed. He half-staggered into the kitchen and put strong coffee on to percolate. If there was one thing he congratulated himself on teaching Kate during the months they had intermittently lived together it was to appreciate strong Italian coffee at pretty well any time of the day or night. When he first met her, he recalled with a slight smile, the convent girl from the north had hardly seemed to know what real coffee was, although he remembered a sticky concentrate called Camp that came out of a bottle which she brewed as a very occasional alternative to strong, dark tea. One advantage of living close to the London docks as a boy had been that delicacies of one sort and another occasionally trickled down among the war-battered terraces where he lived – much as Kate had in

Liverpool – and he had seized what was occasionally on offer. Early in his teens he'd learned there was another way of life that it did no harm to quietly aspire to in his private moments, careful not to let his friends and relations know his ambitions, which they would have ridiculed and treated with contempt.

As he poured the coffee, he sensed that Kate had slipped into the room silently behind him and was sliding on to the second stool at the breakfast bar. He raised the pot and when she nodded poured coffee into the second cup.

'All right?' he asked. She looked at him for a long time with no great warmth in her eyes.

'Did you really have to do that?' she asked eventually. He sighed.

'I really had to,' he said. 'That useless rookie would have made a balls of it, and made sure the guv'nor knew I'd been around and buggered off when I could have helped him out. You didn't have any problems getting back, did you?' Kate shook her head.

'Apart from being ogled by some drunk opposite me on the Tube,' she said. 'Fortunately he got off at Kentish town. I picked up a cab at the bottom of Highgate Hill, no problem. It was all right.'

'But?' he asked.

'But,' she said, draining her coffee. 'I ended up wondering just where we are going together. If we're going anywhere together at all, that is.' She glanced at her watch.

'I have to go to work now,' she said. 'I know it's early, but Ken said he wanted to talk to me this morning. He seemed to have something special in mind.'

'Don't you want anything to eat?' Barnard asked. 'I can make you some toast while you get dressed?'

'I'll get something on the way in,' Kate said. 'Will you be late tonight? We need to talk.' Barnard's face darkened as the tiredness lowered his guard.

'I've no bloody idea, Katie,' he said.

TWO

K ate left Barnard's flat with a sense of relief and then had ample time to stoke her sense of grievance on the Tube as she strap-hung most of the way to Tottenham Court Road. She bought herself a couple of sticky iced buns at a sandwich shop on the corner of Frith Street, and had eaten them before she got to the office. She hung up her coat and glanced towards what she could see of Ken Fellows' office between male colleagues – whose best attempt at a greeting was usually no more than a cursory nod – all busy packing bags and loading cameras, getting ready to go out on assignment. The men were taking their time to adjust to the presence of a female in their midst and Kate guessed that some of them never would, especially the older ones who had come back from the war. They sometimes shared experiences which they seldom spoke of, and certainly not with a woman.

The door to Ken's office was closed, but silhouettes of two people were visible through the opaque glass that separated the boss from the photographers' room. She got herself another cup of inevitably inferior coffee and sat down at her desk, giving more thought to her disagreement with Barnard than to the possible assignment Ken had said he had in mind for her this week. Maybe she should take a break, she thought. She could move back in with her friend Tess in Shepherd's Bush, where she was still paying rent for her room – a precaution that Barnard had always resented but which she had so far refused to cancel. He did not demand any financial contribution from her for his flat, and nothing she'd said had persuaded him to change his mind on that issue, but the idea that she was some sort of kept woman kept creeping into her mind this morning and she didn't like it. One of the changes she'd most valued when she moved from the claustrophobic embrace of Liverpool was the freedom to be her own person, making her own decisions with no one – family, friends or

Catholic Church – making any demands on her. She did not appreciate the idea that she might have exchanged all that freedom for more pressing personal demands from Harry Barnard. Maybe going back to her own place was the answer.

She was so engrossed in her own dilemmas that she was barely aware that most of the photographers had moved out with their cameras and bags of equipment, and Ken Fellows had opened his office door and was calling her inside. She ran a hand through her dark curly hair, then went in and sat in the chair he waved her into alongside a man she'd never seen before, lean and angular with a beard and sharp eyes, who offered her no more than a nod and a ghost of a smile.

'This is Derek Matthews from the new magazine *Topic*,' Ken said. 'He has an interesting proposal for us and I thought you would perhaps be the best person to tackle it. I'm not saying that you're the best or most experienced photographer I've got – don't run away with that impression – but in this case you've a lot of background knowledge which may be very useful. You're the only person here from north of Watford Gap.' Kate managed a nervous smile, wondering what was coming, as Matthews subjected her to a thorough scrutiny before he spoke.

'Ken tells me that you know John Lennon and his wife,' Matthews said. Kate was thrown by the unexpectedness of the question and she hesitated for a second.

'They were at the college of art at the same time as I was,' she said. 'We were hardly close but, yes, I knew them. And then I took some pictures of Cynthia for Ken when she was expecting their baby and was living with John's auntie. I knew her well enough to get through the door when no one else could.' Matthews nodded and glanced at Ken. 'OK, you tell her what we have in mind.'

'You know the Beatles' film is coming out this week, premiere in London and then another in Liverpool on July 10th? *A Hard Day's Night*. It'll be big down here, but it'll be massive up there when it opens. They don't get back to Liverpool much these days now they've decided to live in the south. Anyway, that's almost by the way – that's just the peg to hang a big feature on. Not about the Beatles as such – every paper in the country is besieging them and all the craziness that's going on around them with the hordes of screaming fans. What Derek is interested in is the city itself, and how it's changed and is still changing. I don't need to tell you that Liverpool got heavily bombed during the war, but everyone focused on the Blitz in London . . .'

'Churchill apparently didn't want the Germans to know that the ports were being hit,' Matthews said.

'They weren't just being hit,' Kate said fiercely. 'Liverpool was hammered. I can't remember the actual bombing, of course. I was only a baby. But I remember when I was a little girl I thought that living surrounded by ruins was perfectly normal. And if the streets hadn't been completely wrecked by the bombs, it wasn't long before they sent the bulldozers in to demolish the rest of the houses. We moved to a brand new house when I was about six or seven.'

'You must have heard stories about what went on during the war, though,' Matthews said.

'Some,' she said. 'Some about sailors who'd been lost at sea on the convoys. And stories about what happened to people in the bombing . . .' She shuddered. 'It wasn't just the docks and warehouses they went for, it was streets of houses too, air-raid shelters, everything. And they used incendiary bombs as well as high explosive. Some of the bomb sites are still there, even now. It's said the casualties were much the same as in the East End. But people felt as if they were being completely ignored, and that's still resented. For us kids, especially the lads, the sites were a playground with a spice of danger. They used to swap bits of shrapnel and other bits and pieces they dug up in the ruins. It was horrible, but I suppose we didn't really understand what had happened. Not really. And the adults didn't want to talk about it. They must have seen some terrible things.'

'Apparently the government didn't want Hitler to know how successful the raids had been,' Matthews said. 'The ports were crucial, especially Liverpool with the Atlantic traffic.'

'There may have been good reasons for what the government did, but the bitterness went on for a long time,' Kate said. 'Long enough for me to be aware of it when I was growing up.'

'That's it,' Matthews said. 'That's the sort of storyline I want in your pictures. And how Liverpool came back from all the carnage and recriminations to end up with the Beatles generation. You'll have to do some research for the wartime stuff . . .'

'You can do that here,' Ken said quickly. 'I'll get you into the various archives. But then we want you to go up and get some pictures of the Beatles going to the film premiere. Pictures of all that. There'll no doubt be massive crowds, just like there have been in London and pretty well everywhere they go. But we want much more than that. That's just the peg to hang it on. What we need is some shots of the damage caused by the war and some follow-up pictures of what's happened in the way of rebuilding – some human-interest stuff with people looking back at what happened in the Blitz, and so on. What the changes have been. How Liverpool bounced back. Or maybe didn't for some people.'

'I'd have to spend some time up there?' Kate asked, uncertainly.

'A week or so, I'd say,' Ken said, glancing at Matthews, who nodded.

'It's a good story, worth a lot to us while we're building up a readership,' Matthews said. 'I can't spare one of my own photographers to do the research, so I thought Ken could help. It will be very different from the usual showbiz angle about four likely lads making good. The national paper interviewers have done that to death already. I want something completely different, using pictures no one else has ever seen, or not since the 1940s anyway . . . So what do you think, Kate? Is it something you could handle?'

'Oh yes,' Kate said, with a sudden feeling of excitement. 'I could certainly handle that.'

After Derek Matthews left, Ken Fellows came and stood behind Kate in the now empty photographers' room, putting a hand on her shoulder, then suddenly thinking better of it and redirecting it to stroke his balding head.

'This is big stuff,' he said. 'It's the sort of photojournalism I'd like to get more of, and it just happens you're ideally placed to tackle it because of where you come from. You talk the language. So don't let me down, don't do anything rash. You've got the best part of a week before you need to go up there, so you've plenty of time to look at the archives and select some good stuff from the war and the immediate aftermath.'

'It was grim, but we're a resilient lot, we Liverpudlians,' Kate said. 'A lot of us had to be. And we've got that famous sense of humour, you know. Arthur Askey, Ted Ray, Tommy Handley . . . All those radio shows when I was a kid . . . The radio was always on in the background. What I remember best is that everyone cried buckets when Tommy Handley died. I was quite young and to me he was just a voice on the wireless. I don't suppose I understood most of the jokes. But my mam was devastated, she took his death personally.'

'Radio was very important during the war,' Ken said. 'It kept people going, kept them cheerful.'

'It was never turned off in our house,' Kate said. 'But I do remember, as I got older, how people were determined to put the city back together again. It was as if Hitler would have got away with it in some way if the rebuilding wasn't done.'

'Right, get yourself somewhere to stay before the film premiere and start looking at the archives. I'm sure the local paper will help. What's it called?'

'The *Echo,* the *Liverpool Echo,*' Kate said.

'Call the picture editor and see if he'll point you in the right direction. And Kate, this is a big commission for us – so let's take it carefully. The agency's reputation's on the line here, and if it goes well you won't do your own any harm either. It's a big chance for you to shine.'

'At least the mortuary's cool,' DS Harry Barnard told himself as he and DC Stansfield presented themselves for the post-mortem on the unknown woman whose body had been found the previous evening in Soho Square. According to DCI Jackson, no more senior officers could be spared to attend. But Barnard guessed it was because Jackson had written off the victim as a prostitute, rather than his claimed pressure of work. Watching the routine dissection of a body did not faze

Barnard, but as they approached the hospital he realized that his passenger was looking decidedly nervous.

'Have you done this before, Pete?' he asked.

Stansfield nodded unhappily.

'The boxing trainer. You remember?' he said. 'I didn't enjoy that much.'

'Oh yes, I remember. Well, try not to pass out. It really annoys them. And if you want to throw up, try to get to a sink.' Barnard slid the Capri into a parking bay with a doctor's name on it and led the way to the discreet mortuary door, round a corner away from the main hospital entrance. A technician thrust coveralls into their hands as they pushed through the heavy swing doors. Several people were already around the table in the centre of the room. The pathologist, who Barnard vaguely recalled was a Dr Kent, glanced round at the newcomers.

'DS Barnard and DC Stansfield,' Barnard said as he fastened his coverall. 'We saw the body last night where it was found.' Kent nodded without much warmth.

'I've already made a start on the external damage,' he said. 'Extensive bruising and the signs of strangulation.'

'A sexual assault?' Barnard asked.

'Oh certainly that,' Kent said. 'Moreover, some considerable force was used here. And there are signs that her wrists had been secured in some way for some of the time, although there is no sign of ligaments. They must have been removed.'

'Any indication of the time of death?'

'The weather is very warm. So given that you tell me the body was found almost immediately after it was left out of doors, there would have been no undue cooling before the police doctor took a temperature reading that was low.'

'She seemed cold,' Barnard said, and the doctor nodded.

'Rigor had not set in when she was found, so I would estimate the time of death to be earlier that evening. Can't be more precise than that at this stage.' The doctor moved to the woman's head, and with a puzzled look delicately put a finger close to her mouth.

'There is stickiness here, under the nose and on the chin,' he said. He picked up an instrument and scraped the skin gently, then put whatever he'd collected on to a slide and into an evidence bag.

'Do you think she was drugged?' Barnard asked.

'That's certainly a possibility,' Kent said. 'Alternatively, at some time she might have had some sort of a gag across her mouth to keep her quiet. Tests will tell us more. I've already taken blood for toxicology and blood type, and there'll be more samples from the stomach when I open her up. You'll have to wait for those results, of course.' Barnard was aware of a slight moan from Peter Stansfield, whose face had taken on a faint green tinge even before the doctor touched the array of cutting tools that his technician had arranged neatly for him.

'If your colleague is too frail for this, I suggest he waits outside,' Kent said sharply, picking up a scalpel. 'I can't be doing with hysterics in my lab. It's an unnecessary distraction.'

'Wait for me outside, Pete,' Barnard said. 'Get yourself a coffee or something.' Stansfield scuttled out of the room, leaving the doors swinging behind him and raising again all the doubts that Barnard had entertained about his suitability for his new job. In fact he wondered how Stansfield had coped with his time in uniform as a beat constable if he was such a delicate flower, but guessed that he must have been lucky in the cases he had had to deal with. Given today's performance, a gory road accident could have scuppered his career at any time. There was no doubt he was bright enough for CID, but Barnard was by no means convinced that he was mentally or physically tough enough.

'Sorry about that, doctor,' he said to Kent, who had by now made his first incision in the corpse's chest as the technician readied dishes to receive internal organs. The doctor cast a cold eye in Barnard's direction.

'I expect you are made of stronger stuff, Sergeant.'

'I expect I am,' Barnard said quietly. 'Though whether in the end that's a good thing or a bad thing I'm not too sure,' he added under his breath.

Barnard reported to DCI Jackson when he and Stansfield got back to the nick. He didn't take the DC with him, and he was relieved when Jackson apparently failed to notice his younger colleague's absence. Barnard would not drop Stansfield in the sticky stuff unnecessarily, but nor would he cover for him if he was asked a direct question about his performance, or lack of it, at the post-mortem. However, Jackson did no more than raise an eyebrow, which apparently indicated that he wanted to hear whatever news Barnard had brought back from the hospital.

'The doc reckons she died earlier last night. Probably some time before the body was dumped, and we have an exact time for that from our witness. She was pretty badly beaten up – some of the wounds look as if they amounted to torture. As the doc put it, a considered attack rather than frenzied. She was raped, possibly more than once and possibly by more than one person, and eventually strangled. He reckons her hands might have been tied and she might have been gagged, but confirmation will come from the tests. The same goes for blood group, and whether there were drugs or alcohol in her stomach.'

'She'd hardly have got herself into that position without one or the other,' Jackson said with no sign of sympathy for the dead woman. 'Not if you're right about her wearing expensive underwear and a diamond ring. That's not normal for the usual sort you get on the streets, is it? But if that's the case, why was she dumped right in the heart of Soho?'

'To lead us down a blind alley, maybe,' Barnard suggested.

'And by someone who didn't know that the Vice Squad knows every tart within a mile of Soho Square,' Jackson said sharply. 'And that includes you personally. If that's what they intended, they were unlucky you turned up.' Barnard sighed. He had slept badly on the sofa and watched Kate flounce out of the flat obviously still in a bad mood, but he bit back the retort that it was part of his job to know the prostitutes and pimps of Soho in all their many manifestations. He wondered just how much Kate knew about the unpleasant details of his job, and its occasional compensations, but quickly decided that was an avenue he did not want to explore, with their relationship in such a fragile state.

'Maybe,' he said quietly. 'But if the dead woman was a stranger, maybe whoever killed her was too. After all, she was dumped from a car. She could have come from anywhere in London, or even further afield.'

'Perhaps her killer was not such a stranger not to know what assumptions we'd make if she was dumped in Soho Square,' Jackson said.

'So you agree it might be intended to mislead us?' Barnard asked, convinced he was right but knowing he had no real evidence to support his hunch.

'I don't agree or disagree at this stage. There's no evidence either way. You'd better get an artist in. From what you say she's too badly disfigured for a photograph, but an artist should be able to give us a likeness that we can circulate across London and give to the evening papers. Getting an ID is obviously the first step. We can't do much without that. And have a trawl through missing persons, both for the last few days and ongoing. If the estimated time of death is accurate, she may not have been reported missing yet.'

'Guv,' Barnard said. When Jackson was not linking him too closely to the criminals he was paid to investigate, he had an unnerving habit of trying to teach a man who was not, so far as he knew, even a parent yet – let alone a grandparent – to suck eggs. Not for the first time he wondered exactly how DCI Keith Jackson had come to be appointed to run the Vice Squad when he so obviously found the whole enterprise so distasteful. Although in this case he had some sympathy for the DCI. Like Barnard himself he must have seen his quota of mutilated bodies over the years and, like him, built up defences. But this woman had been so cold-bloodedly used in ways that must have caused her the maximum amount of pain that those defences were not enough.

'We need to catch this bastard,' Barnard said.

'We do, Sergeant,' Jackson said. 'We certainly do.'

THREE

When Kate got back to Barnard's flat that evening, after a suffocating journey on the Northern Line, she got herself a glass of cold water and sat for a moment in his revolving chair contemplating the smart modern home he'd put together for himself. Her mother, she thought, would be astonished by the sleek lines of the furnishing and the vibrant shades of orange and peacock blue, and in all likelihood would hate them. And she might wonder, as Kate did, how a detective sergeant had paid for them. One way or another London was prospering while other places were not; and the prospect of going back to Liverpool, which she no longer really thought of as home, had unexpectedly sharpened the contrast between the northern city that had fuelled Beatlemania over years – without the rest of the country even noticing – and the capital, which had embraced it so noisily in what seemed like only months. London was undoubtedly swinging to the Merseybeat now, and according to the papers even New York seemed to have unexpectedly gone wild for their music. But she wondered if Liverpool really was swinging so wholeheartedly, or ever could or would. After all, it had taken the Beatles years to make their mark there; and the Scousers were nothing if not sceptical when not downright begrudging, always more ready with a sharp put-down than with a compliment. It would be interesting to see what had changed since her move south and whether a city that had had its heart reduced to rubble – as if Oxford Street, Piccadilly and Knightsbridge had been destroyed in a single night – had really recovered.

She finished her drink, then went into the bedroom and pulled all her clothes out of the wardrobe and flung them on the bed. Suddenly she turned on her heel and went back into the living room and picked up the phone.

Tess Farrell answered quickly, sounding slightly distracted.

'Sorry,' she said. 'I've got a pile of marking to do then I'm going to the pictures with my nice history teacher.'

'Is he really nice?' Kate asked. 'Is this really it?'

Tess laughed. 'Too soon to tell,' she said. 'But promising.'

'I . . . we . . . saw *Viva Las Vegas*,' Kate said. 'I wouldn't recommend it, though. But that's not why I rang. I've got a big job on which means going back to Liverpool for a while and I think it would be better if I had my old room back until I go. It will give me a bit more time and space . . .'

'Of course,' Tess said quickly. 'It's your room. You're paying for it. Is this a sign you and Harry are splitting up?' Kate hesitated for a long moment.

'I'm not sure,' she said eventually. 'Maybe. Or maybe I just need some time to think after everything that's happened lately.'

'Well, you know what I think,' Tess said. 'He's too old, too unreliable, too – oh, I don't know – too flash for you. And he gets you into too many dangerous scrapes.' Kate smiled slightly at that, thinking that she had got herself into many of those scrapes herself and had certainly needed Barnard's help to get out of them, but her smile faded quickly as she heard Barnard's key in the lock.

'I have to go,' she said. 'I may come back tonight, but I've got my own key so I can let myself in if you are still out. If I'm going to do this, I think I'd better do it quickly. See you later, alligator.'

'In a while, crocodile,' Tess said, still sounding uncertain. She had always been one of Barnard's fiercest critics, and Kate guessed she wouldn't change her mind now she had spotted a possible crack in the relationship.

Barnard came into the room and flung his coat on a chair before putting an arm round her and kissing her ear. She glanced up at him, trusting that he could not read her mind.

'You don't look very pleased with life,' she said. He shrugged.

'That could be what you call an understatement,' he said. 'DCI Jackson treats me like a criminal half the time and an idiot the other half. How was your day?'

'Ah,' Kate said cautiously. 'My day was very interesting.'

'Tell me,' Barnard said. He went over to his cocktail cabinet and opened the door. 'Do you want a drink?' Kate shook her head, and watched as he poured himself a generous Scotch before sitting beside her on the sofa. 'So what's going on?'

'I have to go away for a bit,' Kate said, hoping she did not sound as nervous as she felt. 'Ken has been asked to do a major feature on Liverpool to coincide with the Beatles' film that's coming out in London this week and in Liverpool on the tenth. He wants lots of pictures showing how Liverpool has changed and how it came to produce a group that's taking America by storm as well as us.'

'How long is a bit?' Barnard asked, and Kate could see he was much more perturbed than she'd expected.

'I'll have to be up there for a week or so. To give me time to see the film premiere and some of the reaction to it, then talk to lots of people about how the city's recovered from the war and the bombing. And I'll have to dig around for pictures of what went on then and what happened to people. Of course I was only a baby during the war, but some of it I know about and there's a lot I can remember. The bombed streets, rationing, never having enough to eat. Tom and me, we had to grow up fast because my mother was pregnant with Annie. He used to take me with him to stand in queues – it didn't matter what they were for. You bought whatever you could and maybe swapped with the neighbours later . . .'

She trailed off, realizing that Barnard was not really listening as he drained his glass quickly and got up for a refill. She hadn't yet told him what he would no doubt regard as the most upsetting element of her news, but it was almost as if he expected the worst.

'I thought it would make sense to move back to my own place until I go away,' she almost whispered. 'Most of my stuff is still there, and there's more space for me to work. It's going to take a lot of time and effort even before I go . . .' Barnard moved closer to her and put an arm round her shoulder.

'What's going on, Katie?' He asked. 'Is this payback time because I messed you around the other night?'

'Of course not,' Kate said. 'It's just that my job is important to me and this is a chance to show what I can do for a national magazine. It's a big opportunity and I don't want to mess it up. I'm going to have to work really hard to do the research before I go north, and then even harder once I get there and when I get back. I need to do this without distractions.'

'Is that what I am? A distraction?' Barnard pulled his arm away and stood up. 'Or is it your idea of a kind way to tell me you want to finish with me? Come on, Kate. You owe it to me to be honest at least.'

'I am being honest,' she said. 'This is about my job, not you. It's important to me. For years people have been telling me that being a photographer is not a suitable job for a woman and I've been trying to prove them wrong. And so far Ken Fellows has been supporting me. I know he had reservations, and the men in the office have even more. They're all still sitting there sniggering, waiting for me to fall flat on my face. But so far I haven't, not professionally at least, and he's offered me a really big chance. I've got to take it with both hands, Harry. That's what I really want to do. And yes, I'm sorry, in a sense you are a distraction. But it's only for a couple of weeks. When I get back we can sort ourselves out. Right now, I haven't got the time or the energy.'

Barnard walked over to the window and looked out at the tree-lined street. There were still some people hurrying home from work and a couple of others were walking in the opposite direction in tennis whites, heading to the club down the road for a knock-up before the light failed. It was a normal evening in Highgate. But he felt that normality had suddenly and unexpectedly deserted him. His voice was husky when he finally spoke, without turning round.

'When you disappeared in Essex and I thought you were probably dead, I realized that I really couldn't do without you, Kate,' he said. 'While I stood there waiting to find out what had happened, I felt as if I was being destroyed from the inside out. I know your job is important to you, and I can see this is a great opportunity. I understand all that. But please tell me you'll come back when it's over and try to mend what's broken between us. Please.'

Kate got up and stood beside him with her hand clutching his.

'I promise,' she said. 'I will come back. And then we'll
see.'

Just over a week later when she hoisted her suitcase on to the
luggage rack and levered herself into the only empty seat in
a crowded compartment on the morning train to Liverpool she
heaved a sigh of relief. She was only barely aware that the
man sitting next to her on the corridor side had given her a
filthy look as he slammed the sliding door shut. People
searching for seats on the busy service were still milling about
in the corridor, and she wondered whether he was afraid a
seventh person would try to cram into the space British Rail
had provided for six.

For the past week she had been just as busy as she had
warned Barnard she would be, trawling through newspaper
and agency picture archives for photographs of the bomb
damage in Liverpool – most of it inflicted in a brutal blitz in
May 1941 – and, more rare, pictures of the rebuilding of the
ravaged city, which she had been only too aware of as she
grew up, with huge areas of the streets lined with scaffolding
and echoing to the shouts and laughter of the builders. She
found photograph after photograph that brought tears to her
eyes – not so much the city's landmarks and shopping streets
in ruins but particularly what remained of the packed tenements around Scotland Road, where she realized she and her
family were very lucky to have survived unscathed when so
many hadn't.

She'd been working in the office during the day and at the
flat in Shepherd's Bush in the evenings, the only respite
provided by two tickets to see the Beatles' film *A Hard Day's
Night* which Ken Fellows had dropped on her desk one
morning.

'You'd better see it down here,' he said. 'I've no idea how
to get complimentary tickets for the Liverpool showing.'

She'd rung Harry Barnard to ask him if he would like to
come with her but he turned her down, sounding distant and
preoccupied. So she went with Tess instead, and they swayed
to the music and laughed at the antics of the four musicians
and Paul McCartney's grandfather, let loose in London, until

Kate almost forgot her problems. Barnard's chilly answer had
upset her, but she refused to let it distract her from the course
she'd embarked on. It was, she thought, almost a test of his
commitment. He had to come to terms with her job and its
demands, in the same way that she had to come to terms with
his, or she could see no future at all for them together.

In spite of her enthusiasm for the task in hand she had found
her research a deeply depressing experience, as well as an
eye-opening revelation, and was obscurely pleased she didn't
have to share it with anyone. Although some of Liverpool's
landmarks had survived, not least the three iconic buildings
at the Pier Head, many others both in the city centre and the
docks had been obliterated. The Customs House, department
stores, historic warehouses on the waterfront and acres of
closely packed streets had fallen victim to high explosive and
incendiary bombs and an occasional devastating landmine.
What must it have been like for her parents, she wondered,
living close to Scotland Road and the docks with two small
children and another on the way, as death rained down? No
wonder they'd never talked about it. For her own part, she
could barely remember their wartime home, as their badly
damaged street had been scheduled for demolition almost
before she started school. A new Corporation house with a
coveted indoor lavatory had been allocated to them in one of
the first newly built terraces, about a mile away, safely beyond
the edge of the Vauxhall slums – a temporary place not big
enough for the O'Donnells, but good enough for them to be
able to wait patiently for a better council house to come up.

More surprising, she thought, was the fact that she had never
heard her father talk about what he did during the war. He
had apparently not been called up and had continued to work
in the docks, although whether that was a reserved occupation,
like being a miner, she was not sure. For whatever reason, the
dockers who remained in the port benefited from extra work
when the conscripts left for the army and navy. Only once
had she heard him comment on the bombing – when he
admitted having helped pull neighbours out of a wrecked house
across the street, although that had only been revealed when
Winny Dempsey, whose house it had been, turned up one day

with a new baby to show off to her mother and it happened that her father was at home as well. Kate reckoned she must have been four or five then because she quite clearly remembered Mrs Dempsey and her mother proudly comparing Winny's child with her sister Bernadette, whose birth she could certainly remember.

The Dempseys had already been rehoused in West Derby, while the O'Donnells, with two extra mouths to feed after her younger sisters arrived, remained in the same dilapidated house where the younger children had been born, waiting their turn on the housing list because their house was still standing – though, as her mother kept complaining, only just. Like many, it had been shored up with huge wooden beams to make sure it didn't fall down around them. So far as Kate could recall, that was the only time she had ever met her former neighbour and she did not think she had ever seen her again. Nevertheless, if she could track her down and persuade her to talk about the Blitz, Winny might have a good story to tell even after all these years.

A whistle blew on the platform and the train lurched into motion, bringing Kate back to the here and now. It was Saturday morning and Tess had come with her on the underground to help with her suitcase, and Kate suddenly recalled what she had said as she hefted the case through the door into the corridor and turned to say goodbye through the open window.

'You need to do some serious thinking,' Tess had intoned solemnly and Kate did not need to be told what she meant.

'I will do some serious thinking,' she said. 'I promise.'

'You can't go on the way you are with Harry Barnard.'

'No,' Kate said, though it was with more a sense of appeasement than conviction.

'Give my love to Marie, if you see her. And to the Cavern, if you go.' Marie had come with them to London in the hope of making it as an actress – but after many failed auditions had gone back home in despair, only to find that success was easier to pin down on home ground after all.

'I'll have a drink in Ye Cracke for old times' sake too, but I don't suppose it'll be the same,' Kate promised, though she did not expect to have much time to revisit her own old haunts around the College of Art. Her camera and her questions would be focused further back in time than that. She had pulled the window up and slammed the door before pushing down the corridor to find a seat, wondering if this really was the turning point Tess seemed to want it to be.

She slept fitfully for part of the journey, tired after several late nights working her way through the collections of photographs she had been able to access in London. But it was true enough that in the south pictures of the wartime bombing concentrated on the East End of London and included very little from anywhere further afield. She was awake again when they pulled into Crewe, and wide awake as the train clattered over the points to take her across the River Mersey and the ship canal and veer west towards what had been home for most of her life. Lime Street station was busy and she had to search for the taxi rank. Ken Fellows had ensured she had an adequate advance on her expenses, instructing her merely to make sure she got receipts for anything she spent on the agency's behalf, and although she was booked into a small hotel not far away in Brownlow Hill she reckoned it was too far to carry her suitcase and decided to indulge herself with a cab.

She smiled slightly as the car made its way past Lewis's department store on one side and the Adelphi Hotel on the other. She guessed that the Beatles might already be there, and wondered whether the day might come when she could afford to stay there too. Eventually she was deposited outside a slightly dilapidated four-storey building which on a faded board outside the front door announced itself as the Lancaster Hotel. She signed in and was shown a small single room on the third floor, where she collapsed on to the bed after carrying her case up three flights of stairs. She might dream of the Adelphi but this, she knew, was much closer to her reality. Hotels had not figured in her family's world, and she felt almost embarrassed to be staying in one so close to home. The room looked clean enough but it was stuffy and the window, which would open only a tiny crack, offered a view of an unkempt back garden and a row of overstuffed dustbins close to what she guessed was the kitchen door. Just as well she was only booked in for bed and breakfast!

She unpacked and lined up her files, which were thinner than she would have liked, and decided that today at least she would have a scout round her old student haunts before making her way to see her mother and possibly her father – though she knew he was only an intermittent resident at the family home – and possibly her sisters. Tom, she knew, had never moved back in with the family after a traumatic spell in London, and she guessed that some of her devout family were busy praying for him to repent his sins while, if he could ever get his hands on him, her father would indulge in a much more physical response.

When she was satisfied with the state of her new base, she picked up a jacket and her handbag, left her key at reception, and headed off up the hill towards the university. She could see that a few more beams had been swung into place on Paddy's Wigwam, the modernist Roman Catholic cathedral which faced off the more traditional Anglican building emerging at a much statelier pace at the other end of Hope Street. It was lunchtime and some of the uniformed boys from the Institute were slipping across the road to chat up the girls at Blackburn House until, as usual, some of the mistresses rushed out to chivvy them away from the railings. She glanced at the art college where she'd spent three years learning her craft and rubbing shoulders with some of the embryonic Merseybeat musicians – including John Lennon, a sharp, funny artist as well as an obsessive guitar player. But the students now looked very young and she turned away, rounded a corner and arrived at the down-at-heel and by no means ancient pub with the decidedly odd name Ye Cracke where she had once spent many hours in the back room making a shandy last as long as possible, while she and her friends put the world to rights and compared the respective merits of the many bands they or their brothers played in. If photography was generally regarded as an odd thing for a girl to be doing, a girl playing – or even singing – in a band was pretty well unheard of.

She opened the pub door and glanced through the smoky atmosphere, but after a couple of years away there was no one

she recognized and by the standards of these lunchtime
drinkers, one or two of them in school uniform, she was far
too long in the tooth and past it. She smiled ruefully and turned
away and made her way past the new cathedral, wondering
what her mother would make of the startling circular design
when it was eventually finished. It was time, she thought, to
go home and ask her mother that and a lot more besides.

Bridie O'Donnell opened her front door before Kate had time
to knock. She looked older than when she'd last seen her, skin
greyer and dark circles under her eyes, and her pinafore was
wrapped tightly round her waist as if to emphasize that she
was losing weight. She gave her mother a hug, and with a
pang of deep foreboding realized just how much thinner she
was.

'Who's here?' Kate asked. 'Is dad at home?' The presence
or absence, intermittent and generally unannounced, of her
father had always dominated even the weather in the O'Donnell
house and Kate felt a guilty sense of relief when her mother
shook her head.

'I don't know where your father is,' Bridie said. 'He's not
bothering with dock work anymore, he says, though what he's
doing instead he doesn't tell me. He just says there's more
regular money in other things. Annie and Bernadette are at
work. They'll be back about six. They've both still got shop
jobs and Bernie's got a boyfriend, a nice Catholic boy called
Gerard from Everton. I'm hoping there'll be a wedding soon.'
Kate nodded. She had no doubt about what her mother and
the parish priest she'd known since she was a small child
would make of her own domestic arrangements in London.
There would be no nuptial Mass for her, she thought, and
quite likely no wedding either, as far as she could see, unless
she really did finish with Harry Barnard. She had never seriously thought he was the marrying kind.

'And Tom? Have you seen Tom at all?' she asked.
Bridie's face closed and she shook her head.

'He doesn't come here,' she said. 'Father Reilly says that's
best. Not while he's an occasion of sin. Last I heard he was
living out in Bootle. He sent me his address, but I don't know

what I've done with it. Your da would kill him if he set eyes on him.'

'Is the kettle on?' Kate asked, changing the subject quickly, with a sigh. She guessed that her queer brother was probably living with someone away from the city centre, where he would be hoping to escape the attention of the police and the suffocating embrace of the Church. 'I'm parched, it's so hot.' Her mother led the way into the kitchen and busied herself warming the teapot and measuring the leaves in – as if they were gold dust, but more likely because she could not bear to meet her oldest daughter's eye. The spectres of the past never seemed to fade, Kate thought, and perhaps never would.

'So tell me again why you're here,' Bridie said, putting the pot on the kitchen table to brew and rinsing a couple of cups from the sink under the tap. 'Are you taking sugar?'

'No thanks,' Kate said. She could still remember the family's excitement when they first visited their new home in Anfield, and she and Tom rushed about turning on taps and flushing the lavatory until their father slapped their legs in a vain attempt to calm them down. The day they had left Vauxhall – where less lucky families were still confined to the slum courts that had survived the war, a dozen families with only one lavatory between them, or in houses shored up, like their own, to prevent collapse – was one of the most exciting she could remember from her early life, and for years the four children had played 'Moving Day' until the memory finally began to fade.

Bridie poured the tea and they sat at the kitchen table to drink it.

'I should have brought you something,' Kate said, feeling guilty as she glanced around the room and recognized the signs of a life still lived too close to the edge. 'I got this big job taking pictures of people who lived through the bombing and of how the Pool has recovered. It's because the Beatles' film is opening the day after tomorrow. Suddenly people want to know what happened here before the bands started. People down there don't know anything at all about people up here.'

'Don't know and don't care, as far as I can see,' Bridie said. 'There's nothing new about that, la.'

'But it is better?' Kate said. 'Isn't it? It looked better when

I came through the centre. Lots of building still going on. That's good, isn't it?'

'Your father's been working lately for one of the construction companies,' Bridie said. 'For a man called Terry Jordan he met during the war. One of ours, at least. There's still them and us even though Labour's taken over the Corporation from the Unionists at last. And they've been pulling down the last of the old tenements down Scotland Road. But it's very slow, and some people are being moved miles out on to the new estates. They don't always like that. It's not the same as the old neighbourhoods where you could always find a friend when you needed one.'

'And a boozer and a betting shop, not to mention a pawn shop,' Kate said bitterly. 'I can't remember much about the war but I can remember living in Scottie Road with an outdoor lavvie and no bathroom. You were pleased to move, don't tell me you weren't. Everyone was. It was like we went to heaven.'

Bridie gave her a thin smile.

'I've always wondered who it was made your brother the way he is,' she said. 'Did that happen in Scottie Road, or was it after we moved? We brought you up so carefully, took you to Mass, to confession, had you confirmed . . . Do you remember that dress I made you? A good Catholic family, that's what we were, and yet look how Tom turned out. Now I'm ashamed . . .'

Kate glanced away from her mother, her expression tense and her mouth dry.

'I don't know how these things happen,' she said, although she had some ideas about that which she would never have shared with her mother in a thousand years.

'I wondered if I could get Father Reilly to seek Tom out, talk to him again . . .' Bridie said.

'Leave it, mam,' Kate snapped. 'He wouldn't thank you. And nor would Father Reilly, I wouldn't think. Just leave it alone.'

'Are you going to Mass down there?' Bridie demanded.

'Not often,' Kate lied, afraid that if she told the truth she might be cast aside like her brother had been. She was, she thought, an out-and-out coward, afraid to share her new life with her mother. Perhaps she should not have come.

FOUR

Harry Barnard rolled over in bed and looked at his alarm clock, which must have gone off without waking him. His head was thumping and his mouth felt like sandpaper from the night before. Realizing with the same sense of shock as every morning recently that he was alone, he rolled the other way and groaned.

'Hell and damnation!' he said to himself as he put a tentative foot on the floor. He reckoned it was probably safe to stand up if he was extremely careful. Still in his pyjamas, and three cups of strong coffee later, he risked shaving, managing not to do himself any serious damage, checked to make sure that all the bottles in the living room were really empty, dressed with difficulty, and then drove very cautiously into central London and parked in his usual spot outside the nick. He picked up another cup of coffee in the canteen, although he knew that it hardly deserved the name, and made his way very carefully up the stairs to the CID office, where he negotiated laboriously to take off his coat and preserve the coffee at the same time.

'God, you look rough,' Peter Stansfield said from his desk at the other side of the room. 'Missing her, are you?'

'Mind your own!' Barnard snarled. If Stansfield, on the strength of a couple of outings together, had appointed himself his best friend, or even worse, his minder, he aimed to disabuse him of that notion very fast.

'Do you want to lend me a hand with these pictures of the dead woman?' Barnard asked irritably. 'They've taken long enough to turn up, so we'd better get them out and about before everyone's forgotten about the poor cow.' Stansfield shook his head quickly.

'I'll leave that to you, mate,' he said. 'I've got enough on. But mind how you go.'

'Fair enough,' Barnard said, thinking that maybe a stroll

round Soho on his own might keep him well away from the
DCI and also do something to improve his hangover. Whether
anything would help to ease the empty feeling he felt inside
he very much doubted, but he put his coat back on and picked
up the sheaf of pictures of the murdered woman – still uniden-
tified and not, he guessed, anywhere near the top of DCI
Jackson's list of priorities. Trawls through lists of missing
persons across London had proved fruitless, and none of the
other forces had reported a missing person of similar descrip-
tion. Whoever she was, she was as anonymous as on the night
she was found. He set off downstairs again, still with a cautious
hand on the banister, aware that he was being watched with
some concern by the uniformed sergeant on the front desk.

'You all right, mate?' he asked. 'You look a bit rough.'

'A touch of food poisoning,' Barnard mumbled. 'Bloody
canteen sausages!'

'Oh yeah?' the sergeant scoffed, but Barnard did not have
the energy to reply.

He headed for Berwick Street market where he bought a
couple of buns and persuaded his stomach to accept them, washed
down by yet more coffee, then began a slow trawl around the
cafés, pubs and shops, showing his sketches of the unknown
woman. The clubs and brothels would have to wait until lunchtime, when they would begin to come back to life and face a
new day already half over. It was there he was most likely to
stumble on someone who knew or had seen the dead woman.
If, being realistic, he was very, very lucky. He did not think that
the woman with the diamond ring had anything to do with the
illegitimate trades of Soho. She did not look the part.

He attempted lunch at the Blue Lagoon coffee bar, where
he often went with Kate if she could be prised away from her
photo agency in Frith Street. But a single bite of his sandwich
told him this was a mistake. He pushed his chair back noisily
and walked out and headed instead for the nearest pub, where
he ordered a beer and a whisky chaser. He knew that wasn't
a wise choice, but he was almost past caring.

It was not entirely true that, as the DCI believed, he knew
every tart within a mile of Soho Square. But he knew a lot of
them, and he worked his way systematically from back-street

door to back-street door where women of all shapes and sizes and colours and nationalities worked the oldest trade in the world, all in harm's way from both misjudged clients and the arbitrary assaults of the law. Resisting the odd invitation to come indoors, explicit as well as implicit, he cajoled his contacts, behind their doors with peepholes to vet visitors and columns of doorbells with no more than a first name beside each, to at least put their heads out into the bright light of day. Then he persuaded them to take a closer look at the sketch he showed them, but not a single one admitted to recognizing the murdered woman. Normally he enjoyed his work in Soho – he liked the glittering anarchic neon-lit nightlife as well as its cosmopolitan daytime bustle – but today's trek was no more than a chore that he struggled to complete in the teeth of his hangover, and it proved as unproductive as he had expected.

He saved one call until last, simply because he knew he could regard Evie Renton, for old time's sake at least, as a safe haven from the women who tried to buy favours the only way they knew how and from the demons inside his head. It was early and she did not yet have on the carefully made-up face with which she would greet clients later. Which may have been why she could not hide her shock when she opened the door to Barnard.

'My God, you look dreadful,' she said. 'Come in, come in. I'll make you some tea.' He took off his coat and slumped into her single armchair, close to the bed from which she looked as if she had only just got up. She left him there then reappeared quickly with a mug of strong tea, into which it was obvious when he tasted it that she had stirred several spoonfuls of sugar. He pulled a face but drank it in the hope it possessed the medicinal qualities Evie seemed to believe it did. Better anyway, he knew, than the alternatives he preferred.

'So what's wrong?' she asked. 'You look as if you've lost a tenner and found a bent halfpenny. Is it that bird you're stuck on? Has she dumped you?'

Barnard managed a faint smile.

'You're too clever by half,' he said. 'She's gone away for a bit, back to blasted Liverpool where she came from. And to be honest I don't know whether she's dumped me or not. If you're really interested, I always thought it was too good to last. But what do I know? Women are a mystery to me.' Evie lit a cigarette and drew the smoke in deeply, even though it instantly threw her into a paroxysm of coughing.

'I'm not sure you're the type to settle down with some provincial lass from the sticks,' she said bluntly. 'Strikes me you need someone a bit more sophisticated than that.' Barnard winced but said nothing for a moment.

'How's that little girl of yours?' he asked eventually.

'Still doing well with my mother,' Evie said. 'And doing well at school.' She shrugged wearily. 'But I don't know if I can go on earning enough to pay her school fees,' she said and Barnard could see the near-panic in her eyes.

'So why are you here?' Evie asked eventually. 'I take it you've not just dropped in for a quickie for old times' sake.' Barnard shook his head and took one of the sketches out of his coat pocket.

'Have you ever seen this woman?' he asked. 'She's the one who was found dead in Soho Square, dumped half-naked under the trees.' Evie looked at the picture closely.

'No,' she said. 'And given her age, if she was on the game round here I'd have come across her, I guess. She's not exactly a spring chicken, is she? Well-fed, though. Which is more than most of us on the game are.'

'She was wearing silk underwear and a diamond ring,' Barnard said. 'So not short of a bob.' Evie raised an eyebrow.

'Interesting,' she said. 'We all do our best to look good when we're working, but I don't reckon there's many real silk cami-knickers round here.'

'So you've never seen her before?'

When Evie shook her head, Barnard leaned back in the chair and closed his eyes for a second. Evie looked at him, her eyes concerned.

'Have a rest here while I go and do a bit of shopping,' she said. 'And there's someone I know who might recognize your victim if you give me one of your pictures. I won't be long.'

Barnard nodded, too weary to argue, and closed his eyes, almost asleep before she was out of the door.

When Evie let herself back into her flat, she found Barnard

stretched out on the bed, face down and dead to the world. She put her shopping away and lay down beside him, putting one arm across his back in a gentle embrace. She did not sleep but synchronized her own breathing with his until, after what seemed like a long time, she became aware that he was beginning to wake. She rolled away, and he turned to face her.

'What happened?' he asked.

'Nothing happened,' Evie said. 'You went to sleep, that's all. You didn't want anything to happen, did you?'

'No,' Barnard said, more sharply than he intended. He sat up, put his feet down tentatively, and slid them into his shoes. 'I'm sorry, Evie. I shouldn't have come.'

'You're an old friend, Harry,' she said. 'Don't worry about it. You've been good to me sometimes when it mattered, but that's all we've ever been.'

'I need to get back to the nick,' he said, glancing at his watch, although the claim was not exactly true. So long as he reported back to the DCI before the end of the day he reckoned he was his own man, which is how he liked it. His job was more about hoovering up useful intelligence than making arrests.

'But I did find out something interesting,' Evie said. She picked up a piece of paper and a pencil and wrote something down.

'This is a friend of mine who used to work somewhere up West for a bit. She gave up because there were men there who wanted her to do things she didn't want to get involved with. Kinky stuff, she said. Nasty. She would be worth talking to, I reckon.'

Barnard put his coat on and put the piece of paper in his pocket.

'I'll do that,' he said. 'And thanks for everything.' He kissed her on the cheek and let himself out. Behind him, Evie dashed a tear from her eye before running a bath, dismissing thoughts of what she might have made of her life if things had been different. It was, she knew only too well, far too late for all that.

Barnard drove along Oxford Street and turned down Park Lane towards Victoria. There were procedures for venturing

out of his own patch, but this was too much of a long shot
to bother with procedure just now. He pulled up outside a
block of council flats close to the river, incongruously sited
cheek by jowl with much more pricey blocks sharing the
river frontage, able to enjoy views of the dirty brown water
rushing by as the tide ebbed and the more distant backdrop
of the Houses of Parliament. He parked on the Embankment
and made his way up the concrete stairs to the address that
Evie had given him and rang the bell. The door was opened
by a middle-aged woman in a flimsy silky dressing gown,
with elaborate make-up, smoking a Russian cigarette in a
holder.

'Did you make an appointment?' she asked sharply with a
trace of an accent that Barnard could not instantly identify.
He flashed his warrant card in her face.

'My friend Evie spoke to you on the phone, I think,' he
said. 'I'd just like a quick word, if you don't mind.' The woman
didn't look delighted to see him, but she waved him inside
and into a living room furnished in the latest Scandinavian
style. Barnard smiled. As a follower of fashion himself, he
knew that the place had not been done up on a shoestring.
There were things he would have coveted if he'd seen them
in Heal's and that he would have been pushed to afford even
on an income more ample than the Metropolitan Police
provided. Whatever this woman did for a living, she must be
doing well.

'A nice place you've got,' he said as he was waved into a
seat and the woman flounced into a revolving chair very like
his own.

'You are? She didn't give me your other name.'

'Alicia will do,' she said, smoothing her hair. 'If my clients
knew I was talking to the police they wouldn't be best pleased.'

'If you're doing what I think you're doing, I don't suppose
they would,' Barnard said. 'You're on your own, are you?'

'I'm not running a brothel, if that's what you mean,' she
said sharply. 'I know the law.'

He pulled the drawing of the murdered woman out of his
pocket and handed it to her.

'She was dumped from a car in Soho Square, strangled and

half-naked. Have you ever seen her before?' Alicia studied the
photograph carefully, then shook her head.

'None of the working girls in Soho know her?' she asked.

'None of the working girls know her. And what little she
was wearing was expensive, including a diamond ring.'

Alicia stubbed out her cigarette and pulled another from the
packet on the table. She offered one to Barnard but he shook
his head.

'I have never seen her before,' she said. 'She is a stranger.'
She lit up and drew the nicotine hungrily into her lungs. 'What
makes you think she is on the game?' she asked.

'Nothing definite,' Barnard said. 'Except where she was
found. And how she's been treated, chucked away like a bag
of rubbish. But that may be what we are intended to think. I
reckon she was taken to Soho Square from somewhere else.
It's secluded there at night under the trees, and she might not
have been found until morning. It was pure chance that the
car was spotted as she was being dumped. It drove off too
quickly for anyone to get a number but apparently it was a
big powerful car, not a clapped out jalopy.'

'But if you are here asking me questions you must think
she was a tart?'

'It's a possibility,' Barnard admitted. 'But she could just as
easily be someone's wife or girlfriend that was surplus to
requirements. Or someone who was picked up – maybe willingly, maybe not – and abused. But there's no one like her
been reported missing, so far at least. It could be consenting
sex that got out of hand. Or it could have been cold-blooded
murder by someone with a big car who thought he could get
away with it by dumping her in Soho – where every other
woman is a tart and when they come to grief those who should
be investigating think the worst and don't try very hard to find
the guilty men.' Alicia nodded and did not dispute Barnard's
analysis.

'Soho's not the only neighbourhood where prostitutes make
a living,' Alicia said. 'You must know that.'

'Evie said you'd bailed out of somewhere you didn't
like,' Barnard said carefully. He knew that if that were true
she would be very wary of repercussions.

'There are places where men are taken to meet women, or other men, sometimes even children,' she said. 'You must know about that sort of thing. These are very often important men, powerful men, who want their pleasures but very, very discreetly . . .'

'I've heard rumours,' Barnard interrupted. 'Is that the sort of place you got involved with?'

'The money was very good,' she said, glancing away. 'When my husband left me without a penny, I found this was the easiest way to make a decent living. But the games these people played were not good. I never heard of anyone being killed but certainly some of the women got hurt, and the children. The men thought they could put it all right with money, compensation they called it. They thought they had impunity – is that the right word? It was vile and it was wrong, and I got out as soon as I could. I rented this flat and now only deal with decent men.'

'But you say these were important men,' Barnard said. 'Did you recognize anyone, perhaps someone you'd seen in the papers?'

'No,' she said, her expression freezing. 'Even if I had, I wouldn't tell you. But most of them were careful to hide their identities. The light would be poor, or they were wearing very little, or sometimes a sort of fancy dress. One or two wore masks to hide their faces. It was very well organized and it was made clear that if I talked about it there would be repercussions. When I said I would not go back, I was told I would be paid a certain amount of money regularly but if I ever told anyone – anyone at all, never mind a detective – it would be the worse for me.' She shrugged wearily. 'I believed them. They were rich, they were well organized and they were involved in various forms of sexual brutality that could have put them in jail if ever revealed. Keeping me quiet would have been easy enough. I would have been just another dead tart who your colleagues would not have wasted much time on. I will never take that risk. So don't imagine that just because you've tracked me down I will talk to anyone about all this. Make what you can of what I've said, but I will never repeat it. I would like to see some of those men suffer, but not at my expense.'

Barnard knew that Alicia's assessment was realistic, and he could find no words to justify the Met or any other police force's entrenched indifference to the victims of the sex trade's punters.

It was not the first time he had seen senior officers less than serious about investigations like this, or been infuriated by the popular newspapers' prurience over the activities of 'good-time girls' and indifference to the risks they ran. The women themselves came to regard violence, and even death, as an occupational hazard. They looked out for each other when they could, because they knew from experience that no one else was looking out for them.

'I could tell you that we're not all like that,' he said. 'Though there's no reason why you should believe me.'

'No,' Alicia said. 'There isn't.'

'Do you know where all this was going on?' Barnard pressed her. 'You could give me an idea about that, surely?'

'Usually I was picked up by car. I never knew where I was taken except that it was to several different places. Going to one place, I was aware we crossed the river, though I don't know which bridge we went over. On other occasions I thought we were merely driving around and didn't actually go very far from here. But I have no idea where these places were. I was taken and brought back, well-paid but threatened that if I said anything out of turn I would find myself in deep trouble. There was only one place I went to more than once – a flat. We went up in a lift and it was quite luxurious. But there are hundreds of flats like that round here.' She shrugged.

'I've made a deal with these people that I'm happy with. It keeps the wolf from the door. I got out, and have found a better way to live where I am in control. I'm not going to put all that at risk.'

Barnard flung himself backwards in his chair in frustration and Alicia spun round in her chair to turn her back on him, gazing out of the window at a string of barges being towed down the Thames that were picking up speed on the ebbing tide.

'I'm sorry,' she said quietly. 'I can't help you any further.

I'd like you to go now, please, and don't come here again. It's too dangerous.'

Barnard walked slowly back down the stairs to his car but did not drive off straight away. He sat smoking and gazed out of the window at the passing cars and at occasional glimpses of the river traffic visible over the embankment wall. He had come to West London at Evie's suggestion and in some ways had discovered more than he wanted to know. Whoever was threatening Alicia had obviously been very effective. He did not think either he or the local CID officers could get any more out of her than he'd done. And it would be very difficult to persuade DCI Jackson that anything he'd been told was relevant to the murder inquiry in Soho he was supposed to be working on – one which had been launched more because the victim looked as though she might be more important than the usual Soho working girl than through any desire for justice for a prostitute. He had, he thought, driven himself into a dead end at the end of which there seemed to be a nameless pit of depravity – possibly reaching into the heart of the establishment – that he was unlikely to uncover without the DCI's support and help from Scotland Yard. And with his record, that would be the day.

When he got back to the nick, he didn't go straight inside. He crossed the road to a phone box, dialled the number of Kate O'Donnell's hotel, and put his coins into the slot when someone answered.

'Do you have a Miss O'Donnell booked in?' he asked. A voice with an accent he could barely understand seemed to say yes down the crackling line, so he ploughed on.

'Could you give her a message, please? Could you ask her to call Harry this evening at home?'

Again the answer seemed to be affirmative, so he thanked the anonymous voice and hung up. He had tried to cut Kate out of his life as that seemed to be what she wanted, but this morning's hangover looked like becoming permanent unless something was resolved between them sooner rather than later. He went up the stairs to the CID office weighed down with a feeling of impending doom.

FIVE

Kate had known better than to ask her mother where her brother Tom was living. But she'd carefully preserved the phone number he'd given her on a remote beach out towards the open sea when caught up in the murder case that had thrown Kate and Harry Barnard together in London. Although he might not still be at that address, at least it gave her a chance of tracking him down.

She checked in her purse to make sure she had enough change to make calls in a red phone box. The pay phone close to the reception desk seemed much too public for this particular encounter, if that was what it turned out to be. She knew how carefully Tom and his friends guarded their privacy, for good reason. Homosexual men might often be tolerated, if not ignored, in central London but up here different and more draconian rules prevailed, in a city where religion was still dominant and the police were sticklers for enforcing the law as and when the mood took them, in spite of promises of law reform.

To her relief and surprise, the number she had kept safe was answered by the familiar voice of her brother.

'Katie? Is that really you?' he asked, sounding tentative as well as surprised.

'It is, la,' she said. 'I'm here for a few days on a job and I thought I couldn't not see you. Mam says you don't often go home.'

'I never go home,' Tom said. 'Dad said that if he ever caught me there he'd thump me black-and-blue, if not worse.'

'You're joking!' Kate said, though she was sure he was not. She took a deep breath.

'Are you doing anything this evening?' she asked. 'Are you going out?'

'No,' he said. 'No I'm not. So why don't you meet me down at the Pier Head and I'll take you to a little pub I know which has Irish music? It would be really good to see you.'

Half an hour later she was standing enjoying a welcome breeze from the river, which ruffled her hair as she watched the ferry pull away from the landing stage to cross the Mersey to the Wirral. It was a sight she had seen hundreds of times, although there had never been enough money for trips to New Brighton to be more than a rare treat. But just standing there, with the towers of the three Graces, the harbourside buildings that had somehow survived the bombing and still dominated the waterfront, made her nostalgic for her child-hood, even though it had in many ways been less than perfect. Suddenly she felt more at home than she'd felt for a long time. After five minutes or so, Tom came quietly up behind her.

'Hello, sis,' he said. 'You haven't written me out of the script, then, like the rest of the family?' Kate turned and gave him a hug.

'Of course not,' she said. 'Why would I ever do that?'

'Lots of people do that,' Tom said.

'More fool them. How are you?' He shrugged, and when she scanned his face more closely she could see telltale lines of strain around his eyes and mouth.

'I'm OK,' he said. 'I've got a job in a little boutique-type shop at the back of Dale Street. A bit like the place where I worked in Carnaby Street. They sell all the trendy gear up here now. Are you going to the film premiere or something?'

'No, I'm not. I'm doing before and after pictures, showing how Liverpool's changed since the bombing.'

'Well you'll see all the dolly birds in their mini-skirts anyway. Having a fantastic time they are with their skirts up to their knickers, driving the Monsignors to distraction. You know the story. And the lads can't get enough of Beatles suits and mophead haircuts. Apparently, when they went to America there were those who loved them and those who thought they were all queer.' He laughed. 'It's certainly changed since we were kids. Anyway, come and have a drink and something to eat. It's great to see you.'

He took her to an unprepossessing pub in one of the back streets close to the docks and the Sailors' Home, where to her surprise a fiddler was playing an Irish reel in the lounge bar with a mainly male audience who seemed to be listening with rapt attention.

'Surprised?' he asked with a grin. 'They also do a good Irish stew, and Guinness to die for. We come here quite a lot for the music. It makes a change from the endless Merseybeat.'

'We?' she asked.

'He's called Kevin,' Tom said. 'You'd like him.' She nodded, but it was obvious he wasn't going to tell her anything more. After his experiences with hostile police in London that was not surprising, and when he asked her if she had a boyfriend she hesitated for a moment before telling him.

'I'm seeing Harry Barnard, the copper who helped us in London.' Seeing, she thought, was a neutral enough word to cover a multitude of sins that would have had Father Reilly foaming at the mouth about confession and contrition and the ever-open doors of hell. Tom was silent for a moment.

'Aren't they all bent?' he said at last, and she could see that he was trying to tame his hostility. 'They certainly seem to be up here.'

'Not as bent as some,' she said carefully. 'You wouldn't have survived without him.'

'Maybe not,' Tom said. 'So I should be grateful. But that's not to say I fancy a cop for a brother-in-law.' Kate laughed.

'It's certainly not got as serious as that,' she said, neglecting to admit that at the moment it did not seem to be going anywhere at all. 'Anyway, aren't they talking about changing the law?' she asked, keen to change the subject.

'Talking seems to be as far as it's got,' Tom said. 'The bizzies up here still enjoy careering round the queer pubs and public lavvies on the off-chance of finding someone to thump. There's no sign that you won't be dragged down the Bridewell and given a good going over at the very least, and a trip to court on top if they're feeling particularly vindictive.'

'So you have to be careful?'

'We're very, very careful,' Tom said. 'That's why I don't come into the city very often, except for going to and from work.'

'And is that why you don't go to see our mam?'

'You've no room to talk on that score,' Tom said, reddening

slightly. 'But in my case it's to keep out of da's way. I don't know exactly what he's up to these days, but he's got some very odd friends.' They made a space on their table for brimming plates of Irish stew, and Kate realized that she was hungry.

'I was going to ask about da,' she said. 'Mam said he's working in construction, which must be better than queuing up at the dock gates every morning hoping to be taken on.'

'The docks are changing, anyway,' Tom said. 'Less shipping, less work. He's probably sensible to move into something different. And he seems to be quite thick with Terry Jordan, who by all accounts is doing very well for himself as a builder, especially now Labour's running the council. Being Irish, he wouldn't have got much of a look in while the Tories were in charge, in spite of being a bit of a local hero.'

'Mam mentioned Terry Jordan,' Kate said. 'What's that all about?'

'I don't know all the details but dad told me about him once when he was in a good mood – drunk probably but not too drunk, you know how he was. This is years ago, before I fell right out of favour. Anyway, da started talking about the war and the bombing when we were babies, which he hardly ever did, so I kept very quiet and listened. He told me about Terry Jordan. He was a bit of a crook, apparently. A spiv. If you had the money and wanted nylons for the wife or something off-ration, then Terry could get it for you. So da said. Anyway, he must have been working in the docks, like da when he wasn't at sea, and the other thing Jordan did was sign up as a rescue man, probably to avoid being called up. Apparently the rescue men went round with the fire brigade, but they were the ones who went into bombed buildings to try to get people out that were trapped inside and crawled into the rubble through tiny holes and cracks. They were generally quite small-built, like da was of course, so I suppose this Terry Jordan was too. Like ferrets, da said. God, that must have been scary!'

'I've often thought that we were actually lucky to have been born when we were,' Kate said. 'We were too young to know what was going on. Think what it must have been like to know you could be blown to smithereens any moment.'

'True,' Tom said. 'Anyway, whatever his sins, Terry Jordan saved a lot of lives in the Blitz. And he got some sort of a medal after one bad night in 1941, dad said. There was a direct hit on a shelter packed full of people. A lot were killed outright, and there was a fire and no way out for the people who were still inside in the smoke. Jordan managed to squeeze in with a hose and got the fire under control, then he used sheer brute force to help move some of the slabs of concrete that were blocking the entrance. He is said to have rescued about a hundred people, and became a hero overnight.'

'So was da seriously a rescue man too?' Kate asked, finding it hard to slot her father into that mould.

'I don't think so, not officially anyway,' Tom said. 'As far back as I can remember, he's always been a drinker and a gambler. I wouldn't have thought he was hero material. He'd be more likely to have been into the black market during the war. I can remember he sometimes came home with unexpected treats for mam, and we had no idea where they came from. I've never really thought about it, but if he was mates with Terry Jordan that may be the answer. And I think sometimes he took a chance and went into damaged buildings with Mr Jordan.'

'And he's still in contact with Mr Jordan, is he?'

'Terry Jordan's gone from strength to strength since the war,' Tom said. 'From Scottie Road to some massive mansion he's built out by one of the golf courses beyond Formby. He probably realized that there would be lots of building work putting the city back together again and bought a small company to cash in. And he's certainly done that. He was on the up way, way back, probably buying his way into contracts one way or another. Certainly using cheap labour – when I was a teenager, there were a lot of Irish workers around, straight off the boats. And since Labour took over the Corporation his signs have been up all over the place. Demolition sites, housing estates, and some big contracts in the city centre even. He must be making a mint. And dad does seem to be working for him, so he must have sobered up a bit. You wouldn't want a drunk six stories up on scaffolding, would you?'

'Terry Jordan might be a good person for me to talk to if he's done a lot of reconstruction,' Kate said, mopping up the last of her gravy with a chunk of bread.

'He might talk to you I suppose,' Tom said. 'You could always tell him who your dad is,' Tom said with a laugh.

'Maybe that wouldn't be a good idea,' Kate said. 'Not unless I can check out what's really going on there. Maybe I'll ask mam.'

'That might be best,' Tom said. 'Now listen to these two.' He waved at the musicians, who silenced most of the noise in the bar as they launched into a plaintive lament. 'They're good.'

Kate O'Donnell's first port of call next morning was the *Liverpool Echo*, the local paper where she had arranged to meet the show-business specialist to get the latest details on the film premiere and perhaps pick his brains on the reconstruction of the city. She was waved into a chair in reception while they rang up to the newsroom to locate him. She had not slept well in the lumpy bed, was regretting a cooked breakfast swimming in grease, and had already decided that the Lancaster was a hotel she would never willingly stay at again. But weighing more heavily on her mind was the conversation she had had with Harry Barnard when she called him at home the previous evening.

Barnard had sounded distracted when he picked up the phone and she guessed he'd been hitting the bottle again.

'How are you?' she had asked. 'Are you OK?'

'As OK as I'll ever be with you up there and me down here, not knowing what the hell's going on,' he said.

Kate sighed. 'Is that why you never contacted me last week?' she asked, trying to disguise the resentment she suddenly felt.

'I thought you wanted to be left alone,' he said. 'You said you had a lot of work to do.'

'I did,' Kate said. 'But it would have been nice to hear from you. I thought you would have liked to come to the film premiere with me.'

'Is this how it's going to be?' he asked. 'You can drop out of my life whenever you feel like it, but I have to keep in touch.'

Kate had fallen silent for a moment. This was a Barnard that she had not encountered before and she felt as though she was being backed into a corner in a way she didn't like.

'You know why I'm here,' she said. 'It's important to me. I'm starting on the serious stuff now. I'll be busy, really busy, for the next few days but I'll try to call you when I get back to the hotel in the evenings. I thought you were busy too, with that murder case you're working on – the woman in Soho Square.'

'Not too busy to wonder how you are, what you're doing . . .' He stopped abruptly. 'I'm sorry to bother you,' he said, so faintly that she'd hardly been able to hear him. 'Maybe we'd just better get on with our jobs. We'll get other things sorted when you come back.' And before she'd been able to reply, he'd hung up.

She had gone up to her unwelcoming room and sat for a long time on the edge of the bed, wondering if she'd just heard a relationship crash in flames and asking herself if she cared. But she knew from the tears which began to flow that she did care very much indeed.

She shook herself back into the present as two men came down the stairs into the *Echo*'s reception area, evidently looking for her. The younger of the two, tall and skinny and bright-eyed, with his jacket slung over his shoulder, held out his hand and shook hers warmly.

'Hello,' he said. 'I'm Liam Minogue, the *Echo*'s Beatles correspondent. If you're planning to write about the Merseybeat, I'm the person most likely to be able to help you. And this is William Jones – Billy – who covers local politics and the Liverpool Corporation, for his sins, because you said you wanted to know about how Liverpool bounced back after the Blitz. That'll mean going back before my time.' His companion was an older man, in a severe grey suit, with his tie done up punctiliously in spite of the already growing heat of the morning. He was portly and florid-faced, his grey eyes distinctly wary above grey bags and veined cheeks. He shook her hand with much less enthusiasm than his younger colleague.

'Good morning,' he said. 'I'll help if I can.'

'I thought you might like a coffee or something,' Minogue said. 'It's probably easier to talk out of the office. The news-room's very noisy with the first edition coming up and the teleprinters hammering away. Is that all right?'

'Yes, of course,' Kate agreed, realizing that the building was shaking slightly with the vibration of the machinery, and she followed the two men out of the building to a café on the other side of the street.

'This is our home from home until the pubs open,' he said with a grin. 'Coffee or tea? And maybe a toasted teacake?'

'Just tea,' Kate said with a grin. 'I indulged in the full English breakfast and I've been thinking it was a mistake ever since.'

'Where are you staying?' Jones asked, and raised an eyebrow when she told him.

'Not one of the city's finest,' he said drily. 'You should ask for the Adelphi next time.' Kate laughed.

'I'm not sure my boss would go for that, la,' she said. 'I'm not working for one of those national newspapers where I'm told people can live on their expenses.'

'Fleet Street specializes in fairy tales, and I reckon that's just one of them,' Jones said dismissively, although Kate thought he looked pretty prosperous himself.

'I thought you were a Scouser when I spoke to you on the phone,' Minogue said, changing the subject quickly. 'How long have you been in London, then?'

'A couple of years. They seem to have got their heads round the fact that women can take pictures, so it looks like it will be permanent.'

'But you never get rid of the accent, they say,' Jones said, with a slightly supercilious tone in his voice. 'Or not without a great deal of effort, anyway.' An effort he must have thought worthwhile himself in view of his own upmarket vowels – more Home Counties than Cheshire, where some of the wealthier Liverpudlians took refuge away from the teeming city. Jones made a show of consulting his watch.

'Perhaps I can help you first,' he said. 'I've got to be at an important committee meeting at the town hall in half an hour, to meet the chairman of planning, and I'm not entirely sure what I can help you with. I know nothing at all about the Beatles or any of this pop-music hysteria. It's pictures you're looking for, I understand. Not really my area either, I'm afraid. I'm more of a words man myself.'

That's me put in my place, Kate thought wryly, but she knew she could not afford to antagonize Jones, as she needed his help.

'Well, you'll probably be relieved to hear that I'm not looking for pictures of the Beatles, or of their film. Those will be all over the papers after the premiere. What my boss wants is a photo feature about how Liverpool has recovered from the war. I'm too young to remember anything about the bombing, although I was born here, but I'm aware of all the rebuilding going on and how everything is still changing. What I'd like is permission to look through your archives and use pictures of what got bombed and what's been rebuilt. My own family's house near Scottie Road got badly damaged and we ended up in a brand new Corporation house in Anfield. My mam was delighted – she was quite made up about it.'

'So you want to show the 1940s and the 1960s?' Jones said. 'Well, there's certainly been a transformation. The Corporation has done a fantastic job getting the city back on its feet again. But there's still a long way to go. It remains to be seen if Mrs Braddock's Labour lot can keep up the pace.' So much for her own family's political allegiances, Kate thought, but she knew better than to get into an argument with Jones when she needed his help. Bessie Braddock, the campaigning city councillor and well-known socialist MP, was well able to look after herself in the rough and tumble of Liverpool and national politics without any help from her.

'Perhaps you could give me a lead on who to talk to, who was involved in the planning and all that, and which of the new buildings have replaced old ones?' she asked.

Jones glanced at his watch again, not disguising his impatience.

'The best thing you can do is talk to the picture editor and ask him if you can look at the archives. You'll find plenty of pictures there. And if you like, I'll ask what records they have at the town hall. Give Minogue here a phone number and I'll get the newsroom secretary to ring you. And if you want more information on specific schemes, you can ring me at work. There were some protests, of course, from people who would have liked the place rebuilt just the way it was before the war – Scotland Road's slums and all, I suppose. Personally, I think in some ways Hitler did us a favour by demolishing so much substandard property. It's incredible the way some people cling to the past.'

'But we lost more than just the slums, didn't we?' Kate said quietly. 'A lot of people died. I'm old enough to remember the wreckage that was left when the war ended, and I can just remember VE Day and the street party we had. After the war, the demolition seemed to carry on and on as if Hitler hadn't done enough. I remember a big fuss about the overhead railway coming down. And the trams going. People were very fond of the trams,' Kate said, recalling clattering journeys through the city when she tried to clamber on to the front upstairs seat beside her brother Tom, feeling as if they were on the prow of one of the ships that still docked within sight of the huddled, insanitary tenements of Vauxhall.

'The overhead railway was bankrupt,' Jones said flatly, 'and the trams were outdated. Nobody's kept trams except Blackpool and they had a special reason to keep them going along the seafront – for the visitors. The big fuss I remember best was over the Customs House, a nice enough building but hardly St Paul's Cathedral and very badly damaged. Some people – agitators of one sort and another, I suppose – wanted it rebuilt, but the Corporation decided against it. In many cases, rebuilding was going to cost more than new build. The builders did very well out of it all, of course. Even people like Terry Jordan, who came from nowhere and made a lot of money in ways I've never fully understood. Anyway, I must go. Give me a call if you need to check anything with me. I have good contacts in the planning department.' He drained his coffee and hurried out of the café. Kate raised an eyebrow.

'Sorry,' Liam Minogue said. 'I thought he'd be more helpful. But he's been fed up ever since the Labour Party got into power here for the first time. Suddenly all his cosy relation-ships with the Tories – Unionists to a man, of course – are

no use to him anymore and he has had to cosy up to the likes
of Bessie Braddock. You'll know what it's like, having lived
here. It's getting better, otherwise I wouldn't have the job I've
got on the *Echo*, but it's all still there under the surface.
Unionists and Freemasons have run this city for generations,
mainly because the Protestant working class has voted for
them. And now they're suddenly out in the cold. That's not
to say our lot are any more straightforward. They could
argue that it's our turn now, and it's fair enough if we're
getting the same sort of finagling wearing a green scarf
instead of an orange one. But the politics are pretty toxic. I
keep out of it myself.'

'Who is Terry Jordan? Mr Jones doesn't seem to like him.'

'He's a local builder who's done well out of the reconstruction, very well in fact for a left footer from Scotland Road.
Billy no doubt thinks he's greased a few palms on his way,
but that's not unusual when big contracts are on offer, regardless of the religion of the people involved. I'm sure it was
going on long before Bessie Braddock took over. There's
always an architect or a planner or a politician ready to help
a contract along. Billy could probably give you chapter and
verse – but he wouldn't, of course, if Unionists are involved.
On the other hand, if he could embarrass the present lot, or
Terry Jordan, I'm sure he would.'

'Sounds like a can of worms,' Kate said.

'Oh yes, it's that all right,' Minogue said.

Kate looked at Minogue over her cup. She could see that
he was older than she was: there were a few strands of grey
in his dark hair and a faint sadness in his blue eyes.

'Were you in the forces?' she asked, wondering if he had
seen more than anyone ought to see. But he shook his head.

'Not during the war, I'm not that ancient. Just national
service in the army afterwards. A pretty boring two years as
it turned out. A lot of people got sent to Germany, but I spent
most of my time in a desk job in Aldershot. I was quite relieved
actually. There were enough ruins here without going over
there to see even more.'

'Do you think your Mr Jones can get me into the city
archives?' she asked. 'I suppose I need to talk to some sort

of planner to match up pictures of the wreckage with the new developments.'

'Although he's not superfriendly, he'll do what he promises,' Minogue said. 'But watch his wandering hands. Are you sure I can't help you with anything to do with the Beatles' film? I could get you access to the four lads and Brian Epstein if you want.' Kate shook her head.

'No, that's not what I want. The whole world will be taking pictures of them. I've seen the film, anyway. My boss got tickets and I went with a friend last week in London.'

'What did you think of it?'

'I thought it was good, very funny. And there's lots of music if you like the Beatles.'

'All right, I'll take the chance to sit down and see it,' Minogue said. 'I wasn't going to bother. Come back to the office with me and I'll introduce you to the picture editor, then we can see where things go from there.'

SIX

During the rest of the day, Kate made better progress than she'd expected. The *Echo*'s picture files were full of images of the wartime devastation that she had been only barely aware of as a small child. For children of her generation, ruins were normal and the local boys and some of the girls used bomb sites as playgrounds and for the retrieval of shrapnel and other relics that were eagerly traded in the school yard. But seeing photos of acres and acres of the city reduced to rubble, taken from the air after the May blitz, brought tears to her eyes. The picture librarian was helpful and indicated which sites had been restored and in what way, and by lunchtime she had a list of suitable subjects for her own photographs. She hoped that with William Jones's help she would be able to glean more information on what had been permanently lost and what rebuilt and who had done the rebuilding.

She called at the town hall to try to locate Jones but was told he was still in the committee meeting, so she spent the rest of the afternoon roaming the city centre taking photographs of the buildings that she knew had been restored or rebuilt, such as the new Blacklers department store and Lewis's, which had been damaged and restored and by the time she was old enough to be a customer had gained an Epstein statue on its façade so explicitly male that it became the butt of ribald Liverpudlian wit. She ended with a walk along the dock road, bereft of its elevated railway and most of its historic warehouses but still a functioning port. It looked bleaker than she remembered, and she wondered how much longer it would survive. She finished at St Nicholas's, the city's sprawling parish church, which had been almost destroyed by incendiary bombs during the war and later rebuilt. The *Echo* librarian had given her a print of the ruin in 1941 and she took several views of the modern rebuilding and the distinctive tower and spire, which had survived the flames.

Feeling more than a little ambivalent about the regeneration which she had taken very little notice of as she grew up, she made her way back towards the city centre and stopped at the *Echo* offices to see whether Jones was back there. A phone call from reception brought him downstairs from the newsroom, pulling his jacket on over his obviously sweaty shirt. 'Come over the road to the Schooner and have a quick drink,' he said brusquely. 'I'm parched. And I've one or two contacts you can talk to if it will help. Minogue says he'll join us in ten minutes.'

Feeling slightly surprised by Jones's change of tone, Kate followed him across the road and into the lounge bar of the pub, where Jones was greeted by two colleagues huddled round a table in a corner so littered with used glasses that they must have been there some time. Jones pulled out a chair for Kate and with a raised eyebrow took her order for a half of shandy before going to the bar.

'You must be the lady photographer,' one of the men at the table offered. 'How did you get into that, then? You must be the only one in the country, aren't you?'

'I trained here at the College of Art,' Kate replied, 'but I had to move to London for a job. You lot at the *Echo* wouldn't have me. And don't say it's not a suitable job for a woman. I've heard all that before and the job suits me just fine.'

'What did you say you were called?'

'Kate O'Donnell,' she said crisply, knowing that she was being slotted automatically into one of the still antagonistic Scouse tribes. 'I was at college with John Lennon, as it goes, but he's made rather more of an impression down south than I have. So far.' They laughed and made space for William Jones, who delivered Kate her shandy with an ironic bow and squeezed on to a stool next to her.

'I can't stop, but I made some notes for you after the planning meeting. These are the details of the major redevelopments there've been since the end of the war – quite a number, as you can imagine having lived here back then – and what the new buildings replaced. Of course a lot of the housing development was on green fields, outside the city limits.'

'Does it tell me who the builders were? I'm thinking they

may have kept blueprints of their plans. Could make good illustrations for my feature.'

'Down here at the bottom of this page,' Jones said. Kate skimmed the list quickly.

'What about Terry Jordan's company?' she asked, not finding the name. Jones glanced round the table and met raised eyebrows. It was obviously a question that surprised the three men.

'He started off quite small,' Jones said. 'He got a few of the big contracts soon after the war and some of us wondered how he'd done that. We reckoned it must have been on the strength of being some sort of hero. But he didn't really take off until his political friends took over the town hall. Funny that. He's landed a few really big contracts since, and I hear he's got contacts in London too. The company is called Macdonald-Jordan Construction. He bought into it and runs it as his own now but has kept the original name. He's looking to get into the development of more new towns. There'll be a lot of money in that. Quite apart from the bomb damage, the Corporation is keen to move people out of the slum housing in the city. There's still plenty of that about. Tenements, outside lavvies, you name it. It's a massive job. And money's tight.'

Kate nodded. She could still remember the worst of it but she was not going to share that with this group who, she guessed, were part of the ascendancy that had left the Irish immigrants to rot around Scotland Road for decades before the war. Just glancing through Jones's lists, she could see that the Corporation had preferred to restore the city centre and build new roads rather than rehouse all the poor. She wondered if Mrs Braddock would do better, but these men would not give her an objective view on that.

'Thanks for all this,' she said to Jones, who was downing his pint. 'It's very helpful.' She saw Liam Minogue pushing his way through the swing doors and glancing round the bar and raised her hand in greeting as Jones got up and bade everyone goodnight. Her two contacts passed each other without any obvious greeting, which confirmed her impression that there was no love lost between them. She wondered why

Jones had bothered to help her, and whether he had an ulterior motive.

Minogue got himself a drink at the bar and slid into the seat Jones had just vacated.

'I can report that the Beatles have arrived safely,' he announced with a mock flourish.

'The Adelphi, I suppose?' a colleague asked.

'More than my life's worth to confirm or deny,' Minogue said with a grin. 'Security's tighter than a duck's arse. And the police say they're on a war footing tomorrow. There's already a pack of girls outside the Odeon. Presumably they're planning to stay there all night. Little idiots.'

'If a daughter of mine carried on like that I'd tan her backside,' one of Minogue's colleagues commented, getting up to leave. 'The best thing that could happen is for there to be a massive thunderstorm tomorrow. That would cool their ardour and send them home to bed.' His colleague joined in the exodus, leaving Kate and Liam Minogue to spread themselves more comfortably.

'Haven't you got a wife to go home to?' Kate asked. Minogue shook his head and Kate was aware again of the shadow behind his eyes.

'I did have,' he said. 'But we got divorced. She has custody of our little girl, so I don't see her very often either. You can imagine how all that went down with the family and the parish priest. It was a mixed marriage, so she had no problem with divorce. And on my side they all shook their heads and said we told you so. So, sorry, maybe you think they're right? I just assumed . . .'

'You assumed right. One of the great things about London is that no one cares what religion you are, or even if you have a religion. And there are no parish priests breathing down your neck, telling you what you can and can't do.'

'Are you married?' he asked. Kate shook her head. 'I've a boyfriend. Though that's a bit on and off at the moment.'

'Come and have a meal with me, then,' Minogue said. Kate looked at him and liked what she saw.

'Thanks, it'll be better than a stuffy hotel room for the evening,' she said. They finished their drinks and Minogue led her back out, holding the door open for her.

'Do you like Chinese food?' he asked. She nodded.

'OK, we'll go to the Pekin. It's supposed to be the best Chinese in town, though I can't say I've had much to compare it with. There're a couple of Indian restaurants opened recently, though I haven't tried them. Someone told me the food was very spicy.'

'I've been to the Pekin before,' Kate said. 'Our tutor took some of us there after we'd finished our assessments at college.'

'Right then,' Minogue said. 'Let's do it.'

'I need to go back to the hotel first to drop my gear off and get changed.' And make a phone call, she thought with a twinge of guilt which she pretended had not happened. But when she dialled Barnard's number there was no reply, and telling herself that she would try again later she went downstairs to meet Minogue in the lobby, fresh in a crisp summer dress, and gave him a dazzling smile.

'Let's go,' she said.

Kate woke early the next morning and lay in her narrow bed gazing at the cracks in the ceiling, reluctant to get up so soon and confused by her own emotions. She'd enjoyed the meal with Liam Minogue, but as the evening went on and it became more obvious that his interest in her was far more than just professional she became increasingly uneasy.

When they left the restaurant he'd put an arm round her waist, but after a moment she pulled away.

'I need to go back to the hotel now,' she told him. 'I need to make a phone call. And I have to be up early tomorrow.'

'I thought maybe we could have a nightcap at my place,' he said. 'I'll see you safely back later.'

'Now would be better,' she replied. 'I really enjoyed our night out, Liam, but that's all it is. I told you, I've a boyfriend in London.'

'An on-and-off boyfriend you said.' He glanced at her quizzically.

'And I'd rather he was on than off,' Kate said, surprising herself with her certainty. 'I'm sorry, Liam.'

He had given up then and walked her back to her hotel, leaving her with a chaste kiss on the cheek. When she tried

Barnard's number again from the phone in the lobby and got no reply she went up to her room feeling even more confused than she had before.

Next morning, after eating a more modest breakfast than she had the previous day, she ventured out into bright sunshine with that hint of water in the breeze that she remembered so well. This was the day of the film premiere and as she walked towards the town centre Kate avoided London Road and the Odeon, where the film was to be shown. But there were already crowds of people heading in that direction, hoping to find themselves a vantage point. It was not, she realized, a good day to be taking pictures of Liverpool's landmark buildings. The Beatles had, it seemed, claimed the city centre as their own.

She decided instead to go home and see if she could locate her father who, she thought, if he really was working for Terry Jordan would be able to tell her where the company was currently working and what it had recently completed. She took the bus out to Anfield and walked, past Liverpool FC's football ground, to the small development of new Corporation houses that had replaced some Victorian terraces demolished by a stray bomb. Her mother opened the door and looked surprised to see her.

'You again, la?' she said. 'Your sisters have gone to work already, if that's who you wanted to see.'

'No, I was wondering if you knew where da was working,' Kate said. 'I want to pick his brains about Terry Jordan and his building firm. Terry Jordan must have been involved in some of the reconstruction after the war, and my contact on the *Echo* says he's still doing well.' Her mother shrugged.

'Last I heard Frankie was working for Jordan on a site for new flats up near the hospital. If you want to see him, you might catch him there. If not, I think they finish about four o'clock. He'll then head for the pub, no doubt. Or the betting shop. He comes home occasionally, but he doesn't generally stop long.'

Kate sighed. 'It doesn't sound as if he's changed much,' she said. 'I'll see if I can track him down. If not, I'm sure there are other ways I can find Mr Jordan. If he's running a big company now, he'll have offices I expect.'

'Will you not stop for a cup of tea?' Bridie asked, making Kate feel guilty. Her mother had struggled all her life, she thought, and tried to do her best for her four children through the hardest of times with little or no support from Frankie. And when push came to shove and Kate, the only one to make it to grammar school, had insisted that she wanted to go to college, Bridie had scrimped and saved to make that possible.

'Put the kettle on, mam,' she said. 'I'm not in that much of a hurry.'

She took a bus back into the city centre then made her way towards the hospital, avoiding London Road where crowds were milling around the Odeon in increasing numbers. To one side of the hospital buildings, she eventually located a building site displaying Macdonald-Jordan Construction's name and a picture of a sunlit block of flats that was obviously being built on the site, with scaffolding up to what she guessed was about sixth-floor level. It looked normal enough apart from a crowd of workers outside instead of inside the perimeter fence, milling around aimlessly and most of them smoking and talking, if at all, in subdued tones. Suddenly the atmosphere changed as a police car arrived, closely followed by an ambulance, and the crowd gave a muted groan.

'What's happened?' she asked one of the men on the edge of the crowd.

'Accident,' he said. 'Some beggar's come down under a pile of scaffolding. Nasty. They're trying to get him out. The fire brigade are round the back.' Almost instinctively Kate got her camera out and wriggled her way to the front of the crowd to take some shots. A couple of uniformed police and two ambulance men carrying a stretcher pushed their way through to the gate and disappeared behind the skeleton of the building. Concentrating on her viewfinder, Kate was surprised to be seized in a tight grip as the crowd shifted. She pulled away and turned round to find her father beside her, with a far from friendly look on his face.

'What are you effing doing here?' he asked, his eyes angry

in a way which reminded Kate only too clearly of the erratic temper that had blighted her childhood. 'Your mam told me you were about because of the Beatles' film, so what are you doing up here? Shouldn't you be at the Odeon with all those effing hysterical lasses?'

'Mam told me this was where you were working,' Kate said. 'It's not the Beatles' film I'm interested in, it's how the city put itself together again after the Blitz. Everyone says Terry Jordan built his business on that. I thought you could maybe help me track down some of the new buildings that I want to photograph and tell me something about Terry Jordan. He sounds an interesting character.' Frank O'Donnell drew a sharp breath and Kate realized that, although in his work overalls and heavy boots he looked the part of a builder, his weathered face was hollow-cheeked and his eyes not just bloodshot but faintly yellow. He looked sick and far older than his years, but she knew him too well to comment on that. If she wanted his help, she would have to tread very carefully.

'Why do you want to know about Terry specially?' he asked. 'This is one of his sites – Macdonald-Jordan Construction – and it'll be just my luck to get the blame for this mess, for some toerag scaffolder who didn't do his job properly. So I don't think I want one of the family in on the act.'

'Macdonald-Jordan Construction,' Kate said. 'Yes, someone told me that. I'd been trying to find a company in Jordan's name with no luck at all. I didn't think from what people have told me about him he'd be as modest as that.'

'He took over Macdonald-Jordan after the war, though I think the old boy is still alive somewhere,' Frank said. 'I've no idea why he never changed the name. Probably didn't want to sound too Irish, especially back in the forties and fifties with the Unionists in charge. You know what it's like. But there's no doubt who the boss is now.'

'I only want to know which of the buildings they were responsible for putting up. Mam must have told you what I'm doing.' Frank hesitated for a moment and Kate wondered just how close he was to her mother in spite of her complaints.

'Terry's done well for himself,' Frank said eventually. 'He's a canny operator.'

'On which side of the law?' Kate asked and her father looked at her sharply.

'That's asking,' he said. 'He's never been an altar boy, hasn't Terry. But I reckon he's built up this business legit, as far as that goes in the building trade. Anyway, he's never been caught. And now I need to talk to him. He won't thank me if I don't let him know what's happened before the bizzies come knocking on his door.'

'Why would the police be so involved?' Kate asked. 'I thought it was an accident.'

'A fatal effing accident as far as I could see, la. The lad broke his neck, I reckon. There'll be questions asked if I'm right, by the police among the rest.' There was suddenly shouting from behind them, where the builders were congregated, close to the fence. Kate and her father turned to see the ambulance crew carrying their stretcher off the site – this time with a body completely covered by a blanket, which told its own story.

'Holy Mother of God!' Frank muttered. 'Come down to the pub with me, girl. You'll only attract attention if you stay here and you don't want to attract attention from the bizzies, you should know that. I can use the phone in the pub. Let the boss know what's going on.'

'Covering your back by the sound of it,' Kate said sceptically, although she followed him through the dispersing crowd, which was waiting for the ambulance to pull away. It did not switch on its siren or blue lights which, Kate thought, said all that needed to say about the fate of its passenger. Leading her down the main road towards the city centre, Frank O'Donnell dodged into the first pub with an open door they came to and looked around for a public phone.

'Get me a small whiskey,' he said. 'Jamesons if they've got it.' He turned towards the pay phone before looking over his shoulder. 'And something for yourself, la,' he added by way of an afterthought. The pub had obviously only just opened and smelled unpleasantly, of disinfectant as much as anything else, but she guessed that Frank needed a drink more than she did so she braved the avid eyes of the barman, who was obviously not used to serving a woman and followed every move she made as she paid and picked up the glasses and carried them to one of the tables and waited for Frankie to finish his call. She could not hear what her father was muttering into the receiver, but the conversation was not long and he slammed the receiver down with some force when it ended. He joined her and picked up his drink and sank half of it in a mouthful.

'They already had the feckin' bizzies round at the office,' he said. 'I knew they would. They've closed off the site for their investigation. Could be closed for days. And the manager wants me to go to the office straight away so they can get my side of the story straight.'

'Surely it was a straightforward accident if the scaffolding collapsed?' Kate asked.

'Nothing's straightforward on a building site,' her father said. 'Terry Jordan takes feckin' labourers straight off the Dublin boat as often as not. You're never sure if they can even read or write. Feckin' tinkers most of them. But Terry's not there. He's in London, apparently, looking for contracts, so they're all running around like headless chickens. The trouble with a man like Terry is that he likes to take all the decisions himself, so when anything goes wrong no one knows what to do.' He looked at his empty glass.

'I'll have another of these before I go and talk to the office.' Kate sat and watched him as he downed his second whiskey more slowly.

'How did you come to meet Terry Jordan?' she asked. She knew the gist of it but not the detail, and wondered how close the two men had been back then. Her father smiled, which ironed the tension out of his face for a moment. But it did not last.

'It was during the war,' he said. 'I knew of him. Most people down Scottie Road did. If you wanted something a bit special and had the money, Terry could usually find it for you.'

'Black market?' Kate asked.

'A little bit of this and that off the boats or from the farms out in the country,' her father said. 'Or maybe he was nicking stuff. I wouldn't know about that. I only really got to know him when he volunteered as a rescue man. They were the real heroes of the blitz and don't let anyone tell you different. You can't imagine the places we crawled into if there was anyone alive under the wreckage. Terry's quite small, makes up for it in energy though, and he could wriggle into cracks in the rubble that hefty firemen couldn't tackle. There was fire, smoke, gas escaping and electric sparks flying. It was a miracle he survived and a miracle we got people out alive.'

'You said we?' Kate said.

'Well, only on and off,' her father said. 'I helped out now and then. But Terry was magic. There was nothing he wouldn't do, especially around Scottie road. He got a medal, you know, for going into a shelter that got a direct hit and finding a way out for the people trapped inside. Or they offered him a medal, anyway. I never heard whether he went up to London to collect it or not.'

'Why wouldn't he?' Kate asked, surprised.

'Oh well, he was a bit hardline back then. Old-style republican. Didn't go much for British royalty and such.' Frank O'Donnell glanced round the empty bar as if the walls might have ears.

'I thought the IRA was dead and buried,' Kate said. Frank put a finger to his lips and patted her on the arm.

'Never mind,' he said. 'You're right, it's ancient history and I never said a feckin' word.' He drained the last of the whiskey and got to his feet.

'Come on,' he said. 'You can ask at the office whether they mind you taking snaps of Terry's monuments. I can't see why they would. They should be pleased.'

They walked into the city centre in silence, avoiding the thickening crowds of Beatles fans, and Frank O'Donnell led her to a modern office block close to the docks. There was a police car parked outside and he groaned.

'They'll want to feckin' talk to me,' he said. 'I should have waited until the coast was clear of them beggars.'

'Were you supposed to be in charge?' Kate asked.

'I was supposed to be the feckin' foreman,' he admitted. 'The usual whacker's off sick. But if they want to know who was working on the site, I haven't had a clue most of the time. Lads come and go. I didn't even know the name of the lad who fell till his mates told me. From Limerick, they said.

Another tinker, I guess. Thick as two short ones. What a feckin' mess.' Kate was surprised at how anxious her father suddenly seemed to be.

'Don't they have a union?' she asked.

'Not on Terry Jordan's sites they don't,' her father said. He glanced at the police car angrily.

'I'll tell you something for nothing,' he said. 'You'll be wasting your time here today. They won't want anyone with a camera mooching around their sites after this. They'll batten down the hatches till Terry comes back. You'll get nothing out of anyone in the office. They're scared silly of the boss.'

'And what about you?' Kate asked.

'Oh, if he wants to lay the blame on me, that's what he'll do. He'll tell the police it's my fault if it suits him. He's done very well for himself has Terry and he won't let anything interfere with that.'

SEVEN

Detective Sergeant Harry Barnard strolled through Soho feeling completely at odds with the world. He had spent the previous evening drinking steadily in the bars and clubs, which were now firmly closed, and had gained a serious hangover that needed a hair of the dog, not easily available at ten in the morning. He had no doubt that if he threw his weight about he could get what he wanted in spite of the licensing laws, but he did not feel fit enough for that. At least, he thought through the fog in his brain, he had rejected the offers of hospitality made by some of the women he'd encountered last night. Which had boosted his morale slightly but done nothing to resolve the problem of Kate's absence. She had left a void he could barely cope with. He was not at all sure how he got back to Highgate, except that he'd woke alone in his own bed and his car was untidily parked outside.

To his surprise he felt a hand on his arm, and spun round close to panic only to find Evie Renton behind him. Evidently off duty at this time in the morning, she was wrapped in a scruffy mac, with no make-up and her hair unkempt.

'You're very jumpy,' she said. 'And you don't look any better than last time I saw you. Worse in fact. Do you want to come in for a coffee? I promise I won't make a pass, though to be honest you don't look as if you're up for it today.'

'What are you?' he asked, managing a faint smile. 'Some sort of guardian angel?'

'I get called a lot of things, but not usually an angel,' she said.

'Go on then,' Barnard said. 'A quick coffee won't hurt before I go and talk to the DCI. That's not something I'm looking forward to.' He had not been able to see DCI Jackson the day before because Jackson had been at the Yard attending meetings, so he had not yet had an opportunity to report on his conversation with Alicia. He was not unhappy to have some extra time to think about what she'd told him, a mixture of the specific and the vague which he reckoned she'd severely edited anyway. And he knew she would not be best pleased if what she'd told him led to more visits from the police. She'd said she was being paid to keep quiet, and if it became obvious that she had attracted police attention the threats might be followed up. Moreover, he'd been well off his own turf, effectively freelancing in Pimlico, and this would not please Jackson or the local nick.

He followed Evie back to the narrow nineteenth-century building where she had her flat, followed her slowly up the narrow staircase and slumped in an armchair until she plied him with strong coffee.

'You look dreadful,' Evie said as she handed him a mug. 'Is she that important, this girl of yours? It's not like you, is it, getting so involved?'

'She's that important,' he said quietly. 'I didn't realize until she went away.'

'Where's she gone? Liverpool did you say? It's not the end of the world, is it? Why don't you go up there and catch up with her over the weekend? You look as if you need some fresh air. It's seaside, isn't it? Sun, sand and fish and chips, like Southend.'

Barnard smiled.

'Not exactly,' he said. 'More docks and big ships, I think. Bolshie beggars always going on strike.'

'Like the East End, then. You'll feel at home up there.' Evie, he thought, in spite of the life she led, had a capacity for optimism that never failed to amaze him.

'I'll think about it,' he said.

'I asked around again about what this woman found dead in Soho Square might have got involved in,' she said. 'A lot of people seemed to have heard rumours about important people looking for a bit on the side, and not just straight sex either. Kinky stuff. But no one seems to know anything definite or who's involved. It's not round here. It's classier than that – Kensington, Knightsbridge, Westminster – and you can be sure that if the nobs are involved they'll move heaven and earth to keep it quiet. Didn't Alicia help you out? Did you go and see her?'

'I did, but she won't say anything on the record. Said nothing very specific at all, in fact. She's got herself untangled from whatever's going on, but she's still much too scared to talk.'

'It might be best to just leave it alone, if you ask me,' Evie said. 'Since Profumo and the scandal and court cases they had last year they'll be even more determined to keep things under wraps, won't they, the nobs and politicians? They won't want another Christine Keeler or Mandy Rice-Davies coming out of the woodwork to cause an embarrassing fuss. You'd be well out of your depth.'

'I need to tell my boss what I've sussed out, if anything,' Barnard said. 'He'll make the decisions on what to do next. As you say, it's probably well out of my league. All we're really concerned with is finding out who this dead woman is. And I'm getting nowhere with that.'

'Maybe just as well,' Evie said soberly. 'Sounds like a can of worms to me. If she'd been a regular on the game round here someone would know about it, and nobody seems to. So go and make up with your girlfriend, why don't you? You've obviously got it bad. Go and say sorry, for God's sake, whatever it's all about, and put a smile back on your face.' Barnard shrugged.

'Maybe,' he said putting his mug down. 'I'm sure you're right.'

Feeling marginally more alert, Barnard finished his stroll around Soho and made his way across Regent Street to the nick. This time he was able to see the DCI straight away. He found the dour Scot with chilly eyes sitting at his desk in his usual pose, his hands steepled in front of him almost as if in prayer.

'Did you find anyone who recognized the dead woman?' Jackson asked sharply.

'No, guv. No one knew her. If she was on the game, it wasn't in Soho. But a few of the toms gave me the same story. They said there were things going on up West that they'd heard about, and maybe she was working there. One of them sent me to see a friend of hers who she thought might recognize the victim. A woman called Alicia – wouldn't give me another name, though I expect it wouldn't be difficult to find – who

told me she'd bailed out of some sort of set-up that catered
for men with kinky tastes. She didn't like what they were
doing, so she got out. She said she never knew where she was
being taken, usually by car, and money seemed to be no object.
And when she said she wanted no more of it, she was paid
to keep quiet and there were a few threats about what would
happen if she didn't. I reckon there might be some connection
with our dead woman. That ring of hers must be worth a lot
of money and she suffered serious damage at someone's hands,
so there might be a link.'

Jackson's expression darkened as Barnard went on.

'Where did you see this woman?' he asked.

'She's got a flat on the Embankment, near Victoria. She was
obviously a call girl and doing pretty well out of it. More
Christine Keeler than street girl. But I didn't necessarily believe
her. She might be covering her own back.'

'And did you have the sense to contact the local CID before
going questioning someone down there? Didn't it occur to you
that they might know all about her anyway?'

'I didn't think it was worth bothering them unless I found
something significant,' Barnard said, knowing that this would
not be viewed as sufficient reason for disregarding protocol.
Jackson drummed his fingers on the desk, which was a sign
that he was very unhappy indeed.

'And did you find something significant? Did she recognize
our victim? Did she know who she was?'

'No, she didn't. But she told me enough about what she'd
got involved in to think our victim might have got mixed up
in that sort of thing, too. Important men looking for thrills –
violent thrills in some cases – and not too bothered about
going too far. Our unknown victim was not just strangled, she
was tortured. Whoever she was and whatever she did, no one
deserves to be treated like that. And how are we to know that
it might not happen again? Men can get a taste for that sort
of thing and you know how it can escalate.'

'You'd think important men with reputations to protect
would take extreme care after what happened to Mr Profumo
and his friends,' Jackson said with obvious distaste. 'You've
put me in a difficult situation, Sergeant. I will have to talk to

CID down there and tell them what you've been up to. And I'll have to take it to the Yard. They aren't going to think your unsanctioned initiative is very helpful. For all we know, they're already looking into these so-called rumours.'

'I suppose so, sir,' Barnard conceded, though he didn't really believe it. The mess the disgraced minister Profumo had got into was more to do with being economical with the truth in the House of Commons than with illicit sex. And although the subsequent prosecutions had provided much entertainment for the nation, there had been very little in the way of an obvious clean-up in high places. The rumours continued, and if anything had become more disturbing.

'Well, you can expect some questions about this woman from the local CID, or even from the Yard,' Jackson said sourly. 'And, Sergeant, if you want to take that sort of initiative in future, please consult me first. Or there may be repercussions.'

'Sir,' Barnard said, feeling he had maybe got off lightly. For all Jackson's faults as a boss, he had always felt that when push came to shove the DCI might be on his side in wanting to mitigate – if only on God's behalf – the harm the sex trade did to so many people. But he did not doubt that there would be pressure from the top to avoid another major scandal swirling around the corridors of power. If it was possible to dismiss the dead woman as just another unlucky tom who'd misjudged her john, there might well be satisfaction in high places. There might be very little he could do to prevent that, but he could at least try.

As he was about to leave the DCI's office, he turned back for a moment.

'I'm going to be away this weekend,' he said. 'I'm going up north to see my girlfriend.'

Jackson nodded abstractedly, about to pick up his phone extension, no doubt already mentally launching damage limitation with the Yard. Barnard shut the door behind himself with rather more force than was strictly necessary.

Barnard went home early and threw some clothes into a holdall. He rang the number of Kate's hotel, starting at about five and keeping on trying until eight, getting more and more frustrated as reception kept on informing him that Miss O'Donnell had not yet returned for the night. He guessed that as this was the day of the film premiere in Liverpool she might be busy, but if she had not been asked by the agency to take pictures of the Beatles he hoped he'd catch her in time to drive to Liverpool to see her that evening. That now looked an increasingly remote possibility.

At half past ten the hotel reception desk finally told him Kate had just come in and passed the call over to her. Immediately he could tell that something was wrong.

'What's going on, babe?' he asked. 'I've been trying to get hold of you all evening.'

'Harry,' she said and the relief in her voice was obvious. 'I've had a terrible day.'

'Tell me,' he said. 'I was thinking of coming up to see you this weekend. I could even bring you back to London if you're likely to finish by Sunday. What do you think?'

'Yes, maybe,' she said. 'That would be good.'

'You're sure?' Barnard asked.

'It's been horrendous here today. First there was an accident on a building site where my da was working. Someone was killed. I didn't see it, but I saw the ambulance crew take the body away. And my da was supposed to be in charge.'

'Your father? I thought you didn't see him and didn't get on with him. What were you doing going to see him at work?'

'He works for one of the contractors who've have been rebuilding the city. You've no idea how it's changed, even since I came down to London. I needed to make contact with Terry Jordan, his boss, to know which contracts were his. I wanted to find out where the offices were, as I couldn't find them in the phone book. I only wanted to ask him that, but it turned out to be the worst possible moment. My father seemed quite scared of what would happen next.

'Then I managed to get a bit of work done for Ken. And later I thought I'd go and have a look at the Beatles going in for their film premiere. They'd pulled out all the stops for them, a reception at the town hall after, loads of guests from all over – Cilla Black, Rita Tushingham, some of the other

bands. Hollywood on the Mersey it was, la, all dead glam-
orous, better than the royal variety performance in London.
But all these people were following the cars down Dale
Street, thousands of them, and then the whole thing got out
of hand and people were getting hurt in the excitement. It
was awful. Little girls were being pulled out of the crush,
some of them needed ambulances, and I nearly got stuck in
the crowd myself at one point. I could hardly breathe.'

'Whoa, whoa!' Barnard said. 'You're all right? You're not
hurt?'

'No, not hurt, not really,' Kate whispered. 'Just shocked, I
suppose. The place went a bit mad for a while. I took some
pictures in case Ken could use them. You never know.'

'Right, that's it then. I'm coming up. There's no point setting
off now. I don't suppose your hotel lets in visitors after
midnight, do they?'

'I very much doubt they let in visitors at all,' Kate said
laughing. 'Liverpool may have the Merseybeat, but they're
still a whole lot more uptight than swinging London. The
Churches make sure of that whenever they can. You hardly
ever see a priest in London but here they're everywhere – all
over the place, especially round here, with the new cathedral
going up just up the hill from where I'm staying.'

'So I'll set off early and be with you in time for breakfast.
How's that?'

'That would be good,' she said, and Barnard could hear that
she was almost in tears.

'Come on Katie, this is not like you,' he said. 'Go to bed,
get some sleep, it will all look better in the morning. I'll be
there, I promise.'

Barnard drove out of London at five in the morning and made
good time up the M1 as far as Rugby, where it ended. He
was then at the mercy of increasingly busy main roads for
the remainder of the journey. He drove into Liverpool after
nine and, having with some difficulty located the Lancaster
Hotel on Brownlow Hill, parked the car outside. He found
Kate in the lobby, looking pale although less anxious than he
expected.

'They stopped serving breakfast at nine,' she said. 'We'll have to go somewhere else.'

'That's not a problem is it?' he said. 'We could go to the Adelphi maybe.' Kate laughed.

'I don't think I'm quite ready for that yet,' she said. 'Even if we could get through the door with all the people who'll be staying there after yesterday. We could go to the café in Lewis's, that's just over the road and they'll probably do you a decent cup of coffee.'

'I could do with that,' he said. 'That was a bloody awful drive once the motorway ended. It's supposed to be going to Yorkshire eventually, but God knows how long that will take to build.'

Barnard stood outside the hotel for a moment looking around.

'What's that thing that looks like a spaceship up there?' He said pointing up the hill to where great spars were forming a circular pyramid shape. Kate laughed.

'That's the new Catholic cathedral,' she said. 'Paddy's Wigwam the Proddies call it, with no respect. Mind you their place is taking forever to finish and is dead traditional. I reckon we'll be done first and I like it better.' They drove down the hill into the city centre and parked in a side street close to Lewis's department store.

'That's pretty full-on,' Barnard said mildly as he surveyed the finer points of the Epstein statue on its frontage. 'You can't be as puritanical as all that in Liverpool if that got public approval. I don't think Harrods would go for it.'

'I think they just wanted something to rival Coventry,' Kate said with a grin. 'I remember the art students at college were very impressed, especially the lads.'

'Yes, I can see they would be,' Barnard said drily. 'Come on then, I'm starving. Let's see what sort of a late breakfast they can manage.' When Barnard had demolished a full English and they were both sipping coffee that did not quite live up to their expectations, Barnard lit a cigarette and leaned back in his chair.

'So what's going on, honey?' he asked. 'You sounded as if you were in a panic last night over not very much. Tell me more.' Kate sighed.

'I was a bit shocked by what happened in Dale Street,' she said.

'But there's more to it than that, isn't there?' Barnard persisted.

'I don't know,' she said. 'All my family are telling me different stories about what my father's getting up to with this builder Terry Jordan. I couldn't track down a Jordan in the building trade, but it turned out the company has another name. He bought into it but didn't change the name, and now it seems to be building on every street corner. My da is definitely scared of Terry Jordan. That was obvious after the accident at the building site. He reckoned he would get the blame for what happened, and if the police are involved it could get very nasty.'

'My guess is that the company would carry the can, not an individual,' Barnard said. Kate nodded, but her eyes were full of anxiety.

'I'm worried about my brother Tom too,' she said.

'Ah,' Barnard said. 'If he was my brother, I'd be worried about him. I told you what happened to mine.' She nodded. She'd been surprised when Barnard had revealed that his younger brother had been so harassed when exposed as a homosexual that he killed himself. She doubted whether anyone else in the police force knew about it. But to her it explained a lot about the man. She took hold of Barnard's hand.

'Will you come out to Anfield and talk to my mam?' she said. 'I'm too close to all this, but if you asked the questions perhaps we might find out just what my da has got himself into with Terry Jordan's company. As far as Ken's assignment goes, now I know what the firm is called I can track down their sites in the city centre and ask Liam at the *Echo* what else they've done since the end of the war.'

'Liam?' Barnard asked, instantly alert. 'Who's he?'

'Just a reporter whose brains I picked the other day,' Kate said quickly. 'He was very helpful.'

'Was he?' Barnard said quietly. 'OK, we'll go to Anfield. Perhaps it would be a good idea to meet your mother.' Kate gave him a sharp look.

'Don't be under any illusions,' she said. 'You're not a Catholic, so you're beyond the pale.'

'Jesus wept!' Barnard said.

'He well might,' Kate agreed.

EIGHT

Bridie O'Donnell answered the door almost as soon as Kate knocked, drying her hands on a tea towel and pulling the strings of her pinafore more tightly round her waist.

'Oh, it's you,' she said, sparing Barnard barely a glance. 'I thought it might be your da.'

In view of the pinafore, which she was wearing over her dress, she had obviously been doing some cleaning. Her face was tired and there were dark-grey circles under her eyes, and Kate could see that her work-roughened hands were shaking. Her eyes swerved away from Kate as soon as she'd waved her into the living room.

'This is Harry. A friend from London,' Kate said as Bridie waved them into chairs, opting for an uncomfortable wooden one close to the door and kneading her hands together in obvious distress, making the dry skin crackle. As she had hardly reacted at all to the arrival of a stranger at her door – whereas usually her first question of many would have been to ask where he went to Mass – Kate knew this was not just her mother's normal anxiety but a serious crisis.

'I'll make some tea,' she said and busied herself in the kitchen aware of the strained silence next door. When she had given all three of them a cup of the strong brew her mother liked, she tried to kick-start the conversation, which had never really got going.

'I saw da yesterday, mam,' Kate said. 'There was an accident at the site where he was working. He was worried about his boss, though I didn't see how da could be blamed.'

'Yes, I know all about that,' her mother said. 'He came round teatime yesterday. Said he was going away until the fuss dies down. I'm worried to death about him.'

'Where's he going?' Kate asked. 'Did he say?'

'No,' Bridie said. 'He doesn't often tell me much.' Kate glanced at Barnard helplessly.

'Going away isn't such a good idea,' Barnard said. 'It more or less guarantees someone will come looking for him. He'll be needed as a witness.'

Bridie slumped back on her chair looking completely drained.

'So what makes you such an expert?' she asked. 'Frank's been coming and going for years, ever since the war. One month he's at sea, the next he's just picking up work at the dock gates – and if you don't know what that's like, you need to talk to someone who does. I thought all that would change when he went to work for Terry Jordan on the buildings, but now this. Father Reilly tells me I have to stick by him, but I sometimes wonder.' Barnard glanced at Kate for a second and she nodded.

'Tell her,' she whispered.

'Tell me what?' Bridie demanded.

'I'm a policeman,' he said. 'A detective. In London, not here, so I know nothing about all this. But if you do see your husband, try to persuade him to go back to his job and help them sort it all out. If he doesn't talk to the authorities, they'll think he has something to hide.'

Bridie gazed at Kate and Barnard, a mixture of shock and fury chasing across her face.

'What are you doing bringing him here?' she flung at Kate. 'You know the trouble our Tom has had with the bizzies.'

'This is nothing to do with Tom,' Kate said. 'I just wanted to know where my father was staying, that's all. I need to see him.'

'And you bring a feckin' policeman here?' Bridie said. 'Holy Mother, you are a stupid little cow!'

'I was with da after the accident,' Kate said. 'He was worried about what his boss would say, but no one thought it was anything except an accident. I don't know why he would think he had to run off.'

Barnard got to his feet with a shrug. He was, he thought, surplus to requirements and would be better out of the way.

'I'll wait for you outside, Kate, if you'd rather talk to your mother alone.' Kate nodded gratefully.

'It might be best,' she said. They heard the front door close behind Barnard, then Kate turned on her mother, almost as angry now as she was.

'Now will you tell me what's going on with da?' she demanded.

'And will you tell him? A bloody copper?' Bridie countered, her face flushed and her eyes full of unshed tears.

'Not if you don't want me to,' Kate said.

'Your father's got his reasons,' Bridie said. 'You know what he's like, he ducks and dives, wheels and deals, just like Terry Jordan used to, though it's never made Frankie any money. As fast as he earns it, he drinks it and gambles it away. Terry's a powerful man in Liverpool now, with friends in high places, and he won't want Frank talking about where they both started.'

'You mean Terry Jordan might have told him to disappear?'

Bridie's lips pursed.

'I'll say nothing about that,' she said. 'But I reckon he'll be out of the country by now if Terry Jordan wants him out of the way. It's not difficult to get on a boat, is it? Not in Liverpool.'

'Ireland?' Katie asked, knowing that her father, of all the family, identified most closely with the Republic.

'Ireland, New York, the South Pole maybe . . .' Bridie said, her voice breaking. 'Now get yourself and your policeman back to London and don't bother about this anymore. There's nothing you can do about your da. There's nothing I've ever been able to do about him. I'm just scared we'll never see him again.'

Kate sighed. 'I wouldn't worry,' she said wearily. 'You know he's a survivor. I've no doubt he'll survive this too, whatever's going on. You could report him missing, but I don't suppose you will as you're so suspicious of the police. I've nearly got enough pictures now for my boss in London, so we'll probably be going back on Sunday night. You've got my phone number at the flat. Even if I'm not there, you can leave a message with Tess.'

Her mother nodded, but Kate could see that this situation had upset her more than anything else she could remember.

'Take care,' she said, but Bridie merely nodded. There seemed to be no spark left in her.

Barnard was leaning against his car smoking. As she closed her mother's front door behind her, he opened the passenger door for Kate.

'Your family has a genius for getting into trouble,' he said mildly. 'The best thing I can do for you is pretend I never heard any of that. I don't suppose I'll be meeting any of the local police any time soon.'

'I don't understand why da's in such a panic,' Kate said. 'But my mother's right. If he wants to disappear, there's no shortage of ways to do so round here. But he never said a word about it to me when I left him at the offices yesterday. But regardless of that, I need to go back there and see someone at Jordan's company. I still need to pin down the buildings they've put up and match them with my old pictures of the ruins. Then I should have enough for Ken.'

'Will there be anyone there on a Saturday?' Barnard asked.

'There might be after what happened yesterday,' Kate said. 'It would be worth a try if it'll save me stopping over until Monday. The planning man at the *Echo* was quite helpful, but I need to confirm things with the builders to be sure. And at the same time I can ask if anyone knows where my da has vanished to. Knowing him, he might be sleeping off a heavy night somewhere. Though I suppose he could be in Dublin by now. It's a long shot, but someone at Macdonald-Jordan might know. I'd like to put my mam out of her misery if I can. If she knows where he is, she'll calm down.'

'Fine,' Barnard said. 'Anything you like if it gets you on your way home.' He glanced at her sideways as he pulled out from the kerb. 'If my place is still home,' he said.

'I'd like it to be,' she said, remembering what she had told Liam Minogue and wanted to tell Barnard. But she still found it hard to put anything encouraging into words, and she could hear how much strain there was in her own voice. She glanced at him as he drove on to the main road into the city and could see how tense he was too.

'Let's leave it until we get back to London to sort ourselves out,' she said. 'I don't think I can cope with it just now.'

* * *

They drove to the office block near the docks where the day before she had stood with her father and realized just how firmly he was under his boss's thumb. And how scared he was of him. The street was quiet and at first they thought Macdonald-Jordan Construction was closed, as it normally would have been on a Saturday morning, but when Barnard looked through the glass street doors he beckoned Kate over.

'There's a light on in there,' he said. 'Someone must be around.' He tried the doors but they were locked, and there was no sign of a bell.

'I don't think you're going to get any joy here,' Barnard said, but even as he spoke a burly man in a camel coat and trilby marched up to the door and put a key in the lock.

'Can I help you?' he asked without much enthusiasm.

'You might be able to,' Kate said, quickly following the newcomer over the threshold and into the entrance hall. 'My name is Kate O'Donnell. My father Frank works for you and I'm trying to track him down. He didn't come home last night and my mam is very worried. Do you know him? Or where he might be?'

The man spun round to face Kate, an unfriendly expression on his face, but Barnard had followed closely behind her and whatever the man had intended to say seemed to freeze on his lips.

'I do know Frankie O'Donnell. I saw him yesterday after the balls-up on our site near the hospital. But I've no idea where he went after he reported what had happened and the police left. No idea at all.'

'And you are?' Barnard asked. 'We know Mr Jordan's away, so we don't really know who to talk to about Frankie. We know he was an old friend of his, from the war Katie says. Maybe we should talk to you instead if you're in charge?'

'The name's Dunne, Michael Dunne. I'm deputy to Terry and in charge while he's away in London. But as I say, I haven't a clue where O'Donnell went after he left here, though I know Mr Jordan will want words with him as soon as he gets back to Liverpool. There's no excuse for sloppy scaffolding.'

'Should it have been checked by the foreman?' Kate asked.

'Of course it should,' Dunne snapped. 'It should have been safe, instead of which we find ourselves all over the front page of the *Echo*, which is certainly not where Mr Jordan will want to be when he's negotiating in London.'

'Did you threaten to sack him, my da?' Kate asked.

'I didn't threaten him with anything,' Dunne said. 'I know he and Terry Jordan go back a long way. And the police merely said they would want to take a formal statement on Monday. That's it for now. Now I really must get on. I'm sure your father will turn up over the weekend. Tell your mother not to worry. He's probably just drowning his sorrows somewhere. We all know he's good at that. It must have been a shock seeing a youngster die like that. But if anyone suggests he's been drunk on the site he'll be in trouble, both with Terry and the bizzies. There's no excuse for that.'

'I'm staying at the Lancaster Hotel,' Kate said. 'If you hear anything about my father's whereabouts, perhaps you could leave me a message there? I don't want to go back to London without knowing he's safe. My mother's in a bit of a state.'

Dunne nodded and turned away, leaving Kate and Barnard standing looking at each other in the echoing hallway.

'It looks as if your father may have had a good reason to disappear,' Barnard said quietly. 'His mate Terry Jordan may not be best pleased with him, and from what you say Jordan may be a hard taskmaster rather than a friend when things go wrong. But the police won't be very happy if he doesn't turn up to make his statement on Monday.'

They made their way back into the street and got into the car.

'What do you want to do now?' Barnard asked. Kate shrugged dispiritedly.

'Will you drop me off at my mother's for a bit? I need to tell her what we found out, which isn't much but might calm her down. If the bosses are expecting him back on Monday, then it's quite possible that's what he'll do. He's not going to want to annoy them more than they're annoyed already, is he?'

Barnard reckoned Kate was being overoptimistic, but maybe

it might make her mother feel better. He glanced at Kate with a rueful smile.

'I need to find somewhere to stay tonight,' he said. 'I don't suppose your place has got any vacancies, has it?'

'I doubt it,' she said without much enthusiasm. 'I got given a poky little room with a single bed because they were so busy with people in town to see the Beatles. I was lucky to get squeezed in at all and most of them will probably stay over to Sunday. They'll all try to pack into the Cavern tonight, and will be fed up because it's so small and sweaty and whatever band is playing won't be the Beatles by any stretch of the imagination.'

'OK, I'll take you back to Anfield and then try to find somewhere to stay. I'll pick you up at your hotel about six and we'll have a meal later. Will that do?'

'Fine,' she said. 'I'm sorry to land you with my messy family in all its glory.'

'It's an education,' Barnard said. Kate laughed and gave him a quick kiss on the cheek.

'Thanks,' she said.

NINE

Kate found her mother busy cooking tea for her sisters, who were not yet home from their Saturday shifts when Barnard dropped her outside the house. The city centre had still seemed crowded as they drove through it, and she guessed that Annie and Bernie might have been held up on the bus home.

'I won't come in,' Barnard said as he pulled up. 'I don't think your mother's very impressed with me.'

'I shouldn't worry about that,' Kate said easily. 'I think she knows I make my own decisions now. I hope she does, anyway.' He kissed her on the cheek before she got out of the car, but he was very aware that she was preoccupied with a lot more than him just now and he drove off quickly without a backward glance as she knocked on her mother's front door.

'So you spoke to someone at the office about Frank?' her mother said dully, as if just to confirm her worst fears.

'The man said he'd expect to see him on Monday,' Kate said. 'I don't think anyone will do anything until then, even if he has done a runner. That's when the police want to take a statement from him, apparently.' Her mother's lips tightened as she turned back to the pan that was bubbling furiously on the gas cooker, filling the kitchen with steam. But before Kate could even begin to reassure her, there was a knock at the door.

'Holy Mother!' Bridie said. 'Have I not had enough visitors for one day and not all of them welcome?' She made her way to the door slowly and it tore at Kate's heart to see how awkwardly she moved. She was becoming an old woman before her time and the blame for that might be partly her own, for disappointing her in so many ways. But, she told herself, it was much more her father's fault for being the unreliable husband he had always been. The voice in the tiny hallway sounded familiar and her spirits lurched even further into gloom. The last person she wanted to see was the parish priest, Father Reilly, and she wondered angrily how much her mother might have told him to bring him so opportunely to the house.

A big man, made more imposing by his black cassock and cloak and black biretta, he ballooned into the room behind Bridie, and Kate sensed that he was not the least surprised to see her there.

'Kathleen,' he said with a bonhomie that jarred with the chilly look in his eyes. 'It's good to see you home again, it is indeed. How are you getting on in the big city? I know your mother misses you.' The thrust was crude but effective, Kate thought, recognizing just how entitled the priest felt when visiting his parishioners' homes and families.

'I'm fine,' Kate said quietly. 'I'm only here on a very brief trip for my work, but it's good to see the family again.'

'Bridie tells me your father has been having some problems at his work,' Reilly said. 'That's a great pity. I thought when he settled down to work for Terry Jordan that would stabilize him with his own difficulties. Did you not hope that too, Bridie?' Kate's mother nodded without saying anything and Kate could see the despair written on her face.

'From what my father told me, Terry Jordan hasn't always been a totally upright pillar of the community,' Kate said. 'Would that be right? Is he really the sort of man my father should be working for? And now da's in trouble over an accident and seems to have disappeared.'

Reilly's fleshy face darkened.

'I think you do Terry Jordan a grave injustice, my dear,' he said. 'Your mother will tell you that he was something of a hero during the war. Isn't that right Bridie? Did he not get a medal for his work as a rescue man?'

'He did,' Bridie said, without much enthusiasm.

'And now Mr Jordan has become a benefactor to the Church. A much valued benefactor. Have you had time to go and look at the progress of our wonderful new cathedral?'

Kate shook her head.

'You should, you should, my dear. It says so much about how we have made our mark on this city at last, after being held back for so many years. Terry Jordan has been a big part of that, you know, and he's been good to your father.'

Kate nodded imperceptibly. She could remember the poverty that remained after the war, and her mother had told her how desperate it was in the 1920s and 1930s. But she could not help feeling that the Catholic Church had contributed to the troubles of her community by deliberately keeping them apart from the rest of the city, so she was not surprised when Father Reilly plunged on with what he no doubt believed was his duty.

'So tell me, Kathleen, are you still going to Mass regularly, making your confession?' The questions came with what was clearly intended as a comforting smile. 'It can be hard to settle in a new parish if you don't know anyone, can't it? Is there a convenient church for you to attend where you live? If you'd tell me where you're based, I could talk to the parish priest to make sure you're made welcome. Where are you? Shepherd's Bush, is it? To be sure, I've heard of it, which is more than can be said of most of the London suburbs. Good Irish stock in Kilburn I know of, but I'm not sure about Shepherd's Bush at all.'

'Don't worry about me, Father,' Kate said, trying to control her irritation. 'I'm fine.' She knew what he was doing as well as he did himself and she would not be drawn into the conversation he was trying to provoke. If she admitted anything approaching the truth about her new life, she knew it would throw her mother into a turmoil that would dwarf her worries about her husband, which were now piling on top of her disappointment about Tom.

'So where are you going to Mass?' Reilly asked, his expression hardening.

'My friend Tess and I have been visiting various churches,' she lied. 'We haven't settled on one we feel at home in yet. I'll let my mother know when we do.'

'A school friend, was she, this Tess? Teresa is it?'

'College,' Kate said. 'You wouldn't know her. We share a flat.' She glanced at her watch. 'I really must be going now. I'm having a meal with a friend tonight and need to get back to my hotel.' She would have stayed longer, but the priest's intrusion had made it impossible to talk freely to her mother.

'Where are you staying, my dear?' Reilly asked and Kate flinched slightly. She had not been away long enough for the memory of how closely and relentlessly priests in Liverpool watched and guarded their flocks to have faded.

'The Lancaster Hotel,' she said reluctantly. 'On Brownlow Hill.'

'Well isn't that a coincidence?' Reilly said, enthusiastic all of a sudden, his eyes gleaming. 'I'm heading in that direction myself, my dear. I'm going to a meeting at the cathedral site. I could give you a lift and drop you at your door.' He turned to Bridie and took her hands.

'I'm sure Frank will turn up again soon, Bridie,' he said. 'I'll remember you both in my prayers and your poor son. With God's help we can still rescue Tom from the sinful influences that have taken over his life. We can always restore a penitent to Holy Mother Church, you know that. Come along, Kathleen.' Kate looked at her mother and knew she could not refuse the priest's offer of a lift without upsetting her even more than she had been already today. She sighed.

'Thank you, Father,' she said. She sat beside the priest in the front of his battered A40, wondering what they could find to talk about that stayed clear of what the Church regarded as her brother's headlong rush to damnation and the similar fate which would await her if they found out about her unmarried liaison with Harry Barnard, whose worst crime of all was not being a Catholic.

Father Reilly lurched erratically back into the city centre and Kate reckoned thankfully that he was sufficiently unsure of which gear he should be in to find the energy for conversation of any kind, least of all a pastoral one. But she was taken by surprise when she realized that he was driving past her hotel without apparently any intention of stopping.

'The Lancaster is back there,' she said loudly, but the priest merely accelerated to go more quickly up the hill towards the university and the skeleton of the Cathedral of Christ the King.

'I thought you might like to see how the cathedral is coming along,' he said. 'I think I can get us a look inside.' Kate took a deep breath, guessing that this was a carefully contrived opportunity for Reilly to grill her more energetically about her lifestyle than he had been able to do in the company of her anxious mother.

'You'll make me late for my date,' she objected as he squeezed the car into a parking space close to the building site.

'Come along, my dear,' Reilly said, heaving his bulk out of the car, his cassock billowing in the sharp wind coming up the hill from the estuary. 'If I can find him, there's someone I'd like you to meet. But if he's not in, we can have a look at the building anyway. And we can have a little chat about what I suspect is your drift away from the Church, which will cause your mother as much grief as your brother's behaviour. Believe me, I can sniff out a lack of truthfulness, a want of humility, when the faithful decide they are as good a judge of what they should do as their spiritual advisers. There's two thousand years of wisdom in the Church, and your puny conscience is no match for that. I'll not have Bridie damaged again, young lady.'

Kate felt trapped between her rising anger and the knowledge that Father Reilly had the power and the ruthlessness to use his perception of her backsliding to make her mother's life a misery. She bit back her protests and followed the priest in the direction of the cathedral, down a side alley close to the perimeter fence towards a small prefabricated building where a light gleamed through a window partly obscured by building dust. He knocked on the door, and opened it when a voice called him to enter.

'Father Dominic,' Reilly said. 'I'm a bit early for the meeting to be sure, but I wanted to bring this young lady up here with me beforehand. She's one of my parishioners living in London now and she's losing touch with her roots and, I suspect, with the Mother Church. I thought if we could show her something of the new building here it might strengthen her faith, quell any doubts she's having, and impress upon her how the Church is going from strength to strength in her own home town.'

A tall thin man in clerical dress stood up at the desk and waved them inside, though there was no sign of a smile, only what looked like slight irritation at being disturbed and distracted from the heap of papers on his desk. His face was sallow, his hair iron-grey, and his eyes like cold-blue ice.

Father Reilly ploughed on, apparently undisturbed by the chilly reception.

'Kathleen, this is Father Dominic, one of the archbishop's right-hand men and in charge of the wonderful progress of our Cathedral of Christ the King. Kathleen is the daughter of Francis O'Donnell, who works for Terry Jordan's company.'

'You know Terry Jordan, do you?' the priest asked, a faint indication of interest crossing his face. 'A remarkable man.'

'No, I don't know him,' Kate said quickly. 'My father works for him but I've never met him, at least as far as I know. Maybe he came across me when I was a small girl, but never since. I only heard his name in connection with the rebuilding of the city after the war, which is why I'm here. To take some pictures for a magazine of the changes that have happened since the bombing.' His interest apparently aroused at last, the cleric's eyes brightened.

'Well, we escaped a direct hit here, thanks be to God,' he said. 'And the cathedral will be one of the landmarks of the renewed city when it's completed, which will not be long now. A major landmark, if not *the* major landmark, wouldn't you say Father Reilly?'

'Oh definitely,' Reilly said quickly.

'And I'm sure the archbishop will be interested in the assignment you're doing, Miss O'Donnell. Liverpool's suffering is not as well known as it should perhaps be. For very good reasons, I'm sure. Mr Churchill wanted to conceal the damage being done to the ports. The Church was set back like everyone else, so you certainly should be aware how generous Terry the clinic has been in the help he has given to this project and others.'

'Has he been involved in the building work here?' Kate asked.

'Not as such, no,' Father Dominic said. 'His firm was not large enough to be a bidder when the tendering was done after the war. But as a fundraiser he has been magnificent. A true defender of the faith in the building trade and a generous contributor himself. Very generous indeed. From the sound of it, he has been considerably more loyal to where and what he came from than some members of your family, which will be a grief to us all and to the Lord Jesus Christ and his Holy Mother. A pity. But perhaps this is something you can work on with Father Reilly while you are here. It would be remiss of us not to try to return you to the faith of your fathers.'

Kate tried to damp down the anger that threatened to overwhelm her, not only at the unwanted intrusion into her own life but also the fact that this man evidently knew about Tom – knowledge which could only have come from the parish priest. She swallowed down an angry retort and turned to Father Reilly.

'I don't have much time, Father,' she said. 'If you want to show me anything of the cathedral, perhaps we had better get on with it.' The two priests exchanged a glance and Reilly nodded. 'May I borrow the key?' he said.

'Do you have your camera here with you, Kathleen?' he asked. 'If we go to the viewing platform you'll get an excellent view of the whole site, especially of the recent work on the crown – the Crown of Thorns, of course, and the crowning glory of the architect's design. There are those who dislike it. No doubt you'll have heard it called Paddy's Wigwam. But that's Protestants for you, always seeking to disparage.'

Kate nodded and said goodbye to Father Dominic, who was watching them leave.

'God bless you, my child,' he said. 'I will remember you in my prayers.' Kate thought that sounded more like a threat than a promise, but she nodded and followed Father Reilly out of the door. He led the way to the cathedral itself, where he unlocked a door and took her up some steps leading to a viewing gallery that gave an extensive view of the building work.

'It's very impressive,' she said, gazing at the soaring circular centrepiece of the structure. 'Reaching to heaven, I suppose?' Reilly looked at her sharply.

'I'm sorry to hear you so cynical, my child,' he said.

'I have good reason,' she said, and quickly made her way

down the steps again, not wanting to elaborate. 'I'll make my own way back to the hotel,' she said. 'And please don't pester my mother about me or Tom. She's not responsible for the paths we have taken.'

'I'm sure she will remember you both in her prayers, as I will,' Reilly said, obviously angry as she turned away and began to march determinedly back towards Brownlow Hill and her hotel, where she hoped Harry Barnard would be waiting. The sooner she got away from Liverpool and its memories the better, she thought. It had been a mistake to come.

TEN

'Is there anyone in CID I can talk to?' Harry Barnard asked the bored-looking uniformed sergeant on the front desk at Liverpool's main central police station, flashing his warrant card, which at least encouraged the sergeant to sit up and take notice.

'I think I saw the DCI go upstairs,' he said. 'Everton are playing some friendly game at Newcastle this afternoon, so he'll be at a loose end waiting for the result in half an hour. What's it about?'

'A missing person,' Barnard said. 'Ask him if I can have a word, would you?' The sergeant conducted an ostentatiously careful study of Barnard's warrant card, then made a call on the internal phone and evidently received an affirmative answer. He pointed the visitor towards the swing doors that led to the rest of the building.

'Up to the top of the stairs,' he said. 'DCI Strachan will meet you there.' Barnard followed instructions and on the landing found a heavily built man in his fifties wearing slacks, a tweed sports jacket and a patterned sweater. His hair was red, his face sweaty and an unhealthy shade of pink, and his accent placed him squarely in Belfast – to such an extent that Barnard had difficulty unscrambling his tortured vowels. With an anxious expression, Strachan glanced at his watch.

'What's the score?' Barnard asked, recognizing the symptoms of second-half anxiety which Chelsea put him through often enough.

'They were two-nil down last time I heard,' Strachan said. 'It's only a friendly, but even so . . .'

He cast a questioning eye over Barnard.

'You're a long way from home, Sergeant,' he said. 'To what do we owe the pleasure of a visit from the mighty Met?'

'Nothing official,' Barnard said quickly. 'My girlfriend's back home in Liverpool taking some photographs for a magazine article and she's worried about her father. He was working on the building site where there was an accident yesterday and he seems to have vanished since, so the family's anxious. I said I would see if I could find out if you had come across him at all.'

'Her father is who?' Strachan asked and Barnard thought he could see a spark of interest in the bright-blue eyes beneath the sandy brows.

'Frank O'Donnell. He was the foreman on the site, apparently, and he's not been home since the scaffolding came down taking some builder with it. Have you had any reports about him? It would set my girlfriend's mind at rest if I could locate him for her. I guessed you'd want to interview him about what happened at the building site, so thought you might know where she can contact him.'

'If I know anything about Irish builders on the weekend, he's probably lying dead drunk outside one of the dozens of boozers down the Scotland Road,' Strachan said dismissively. 'You can have a quick look at the incident book if you like, but I've not heard anything about O'Donnell. I expect someone would have let us know, as I'm sure we'll want a statement out of him on Monday. Who did you say he was working for?'

'I didn't,' Barnard said. 'But his daughter says he was working for Terry Jordan's company.'

'Was he now?' Strachan said. 'Well, that's a flourishing firm these days, in spite of being run by a dodgy Fenian bastard. I'd not imagine they were cutting corners to save a few bob – they're too big for that nonsense now they're thick with the new regime at the town hall. So I shouldn't think O'Donnell's got much to worry about. His boss is well in.'

'With you?' Barnard asked and then realized that this was not a question Strachan might want to answer. The DCI's reddening face confirmed his feeling as he wiped a film of sweat from his forehead.

'There was a time when no one at the town hall would pass the time of day with Fenians like Jordan, but things have changed since Bessie Braddock and her friends took over. Isn't there a saying about lunatics taking over the asylum? Things are better ordered in Belfast. And in this station too while I've got anything to do with it. Anyway, have a look in the incident book and see if your man has been noticed. As I said, we'll be expecting to talk to him on Monday, so we'll not have any interest in his whereabouts till then. Ask the desk sergeant to show you what you want to check.'

'Thank you sir,' Barnard said and turned away in the direction of the stairs. DCI Strachan watched him until he was out of sight, then went into his office and dialled an outside line and waited some time for the connection to be made.

'Dave Strachan in Liverpool,' he said when the connection was made. 'How come I get a detective sergeant from London sniffing around here looking for Frankie O'Donnell? What's that all about? Is it down to you lot or what?' He listened to the voice at the other end of the line for some time before saying, 'right, I'll see what I can do.' And then hung up abruptly. The phone rang again almost immediately and he glanced at his watch.

'Three-nil?' he exclaimed angrily. 'Useless tossers. They say it's only a friendly, but at this rate they'll have Liverpool winning the bloody cup next season.'

To Kate's relief she found Harry Barnard waiting for her in his car, parked outside the hotel. She opened the passenger door and slumped into the seat with a sigh.

'You look frazzled,' he said. 'What happened?'

'Oh just stuff,' she said. 'My mother's parish priest turned up and started hassling me about whether or not I was going to Mass in London. I'd forgotten how entitled they feel to nag the backsliders. Especially Father Reilly, who must have known me since I was a babe in arms. And of course the fact that Tom is what Tom is makes my mother feel very exposed. Anyway, I lied my way out of trouble to save my mam's embarrassment and then he offered me a lift back to town which I stupidly accepted and he took me up to see the new cathedral, instead of dropping me here as he'd promised. And we had to talk to some senior man as well, so there were more interfering questions, as if they owned me. Which I suppose they think they do.'

Barnard looked at her for a long time.

'Why do you resent them so much?' he asked. Kate looked down at her hands for a long time before replying, her face pale and closed.

'How much do you know about the Catholic Church?' she asked at length. Barnard shrugged.

'Not a lot,' he said. 'When I was a kid we were hardly aware of Catholics. They went to different schools, so I don't think I ever met any. Where I lived there were lots of Jews and they came in for some stick in the East End, but I don't remember much about Catholics.'

'Well Liverpool was different,' Kate said. 'There were lots of us and nobody liked us very much, mainly because most of us were Irish. And since the Protestants were Ulster Unionists, it was political as well as religious. Anyway, the Church made every effort to keep us separate and tightly controlled, so it wasn't just the Prods who were being stand-offish. And on the whole, people put up with it. They felt protected by the Church when no one else would protect them. In return, I suppose, no one made waves, no one asked questions. That wasn't just discouraged, it could be jumped on from a great height. So if anything went wrong inside the Church, it would not be talked about.'

'And things went wrong for you?' Barnard asked, realizing that Kate's hands were shaking and she had gone very pale.

'You have your first confession and communion when you're about seven or eight, when you're supposed to be old enough to understand what it's all about. Before that there are classes to prepare you for the big event – and it is a big event, with the boys in white suits, the girls in bridal dresses, presents, parties, and all the family celebrating. My mother was busy with the two little ones, and I can't remember my father taking much interest if he was there at all. So when it all went wrong I didn't know who to tell, who to talk to, or who would believe me.'

'How did it go wrong?' Barnard asked quietly. 'What was the problem?'

'Father Jerome was the problem,' Kate said. 'A young priest, Father Reilly's assistant, who took some of the classes. He began to keep me and Tom back when the others had gone home. He said we both needed some extra help with the catechism and when we were alone with him he began to behave oddly, said we were to treat him like a big brother, a big brother in God. And then in the holidays we went with a few of the others on a special visit to a Catholic boarding school, although my mother said she couldn't afford it. But somehow we got paid for by someone. It was only later – when Tom told me what happened during that visit – I guessed it was Father Jerome who'd paid.'

Barnard knew instinctively that he was not going to like what Kate seemed determined to tell him.

'So what did happen?'

'Father Jerome was always very friendly. I thought he was wonderful because I'd never had much attention from my dad. If you were upset, Father Jerome would put an arm round you, try to cheer you up. Boy or girl, it didn't seem to matter to him. But after that trip Tom went very quiet and seemed to be avoiding people at the classes – not just Jerome but all the priests. He seemed to have frozen up inside. He wasn't the same.'

Barnard gripped the steering wheel, his knuckles white, anger threatening to overwhelm him though he knew that was not what Kate needed just now.

'He told you, though, in the end?' he asked quietly.

'He told me, much later on, that Father Jerome had been pestering him all through the classes and that on that trip, when we were away from home, he used to come for him at night.'

'He interfered with him, raped him maybe?'

'I was too young to even know that word, but it sounded as if he did. Tom was even more confused than I was. Not long after, Father Jerome moved on to another parish and we didn't know who to tell, or even if there was anything to tell. We hadn't got the words to talk about it.'

'And no one would have believed you, anyway,' Barnard said bitterly, thumping the steering wheel. 'Two young children against the might of the Catholic Church? Not a chance! And then?'

'We got all dressed up and made our first communion and

got our missals and rosaries, and in the photographs both Tom
and I look miserable. I knew something was very wrong, but
I didn't really understand what it was at that stage. Later –
after he told me, in detail – I tried to have as little as possible
to do with the Church, but it's not easy in a tight-knit community like Scottie Road. My father was not around much and
my mother was preoccupied with my sisters. Bernadette was
a sickly child, and until the Health Service started you had to
pay for doctors . . .'

'So you bottled it up?'

'We both did. And as soon as I could, I stopped going to
Mass and tried to find a way to get out of Liverpool. Tom did
the same.'

'Less successfully than you did,' Barnard said.

'And he had more problems with sex later. As you know.'

'You think the two things are connected?'

'Maybe,' Kate sighed. 'How can you tell? Anyway, that's
enough of this old history. There's nothing can be done about
it now. I'll go and get changed.'

Barnard sat for a moment in silence, breathing hard until
the shock of what Kate had told him dissipated slightly. It was
commonly accepted – tolerated even – that there were men
who sought out children for their gratification. Choir masters,
scout leaders, boarding-school teachers were routinely mocked
and suspected, but little or no action was demanded. In the
sleazy world of vice, with which he was only too familiar,
child victims sometimes emerged and were dealt with without
much sensitivity. But he had never heard an accusation against
a priest before. And he very much doubted whether Father
Jerome could be traced all these years later. The Church, he
guessed, would look after its own.

He twiddled the tuner on his car radio but found nothing
much of interest apart from the news. He'd cheered on the
latest attempts to break the BBC's domination of pop music,
which had until recently remained unchallenged, but needless
to say there was no access to Radio Luxembourg or the newly
fledged Radio Caroline on a radio as limited as his. He was
surprised when Kate reappeared, still wearing the same clothes
and looking furious.

'Problem?' he asked.

'Someone's been in my room,' Kate said. 'I picked up the key in reception but when I got upstairs my door was unlocked, and my stuff's been spread about all over the place.'

Barnard got out of the car.

'Have they taken anything?' he asked.

'Difficult to tell,' Kate said. 'Come up and have a look. They can't object to letting a police officer in, can they?' He followed her back into the hotel and stopped at the reception desk with his warrant card in his hand.

'Someone's been into Miss O'Donnell's room while she was out,' he said. 'I'll take a quick look round to see if anything's been taken. You didn't see anyone you didn't know going upstairs did you?' The pale girl in a mini-skirt and tight-fitting sweater shook her head.

'Do you want me to dial 999 for the bizzies?' she asked, a faint spark of interest in her eyes.

'I'll have a look first,' Barnard said. 'I don't suppose you'd want a fuss if nothing's been stolen.'

She nodded doubtfully and watched as Kate led the way upstairs to her small room on the third floor.

'You know me,' she said, trying to keep her agitation at bay. 'I'm a fairly tidy person. I put my personal stuff in the chest of drawers and tucked the suitcase under the bed. And look at it now!' Her belongings seemed to have been flung anywhere and everywhere across the bed and dressing table, her make-up and hair gear upended on top of the chest.

'Is anything missing?' Barnard asked. 'Any of your photographic stuff?' Kate shook her head.

'I had my camera with me and the exposed films. All in my handbag. If that was what they were looking for, they won't have found anything. But why would they be looking for them? What would anyone want with a series of pictures of buildings that aren't not very interesting except in the context of what they replaced? Not many of them are even very beautiful. They wouldn't win any architecture prizes, except perhaps for the Catholic cathedral and that's not even finished yet.'

'And nothing else is missing? You didn't leave any money up here?' Kate looked at him in astonishment.

'You don't know much about this city if you can ask that. Things may be looking up, but that doesn't mean you don't have to nail anything valuable down any more. When I was at college, some of my mates lived in digs and they were always getting things nicked. The scallies used to make regular raids and nick expensive gear – cameras, musical instruments and stuff.'

'So do you want to report it?' Barnard asked. Kate shrugged and began to gather up her possessions and pick up the bedclothes, which had been flung on the floor, but then she drew a sharp breath.

'What?' Barnard asked sharply and Kate, pale-faced and shaking, pointed beneath the blankets at a dark-red stain.

'Is that blood?' she whispered. Barnard picked up the thin wool and felt it, and then sniffed it cautiously.

'It's damp, so it's recent,' he said. 'But no, it's not blood. Some sort of paint, I think. But it says one thing – someone was very keen to give you a scare. Have you any idea who that might be?'

Kate shrugged.

'I don't know . . .' she said. 'First my father disappears and now it seems someone's got it in for me, but I don't know why.'

'I nearly forgot to tell you,' Barnard said. 'I called in the nick to see if they had any idea where your father was.' Kate looked at him in astonishment.

'That was a brave move,' she said. 'And maybe a dangerous one. I don't think you understand the relationship between the police and the Irish up here.'

'It sounds a bit like the police in Notting Hill and the West Indian community.'

'More or less,' she said. 'Though it's been going on longer here. Much longer. We were the West Indians a hundred years ago, when people came from Ireland to escape the famine.'

'That's all old history, surely?' Barnard said, before realizing that for Kate's family it probably wasn't.

'Maybe,' Kate said. 'I'll tell you when I find out where my father is.'

'Well, they weren't completely unhelpful,' he said quickly.

'They let me have a look at their incident book, and the details of the accident are all in there. Including your father's name as a witness. He's down to be interviewed on Monday morning. They're not really interested in where he is between then and now. But at least they'll take an interest on Monday if he doesn't turn up. I guess that's the best you can hope for in the meantime. Sorry if that's not much help.'

'It won't cheer my mother up much, will it?' Kate said.

'Come on, let's get out of here,' Barnard said.

They drove back down the hill into the city centre and parked near the Pier Head. It was still busy.

'Do you fancy an Irish pub?' she asked. 'I went to one with Tom. There's music and the food's good.'

'Let's give it a try,' Barnard said easily and Kate led the way into the narrow streets behind the docks. They were early enough to find a table, and by the time their food arrived the musicians were tuning up and the noise was loud enough to make much conversation impossible. Which, Kate guessed, suited Barnard as well as it did her. She was too preoccupied with her family's problems to give any thought to her own, and she knew that she had shocked him by telling him why she had abandoned the Church. But when the musicians took a break and conversation stood a chance again, Barnard glanced at her inquiringly.

'I have to drive back to London tomorrow,' he said. 'I'm due back at work on Monday morning. Are you coming with me?'

'I can't,' she said, pushing the unfinished remains of her meal round the plate to avoid Barnard's eye. 'I haven't finished everything I want to do for Ken, and anyway I want to make sure my da has surfaced again on Monday morning. I need to know he's OK before I come back.' Barnard nodded.

'I suppose that all makes sense,' he said, 'though I miss you, Katie. I took a room in a pub in somewhere called Toxteth if you'd like to come back with me.'

Kate's eyes filled with tears.

'I don't think so,' she said. 'Not tonight.'

'Does that mean not any night?' he asked, his face gaunt and his eyes full of anxiety.

'I don't know, Harry,' Kate said. 'I'm sorry, I really don't know. Come round in the morning before you set off. Don't go without saying goodbye.'

'Would I?' he said in mock outrage. But Kate was not sure she believed him.

ELEVEN

K ate was wakened by the sound of hammering on her bedroom door. She had slept only fitfully and pulled the eiderdown around her shoulders as she slid back the bolt and opened the door. She was astonished to see her sister Annie outside, looking red-eyed and tearful.

'What is it, la?' Kate asked, suddenly terrified. 'Is it da? Or our mam? Are they all right?'

Annie pushed past Kate and sat down on the edge of the bed, tears running down her face. Annie, her first sister, with her copper hair and pale complexion, the baby she had adored from the moment she saw her cradled in her mother's arms, looked as if she had been almost destroyed by something no less devastating than a death.

'It's our Tom,' she said. 'His friend Kevin came to our house very early this morning and told us the police came for Tom before first light. They took him away to the Bridewell in handcuffs, but wouldn't say what he's supposed to have done.'

'Was da at home?' Kate asked, dropping the eiderdown on the floor and beginning to get dressed quickly.

'No, thank God and all the saints,' Annie said. 'Mam said to fetch you and your boyfriend. If he's a bizzy he might be able to find out what's going on, mightn't he? He should be able to help. That's if he's not another one who hates what Tom is. Is he as bad as the rest of them? Don't say he is, Katie. Please don't say that.' Annie was on the verge of hysteria, and after pulling on her coat Kate put her arms around her and sat beside her on the edge of the bed.

'Calm down, calm down,' she said. 'Harry's not as bad as the rest of them, I promise. He has his own reasons not to be. He said he was staying at a pub in Toxteth called the Legs of Man. Come on. We'll find the phone number and see if we can get hold of him. He's got a car, and anyway he'll tell us what to do. Or maybe what he can do. They should listen to him at any rate.'

Annie wiped her eyes and blew her nose hard, her face chalk white beneath the freckles.

'All mam could think of doing was getting hold of Father Reilly, but I don't think he would be much help at all.'

'I can't think of anyone Tom would less like to see, except possibly the Pope,' Kate said angrily, ignoring Annie's expression of shock. 'Come on, let's go down and get a phone book. I can't think of anyone else in this bigoted city who's likely to want to help Tom except Harry.'

To the two sisters' relief, Barnard arrived at the Lancaster Hotel much more quickly than Kate expected.

'I was checking out anyway and planning to take you out to breakfast,' he said with a ghost of the smile that had unfailingly bewitched Kate not so long ago. 'And this must be Annie,' he said, taking in the auburn-haired young woman who was clinging to her older sister as if to a life raft. He glanced around the hotel foyer and spotted the dining room, littered with dirty dishes but thankfully empty.

'Come on,' he said. 'I need some coffee at the very least, so you can tell me all about what happened and we'll decide what we can do about it. Though you do realize that if the police decide to take against what boys like your brother get up to, they can pretty well buy in the evidence they want to make it stick? No one wants to be tarred with that brush anywhere, and I should think especially not in this town.'

Barnard was persuasive enough to tempt the pretty waitress into providing not only coffee but toast as well, though when he sampled the coffee he soon pushed it away in disgust.

'You'd think a sea port would know what coffee was supposed to taste like!' he complained. 'Anyway, Annie, for a start can we talk to Tom's friend Kevin to find out exactly what happened and what the arresting officers said? They must have had some pretty good excuse to drag him out of bed in the small hours.'

'Kevin said he was going down to the Bridewell to see if he could find out what was going on, but it would be better if we go too.'

'They won't need much of an excuse to arrest Kevin as well if the mood takes them,' Barnard said, making no attempt to soften the message. 'If they're anything like the Met, there are always a few people on duty who like nothing better than to round up a few queers to provide a bit of entertainment on a dull shift. And you can be sure that some of them'll claim to be doing God's work as well as upholding the law.'

They finished their breakfast in silence, then Barnard ushered them out and into his car. Sitting beside him, Kate guided him through the quiet Sunday morning streets, past the shuttered shops and the debris of the night before's partying. Though the Beatles euphoria seemed to have subsided, there were broken bottles in the gutter outside several pubs and a few groups of young people weaving unsteadily through the detritus.

'That's the police station,' Annie said and Barnard slowed down, reluctant to park his bright-red car too close.

'And that's Kevin,' she said pointing to a thin young man in a duffel coat with the hood pulled over his head obscuring his face. He was standing uncertainly on the pavement opposite the police station, watched closely by two uniformed constables from the top of the entrance steps.

'You'd better bring him over, Kate,' Barnard said quietly. 'Make it look as if you're his girlfriend or something. You can't be too careful.' Kate got out of the car and crossed the road, aware of the watchful eyes of the police officers. She put a hand on the man's arm hoping fervently that they were right and that this really was Tom's boyfriend.

'Kevin,' she said quietly. 'I'm Tom's sister. We heard about what's happened. Give me a quick hug as if we're old friends, and we'll take you somewhere where we can talk.' His eyes, half-hidden beneath his hood, gave Kate a haunted stare.

'You're Kate?' he whispered. 'He told me he'd seen you the other night. But isn't your boyfriend a bizzy?'

'Not here,' Kate said. 'In London. Things are different there. He helped Tom when he came to London to work and found himself in a bit of trouble. Come on, quick, before those beggars on the steps come over. You don't want to end up

inside with Tom. Give me a kiss and look as if you mean it.'
She put her arms round his neck and he gave her a half-hearted
peck on the cheek.

'What the hell did we do to deserve this?' he asked as he
got into the back seat of Barnard's car alongside Annie.

Barnard accelerated away without answering directly.

'Where can we get decent coffee at this hour on a Sunday
morning?' he asked as he scanned almost empty pavements
and shops and cafés and pubs with 'Closed' signs firmly in
place. It was a city very definitely not open for business, with
the only people out and about heading for church or chapel
with determined looks on their faces. Having been taken over
by hysterical music fans of the Merseybeat generation only
two nights ago, the city had now turned its face against frivolity
in favour of prayer.

'We could go back to our house, but if our da turns up he'll
go doolally,' Annie said gloomily.

'And our place is right out beyond Bootle . . .' Kevin said
even more tentatively.

'Try Lime Street station,' Kate said. 'The buffet in there
should be open. And even if it's not, there are places to sit.
We need to make some urgent decisions about Tom. Like how
do we get him a solicitor?'

The station was quiet and they found an empty table in the
buffet. The two men went to the counter to order drinks,
leaving the sisters staring disconsolately at each other across
the tea-ringed Formica.

'Could he really go to prison?' Annie whispered.

'I think so,' Kate said. 'Harry will know the worst that can
happen.' Though he would not, she was sure, tell Annie what
he knew from personal experience – that there were outcomes
worse than those the law could impose on Tom, worse than
sending him to gaol.

'I thought tea might be safer than coffee,' Barnard said,
handing four cups around. Kevin took his with shaking hands.
Kate tried to gauge from Harry's expression what he was really
thinking, but Annie was even more adept than she was at
picking up unspoken signals.

'What's the worst that can happen to him?' she asked

Barnard. 'Don't mess us about. Tell us the truth. We need to know what we're up against.'

'It depends whether they charge him and what they charge him with,' Barnard said carefully. 'Kevin, when they picked Tom up did they give you any idea what they thought he'd done?'

Kevin shook his head.

'They broke the front door down, shouting and screaming about poofs and perverts, and had him out of the place in handcuffs almost before I could get out of bed and put some clothes on.'

'They didn't want to take you with them?' Barnard asked. Again, Kevin shook his head.

'One of them asked me how old I was, and when I said I was twenty-two they seemed to lose interest.'

'That sounds as if they would have liked to charge him with seducing kids, which could put him behind bars for a very long time. But they can't stop you giving evidence for the defence, and if you've been together for a while such a charge might be hard to prove. Tell me, how long have you been together?'

'About eighteen months,' Kevin said quietly. 'We moved out of town to get away from the queer scene. We just wanted to be on our own, live a normal life. And now this. Why can't they just leave us alone?'

'What you do is still illegal though it's years since the report that recommended changing the law, and we still don't seem to be getting any closer to changing it,' Barnard said. 'And you all know where the opposition's coming from – the Churches of every shape, size and persuasion.'

'It's not just the priests, though,' Annie said, glancing at Kate. 'Our parents will be mortified if Tom ends up in court. My mother will die of shame. No amount of Hail Marys will make her feel better. She'll think it's her fault. She thinks everything's her fault.'

'I'll go down there and see what I can find out,' Barnard said. 'I'm more likely to get in than family are. If they're serious about charging him, they won't let any of you near him.' Kate shuddered. This was not the first time Tom had run into difficulties with the police and she feared that this time it would end less happily.

'Stay here,' Barnard said. 'Have a slap-up breakfast, and I'll be back as soon as I've found out what's going on.'

Harry Barnard walked into the nick with more apparent confidence than he felt. There were suddenly too many questions around Kate's family for it all to be just coincidence. Her father's disappearance could have been down to a drunken binge, but someone had ransacked Kate's hotel room and now Tom, the most vulnerable of all, was in deep trouble. He could think of no reason why Kate's assignment could have provoked this sort of reaction. It was more likely that the roots of the problem went way back and started here in Liverpool, not with Kate's visit.

There was a different sergeant on the front desk this morning, so Barnard showed his warrant card once more and asked if it was true that Tom O'Donnell had been brought in for questioning.

'The poofter? What's it to you, whack?' the sergeant asked, his expression deeply unfriendly.

'I know his sister and she's anxious about him,' Barnard said. 'Has he been charged? And if so, with what?'

'He'll be in court Monday morning,' the sergeant said reluctantly. 'That's all I can tell you, whack. You know the score.'

'Can I see him? Just for a couple of minutes?' Barnard persisted.

'Not on your life. It's more than my job's worth just talking to you.' But before Barnard could make any further attempt to persuade him, he was aware of the main doors being flung open with a crash and he turned to face DCI Dave Strachan bustling in with a senior uniformed officer close behind him. At the same moment, another uniformed sergeant appeared from inside the building, looking very anxious indeed.

'I've sent for an ambulance, guv,' he said. Strachan, red-faced and furious, glanced at Barnard and then at the newcomer before turning back to Barnard.

'What the hell are you doing here?' he asked, grabbing hold of Barnard's arm and almost pushing him through the door in the direction of the main offices.

'This is a detective sergeant from the Met,' he said to his colleague. But further explanation was prevented by the arrival of an ambulance, its bell clanging, and the appearance of two ambulance men in a hurry, carrying a stretcher.

'Where's the casualty?' one asked. In the mêlée that followed, Barnard found himself ignored for a moment while all the local officers hurried into the bowels of the building, downstairs to the cells. He followed as unobtrusively as he could, and watched as the ambulance staff hurried through the open door of a cell and attended to a figure sprawled on the floor. He could not see a lot but enough to recognize Tom O'Donnell, who did not seem to be moving and was, he thought with horror, quite possibly not breathing.

'Jesus wept!' he muttered under his breath, pressing himself against the corridor wall and hoping that everyone's attention was directed into the cell, leaving no one to notice his presence. But that could not last. He watched as Tom was lifted on to the stretcher, and as he was carried past him towards the stairs he could see that his head and face were bleeding and his eyes were closed.

Inevitably Strachan saw him as he followed the stretcher out of the cell, and his face distorted with fury.

'How did you get down here?' he snapped. He turned to the sergeant who must have been in charge of the cells. 'Arrest this man for interfering in police business,' he said. 'Put him in a cell and I'll talk to him later.'

'Sir,' the sergeant said, turning a deeply unfriendly eye in Barnard's direction, and Barnard knew that offering any resistance might mean he would be the next person carried out of the custody area. With a groan he sat down on the hard bunk towards which he'd been pushed, and shrugged resignedly as he listened to the door being locked. He had, he realized, walked into a nest of vipers and would be lucky to come out of it with either himself or his career intact.

After an hour Strachan reappeared, with the custody sergeant in tow. Barnard made to stand up but Strachan pushed him back on to the bunk and hit him hard across the face, so hard that his head snapped back and made contact with the brick wall. Half-stunned, he put up his hands to protect himself, but the sergeant grabbed his arms and pushed him against the wall, allowing Strachan to aim more blows at his head and body.

'For Christ sake!' he yelled in an interval the DCI seemed to need to get his breath back. 'What's this for?'

'It's for poking your nose in where it's not wanted,' Strachan said. 'And now I'll tell you what's going to happen. I'm going to get hold of your boss in London, and make an official complaint about your behaviour and ask them to come and fetch you. And you'll go back to the Met in handcuffs, facing a charge of being involved in an attempt to pervert the course of justice by trying to aid the escape of a prisoner. It's that or I keep you here and charge you with being Tom O'Donnell's lover. Your choice. Either way you'll end up behind bars.'

'You're joking!' Barnard exclaimed, and immediately regretted his lack of caution as Strachan hit him again and again until the custody sergeant put a restraining hand on his arm.

'Maybe not a good idea to send two to hospital in one morning. We're not in Belfast now, sir.' Strachan nodded reluctantly.

'You're probably right, Sergeant,' he said. He turned back to Barnard. 'So let's get rid of you. You'll stay here until I can arrange to get you back to your home turf, Sergeant bloody Barnard. And don't let me catch you within a hundred miles of the Pier Head ever again.'

By eleven, Kate had lost patience. The three of them had picked at breakfast and drunk more tea, and as Barnard had not yet returned she decided it was time to try to find him.

'I'm not going near the Bridewell,' Kevin had said fiercely. 'If I show my face there, they'll have me inside too.'

'I'll come with you,' Annie said. 'Then I need to get home and tell our mam what's going on.'

The three of them walked down the hill towards the city centre. Before they got as far as the police station, Kevin stopped.

'I'll get the bus home,' he said. 'I daren't go near the bizzies. But we've got a phone. I'll give you the number, and can you let me know what's going on?' He looked so defeated that Kate gave him a hug, before putting the slip of paper with his number on into her bag.

'I'm really glad you're with Tom,' she said. 'As soon as I know anything at all I'll ring you. I promise.'

The sisters stood transfixed by the sheer unexpected complexity of what had happened, as they watched him walk away, shoulders slumped, towards the buses at the Pier Head.

'Wherever Harry is, his car won't be far away,' Kate said at last. 'And it's pretty noticeable.' They found it quite easily, parked just a street away from the police station with no sign of Barnard himself.

'Do you reckon he's still talking to the police?' Annie asked. Kate shrugged.

'I've no idea,' she said, pulling the door handle, expecting the car to be locked, and was surprised when the door swung open. She peered inside and could see nothing out of the ordinary apart from a manilla folder that must have slipped half out of sight under the front passenger seat. From the scruffy state of it, she guessed that she must have been resting her dirty shoes on it, without realizing, the last time she was in the car. She turned to Annie.

'You get off home, la,' she said. 'Mam will need to know what's going on. I'll wait in the car for a bit until Harry turns up. You can leave a message at the Lancaster Hotel if you need to. We'll go back there eventually I expect. Ring from the call box anyway. I should be able to tell you what's happened to Tom by then. We have to keep in touch.'

Annie flung her arms round her sister for a moment. 'Take care,' she said. 'I'll talk to you later.'

'I shouldn't think Harry will be long now,' Kate said, trying to infuse some reassurance into her voice as Annie turned away and headed for the Anfield bus. Like Kevin, she looked a forlorn figure as the wind from the river blew her hair into a red halo around her head. Something, Kate thought as she slipped into the driving seat to get out of the rising breeze, was very, very wrong. And with Harry Barnard missing, she had not the faintest idea what it was.

She succeeded in turning the radio on and listened desultorily to the Light Programme, which did not seem to have noticed the existence of rock and roll, let alone the Merseybeat, and to relieve the boredom she picked up Harry's folder and noticed the Metropolitan Police insignia on the front. She knew she had no right to pry, but curiosity eventually got the better of her and she flipped it open only to feel a sense of anticlimax when she realized that all it contained was a sheaf of copied sketches of a woman with no indication of her identity or even, given the wooden features of the portrait, whether she was alive or dead. She suspected, after gazing at it for a while, that the latter was more likely and it had quite possibly been drawn from a body on a pathologist's slab. She shuddered, realizing it was probably the woman who'd been found in Soho Square. She peeled off one of the sketches from the bundle, folded it up, and put it into her bag. It would be an interesting if macabre contribution, she thought, to the archives Ken Fellows had at the agency, though she realized it could never be published unless the police circulated it themselves.

Finally, feeling too frustrated to sit still any longer, she flung herself out of the Capri and made her way towards the police station. The sergeant on the front desk glanced up as she approached.

'What can I do for you, darling?' he asked, his eyes undressing her as she stood uncertainly in front of him.

'I wonder if a copper called Harry Barnard has come in here this morning? He's my boyfriend but he's not from here, he's up from London, and I've lost track of him.'

The sergeant's expression turned furtive, and he glanced at the door leading to the interior of the building before he replied.

'What makes you think he'd come here, petal?' he asked.

'He was going to ask about my brother,' Kate said. 'Tom O'Donnell. I think he was arrested this morning.'

'I've never heard of either of them, pet,' the sergeant said. 'I've only just come on duty, but we wouldn't give out information like that, anyway. Your man would know that.' It was as if a shutter had come down, and although Kate knew the sergeant must be lying it was obvious that she was not likely to be able to persuade him to tell her the truth.

'So do you know if my brother's all right? He was brought

in early this morning and my mam needs to know what's going on.' If anything, the sergeant's expression became even more distant.

'I wouldn't know anything about that,' he said. 'I told you, I've only just come on duty. If he's been charged he'll be in court tomorrow morning, I expect.'

'Someone must know where he is,' she countered. 'People can't be dragged from their beds and just disappear.'

'I think maybe you'd better go home, miss,' the sergeant said, his tone harder now, and Kate was conscious of people coming through the swing doors behind her. She turned on her heel and hurried out.

'Who the hell was that?' DCI Strachan asked.

'Says she's O'Donnell's sister,' the sergeant said. 'Looking for him, and for some friend of hers from the Met who's left her in the lurch.'

'You didn't tell her anything, did you?' Strachan demanded.

'I didn't know anything to tell her, did I, sir?'

'Nothing at all,' Strachan agreed. 'And don't you forget it.'

TWELVE

Affter her fruitless visit to the police station, Kate went back to Barnard's car and stood indecisively beside it. But it did not take long for her to decide that the only place for Barnard or anyone else to contact her with any chance of success was the Lancaster Hotel. She walked back through the city centre, which was still uncannily quiet after the excitements of the last few days, and wondered if there would be another film premiere in the Beatles' home town if they made another film. Or whether the quartet, who seemed to have settled in the south when they were not globetrotting to concerts around the world, had now effectively left the Mersey and the Merseybeat and the faltering docks behind. Her brief acquaintance with John Lennon at the College of Art had never given her the feeling that he was closely attached to battered old Liverpool, still trying to put itself together again after the war. He'd always seemed to have his eyes on something else entirely. And who could blame him now it looked as though he had achieved it in spades? There would be those who begrudged his success, but she was not one of them.

She took a detour up Matthew Street but the doors of the Cavern were tightly closed, the posters outside beginning to look wind-blown. The underground club where she and so many of her Liverpool friends had sweated so many deafeningly claustrophobic nights away was becoming a blurred memory, effectively cut off from her own new life in London. Those days, she suspected, were over and would not be coming back either for her or for the bands who'd made a success on a bigger stage, however loyal their fans up here might be.

Before she started to climb Brownlow Hill to the hotel, she looked up to where the stark struts of Paddy's Wigwam were just visible amongst the surrounding buildings along Hope Street and thought of the two priests who had so arrogantly tried to reorganize her life for her. What made them think they held any sway over her after all this time? How dare they interfere! It was not just for the Beatles that Liverpool was over, it was over for her too.

The receptionist glanced up from the register as she walked in.

'I've got a couple of messages for you, Miss O'Donnell,' she said.

The first was from Harry Barnard, simply saying he was going to the police station to find out what had happened to Tom. The second, from her sister Annie, left at reception a couple of hours later, answered that question in a way that filled Kate with horror: Tom had been taken to Casualty, and she was on her way to the hospital to find out how he was and why he had been rushed there by ambulance.

Kate felt breathless with anxiety. She turned to the receptionist, who was looking at her with concern.

'You've gone white as a sheet,' she said. 'Is it bad news, la? Are you all right?'

'Not really,' Kate said. 'If anyone else calls for me, could you tell them I've gone to Casualty to see my brother Tom? He's been rushed into hospital apparently.' Breathing heavily she turned away, and then had second thoughts as her brain struggled with this sudden new calamity.

'Could you ring for a taxi, please?' she asked the receptionist. 'I need to get there as soon as I can.' She looked in her purse and reckoned she had easily enough of her quite generous expenses left to cover the fare. Ken Fellows, she thought, would understand and she watched as the young woman made the phone call. 'Ten minutes,' she said as she put the receiver down. The cab arrived more quickly than that, and in less than ten minutes Kate was walking fearfully into the Casualty Department, where she saw her sister and her mother slumped on hard chairs in the waiting room.

'How is he?' she demanded. 'Have you seen him? Is he all right?' As Bridie wiped away tears, Annie turned to her sister angrily, eyes flashing and cheeks flushed.

'No, he's not all right, la,' she said. 'The nurses took me in to see him and he looks as if he's been in a car crash. He was hardly conscious. I don't think he recognized me. They said they were waiting for a different doctor, one of the top doctors. Then we were just holding his hand when two bizzies in uniform came rushing in and said he was still under arrest and we were not allowed to talk to him. That's if he could talk anyway, I said, and they told me to feck off or they'd arrest me too. And our mam had hysterics and they bundled us out of the cubicle as if we were criminals. Then another officer came and pulled us out here and wouldn't answer when I asked him what had happened to Tom – not even when I screamed at him. They must know, but they won't say.'

Kate looked at the curtains pulled around one of the cubicles.

'Is he in there?' she asked, and Annie nodded silently. Kate marched across the space between the waiting area and the treatment cubicles and pulled the curtain back to reveal a doctor and two nurses busy around the bed, where she just caught a glimpse of her brother before the two police officers standing at the head of the bed noticed her and rushed in her direction. One was the senior officer she'd seen at the police station when she inquired about Tom. He looked even less friendly now than he had back then. Although they had not exchanged a word then or now, she sensed that the man must be Tom's most senior tormentor and a threat to her entire family.

'What happened to him?' she demanded loudly, so that the medical staff would hear her. 'There was nothing wrong with him when he was taken away. So what happened?'

'An accident,' DCI Strachan said equally forcefully. 'He was playing up and fell down some stairs on the way to the cells. Entirely his own fault for behaving like a fool.'

'My brother's not a fool,' Kate said flatly. 'And he looks to me like he's been beaten up. You don't get bruises like that from falling down stairs.'

Strachan came towards her and, taking hold of her arm in a vicelike grip, pushed her through the cubicle curtains.

'This man is under arrest,' he hissed close to her ear. 'And you have no right to be here. So get out, now. Get out, or Sergeant Davies here will arrest you and you'll see the inside of a cell yourself – and I promise you, you won't like that.'

Feeling defeated, Kate and Annie sat one on each side of their mother again, leaving Tom white-faced and unmoving, until eventually one of the doctors left the cubicle where he was being treated. He glanced in their direction and Kate seized the opportunity to question him.

'How is he?' she asked. The doctor looked embarrassed.

'You're what? His sister?' he asked and Kate nodded.

'I've insisted we keep him in,' he said. 'He's concussed and I'm not happy about the head wound. Plus we need to X-ray his arm, which looks as if it might be broken. We'll deal with all that and keep him here at least overnight. Apart from that, it looks mainly like bruising. Nothing too serious – maybe looks worse than it is, but you can never be sure.' He glanced behind him to where DCI Strachan was standing, glowering from the cubicle entrance.

'The police don't want you to talk to him at the moment,' the doctor said. 'I'm sorry but they're within their rights, I think. And in any case, he's not very coherent. If I were you, I'd go home and phone in the morning to see how he is. We'll look after him, I promise.'

Kate nodded wearily.

'Thank you,' she said. 'It doesn't look as if we've got any choice, does it?' But as she turned away, one of the nurses called the doctor back to Tom's bedside and it was obvious from the flurry of activity which followed that something was seriously wrong. From where she stood, it looked as if Tom had lapsed into unconsciousness again.

The doctor came back towards her as porters rushed into the cubicle and began to wheel the bed out, with DCI Strachan following close behind, still fuming. 'We need to operate to relieve some pressure on his brain,' he said. 'I'm sorry, we'll do our best.'

Kate turned to Annie and her mother.

'We'd better call Kevin,' she said. And as her mother made to protest she turned on her. 'He's entitled,' she said. 'You might not like it, but he is. At the very least he's a close friend, though you know he's more than that.' Her mother nodded reluctantly.

'Then see if you can find your effing father,' she said. 'He's entitled too.'

'Have you any idea where he might be holed up?' Kate asked.

'No, but I reckon Terry Jordan will know,' Bridie said. 'They seem to be thick as thieves again these days.'

'He's in London as far as I know,' Kate said. 'I won't be able to contact him there.'

'Then ask Carmel, his wife,' Bridie shot back. 'I don't reckon there's much she doesn't know about what he gets up to. She wouldn't have married him otherwise, would she? They live out by a golf course, close to the sea, in Formby. Very la-di-da they are these days.'

As she left the hospital, Kate struggled to come to terms with the idea of getting out to Formby on a Sunday afternoon. But she didn't argue, there didn't seem to be much point adding to the family's anxieties. And if she could find Harry Barnard, no doubt he would take her in his car. The key to it all, though, was finding Barnard.

Harry Barnard shot to his feet as the cell door crashed open and DCI Strachan stormed in. 'Right,' he said. 'You're on your way back to London. I've spoken to your boss. Told him what's been going on up here and that I want you off my patch. And as it happens, he wants you back there urgently.' Barnard ran his tongue over his lips, which he realized from the metallic taste must be caked in dried blood.

'Did he say why?' he asked through swollen lips.

'No,' Strachan said. 'Just that he needed to talk to you today. First thing you need do is get cleaned up. And Sergeant—' Strachan pushed his face into Barnard's until there was barely an inch between them. 'If you think you can run complaining about me to the Met – or anyone else for that matter – think again. I warned you what I could charge you with, and that still stands. My reputation up here is rock solid and complaints from a few Fenians won't touch it. In fact with the people who matter that could actually improve it. And my reach is long. From the sound of it, DCI Jackson has got his own bones to pick with you. Did you come up by car?'

Barnard nodded wearily, realizing just how thorough a beating he'd been given.

'Are you fit to drive?' Strachan persisted.

'Not right now,' he said, only too aware that the DCI's face was going in and out of focus alarmingly.

'Right, I'll get one of my DCs to drive you in your own car. Smarten yourself up and you can call your boss and tell him what's happening. We'll skip the handcuffs, but if you give my driver any trouble I'll throw the book at you. Understood?'

'Understood,' Barnard said. 'Can I contact my girlfriend? She'll wonder what the hell has happened to me.'

'That's the O'Donnell girl, is it?' Strachan asked. 'The one with the nasty little pervert for a brother? She's nearly as much of a pain in the neck as you are. Is she expecting to go back with you?'

'No,' Barnard said. 'She's here on an assignment and it isn't finished yet.'

'Leave her a message,' the DCI said. 'Where's she staying?'

'The Lancaster Hotel,' Barnard said, knowing that Strachan would store that bit of information away and would have no compunction in using Kate as a guarantee of his own good behaviour.

'Tell her to keep out of my hair,' the DCI said. Barnard's shoulders slumped.

'Let's get on with it then,' he said. The thought of facing DCI Jackson back at his own nick seemed an infinitely preferable option to remaining in the clutches of this Scouse monster who inexplicably thought he'd found himself on the right side of the law.

Kate walked back to the side street near the police station where she'd last seen Barnard's car parked. To her horror she found it had gone. She stood looking at the empty space, wondering what to do until she remembered that when Tom returned to Liverpool after his ill-fated attempt to move to London his friend Declan had taken her, in order to meet Tom, on a local train that followed the Mersey shore towards Southport. If the service was running on a Sunday, it would undoubtedly go through Formby. And if she could get that far, she just might be able to track down Terry Jordan, or at least his wife, in their lair.

The station was not busy and the man in the ticket office was helpful.

'I need to get to somewhere near Formby Golf Club,' she told him. 'Which is the best station to go to?'

After a journey that gave her time to think a bit more coherently about what was happening, she came reluctantly to terms with Tom's situation but was left agonizing about why and where Harry Barnard had so unexpectedly vanished. The only conclusion she reached was that DCI Strachan, who she firmly believed was responsible for Tom's injuries, must be involved with Barnard's disappearance too.

When she finally came out of the station at Freshfield she found herself faced with a number of large houses in extensive grounds and a road leading away to the right helpfully named Golf Road. Even from where she stood she could see the manicured links stretching away to the dunes that lined the shore and could glimpse the grey waters where the river met the shallow sandbanks and the sea. Looking down the rows of substantial houses to her left, she decided that there was no way she was going to track down Jordan by knocking on those palatial front doors, so she set off up the road to the golf course, hoping she might find someone there who knew Terry Jordan or his wife. From what she had heard about Jordan, she did not think he would be unknown to other members of the club. But what she had left out of account was that this was a club without lady members, and she attracted increasingly quizzical looks from the men, some of them wearing plus fours, that were hurrying in and out of the facilities followed by caddies carrying their heavy golf bags or pulling them along. As she approached what looked like the main club house, a man in a navy uniform stopped her and asked her business in an aggressive tone.

'I've a message for Mr Terry Jordan,' she said. 'There's no reply at his house and I wondered if he was here.' The man hesitated for a moment.

'I've not seen him today,' he conceded as if even this admission was more than his job was worth. 'But Mrs Jordan was here for luncheon with some of her friends. Ladies are admitted to the social facilities as guests.' He made it sound as if he did not really approve of that amount of latitude being offered to what he would no doubt call the weaker sex.

'Is she still here?' Kate asked. The man looked behind him to where various groups were emerging from the club house, most of them in a cheerful, even merry, mood after, Kate guessed, copious drinks and a substantial Sunday lunch.

'She's the lady in the blue dress,' her informant admitted in a whisper, unbending for a moment. 'But don't tell anyone I told you, la.'

Most of the group got into cars but Mrs Jordan waved them off and began walking slightly unsteadily towards the gates. As she approached, Kate was able to fall into step beside her.

'Mrs Jordan?' she asked. 'I'm Kate O'Donnell. I think you know my father, Frank.'

The woman stopped and gave her a deeply suspicious look.

'So what if I do, dear?' she asked, her accent pure Scotland Road, untouched by her wealthy surroundings. 'What is it you want?'

'He works for your husband,' Kate said in a rush, 'and he seems to have disappeared. My brother's in hospital very ill, so we need to contact my da and thought maybe Mr Jordan would know where he is. They're old friends from the war, I think. I'd be very, very grateful if you could help me find him.'

Kate realized that Mrs Jordan was swaying slightly, and her eyes were glazed as if what she had heard was difficult to take in. The older woman put a hand on Kate's arm and held on tightly.

'I think we'd better go home if you want to talk,' Mrs Jordan said. 'It's only just round the corner. I wonder if I misunderstood what you just said. I thought you meant . . .' She hesitated. 'Oh, never mind. Come back with me and tell me all about it. I'd not say no to the company. My husband's actually gone off on one of his jaunts.'

'That would be good,' Kate said and they made their somewhat erratic way down the road, with Kate steering her companion out of the way of the cars still leaving the club, until Mrs Jordan veered to the right and came to a stop outside a pair of substantial gates at the end of a broad drive with a low ranch-style house visible at the end of it.

'Come in, come in,' Mrs Jordan said when they finally made it to the front door and she succeeded, after several attempts, in inserting the key into the lock. She led the way into a large sitting room facing on to the back garden, which itself looked out over the rolling golf links where some men were still playing.

'Wonderful!' Kate said, thinking of the cramped tenements where Jordan himself, if not his wife, must have grown up. She realized that Mrs Jordan had veered across the room to a massive cocktail cabinet where she was busy pouring herself a drink.

'Housekeeper's off today. Do you want something?' she asked, waving a bottle of gin in Kate's general direction. 'G&T?' Kate shook her head. It might be wise, she thought, to pin the lady down before she could drink much more and perhaps fall down senseless, as she had seen her own father do more than once.

'They told me at his office that your husband is away in London,' she said, 'and I wondered if you knew about the accident at the building site where my dad was the foreman and where he might be. An Irish lad was killed, and no one's seen my da since. He's not come home, he's simply vanished. And now my brother's in hospital seriously ill, so we really need to contact my da.'

Mrs Jordan sank into the embrace of one of the enormous sofas, slopping her drink down the front of her blue summer dress. Some slight spark of understanding entered her blue eyes.

'Frankie O'Donnell . . .' she said. 'Is he your father? Or you think he is, anyway? In my experience you can never be too sure.'

Kate opened her mouth to protest at this unexpected slur on her mother, then thought better of it. Mrs Jordan giggled and slopped her drink again. 'I haven't heard about an accident at all, but I remember Frankie from the war. He used to help Terry now and then when he was a rescue man. Burrowing into all those ruins like rats. That was before we were married, of course, and before Terry went legit in the building trade. I don't suppose I'd have looked at him in those days. He might have been a part-time hero, but he was a bit of a spiv too. Always on the make. I don't know how he got away with it. It was good practice, I suppose, for what he's been getting away with since.'

Kate was startled by Carmel Jordan's candour, but hesitated to ask what she meant.

'Never mind!' Carmel added, evidently realizing, even through the alcohol fumes, that she'd said too much. 'Anyway, I can't complain, can I?' And she waved an expansive hand around the vast sitting room.

'My da's been working for your husband on the building sites recently,' Kate said. 'Did you know that, Mrs Jordan?'

'I did. Terry's mentioned his name once or twice. I knew he was back on the scene in spite of the booze.'

'He's supposed to talk to the police tomorrow about how this lad got killed. It'll all get very complicated if he doesn't turn up. And he doesn't know that my brother is in hospital . . .' Kate faltered slightly and Mrs Jordan put a hand on her knee.

'Call me, Carmel,' she said, nodding slightly, and took another drink. 'We don't stand on ceremony here. I leave that to Terry and the la-di-da friends he's making these days all over the place. He built this house for entertaining, he said. Entertaining and for the children that never arrived. But I don't like entertaining.' Kate realized with embarrassment that there were tears coursing down Carmel Jordan's face, making runnels in her heavy make-up and smudging her lipstick.

'I'm sorry,' she said, feeling helpless in the face of grief she didn't understand and could do nothing about. Carmel finished her drink in one and her face suddenly contorted.

'I wouldn't mind if he didn't humiliate me with his bloody women,' she said. 'Terry, I mean. He's always got some floozy on the go.'

'At least my da didn't do that,' Kate murmured.

'The worst thing was we were having a row one night and he told me one of them had had his child. I could have killed him. For all I know, he's got dozens of little bastards scattered about the place. But he's indestructible, is Terry. It was obvious in the war – he should have been killed a dozen times bulldozing his way through the ruins the way he did, but he was never even seriously hurt. He came out of it a hero, and there was no gainsaying him in Liverpool after that. Thought he was invincible. And maybe he is. One of my friends told me he'd taken his latest bit of fluff to London with him on this trip. Doreen Darcy she calls herself. How brazen is that when he's talking to some Church bigwig about developing land they own? Who'd ever have thought he'd be in deep with the Monsignors, the Corporation, the planners . . . Anyone who's anyone with a bit of influence, it looks like. You'd think he'd rebuilt the bloody city all on his own, though it's true he's rebuilt more of it than anyone would've expected when he started. And now some minister in London is ready to eat out of his hand, apparently. If I hadn't listened too hard to the bloody Church, I'd have divorced him years ago and dented his reputation. Trouble is I like my little luxuries too much to give them up.' She lay back on the sofa with her eyes closed and Kate was afraid she was falling asleep as she began to breathe laboriously, her heavily bejewelled hands laid across her breasts as if she was practising for her own burial.

'So you've no idea where my da might be?' Kate persisted. Carmel opened her eyes blearily.

'I've not seen him, dear,' she said. 'Not for years. I do remember him vaguely, but I don't take much notice of Terry's business. If your da's blotted his copy book, he's most likely have taken the first boat out, isn't he? He'll know Terry won't help him if he thinks he can avoid the blame for a nasty accident himself.'

Kate sighed heavily.

'I'll get back to the hospital, then,' she said. 'Thank you for trying to help.'

'I'm sorry for your troubles,' Carmel Jordan said. 'I'll remember your poor brother in my prayers.'

Much good that will do, Kate said to herself as she made her way out of the rambling house. She'd come all this way and gained absolutely nothing. And her worst fear was that for Tom it might already be too late.

THIRTEEN

F eeling sick and desperate, Kate took the train back to the city. Her first instinct was to go straight to the hospital, but as she was close to the police station she thought she would call in there to see if she could track down Harry Barnard. The sergeant on the desk looked at her as blankly as his predecessor had done earlier.

'Never heard of him,' he said, his eyes so opaque that she knew he could only be lying.

'Well thanks,' she said and turned on her heel. She hurried back to where she had last seen Barnard's car and her heart lurched when she saw that there was still no sign of it. Harry could be looking for her, she thought, although she did not really believe it and in any case she knew she could not leave her family any longer. She needed to know how Tom's operation had gone and confess to her mother and sister that she had made no progress in finding her father. She half walked and half ran the rest of the way to the hospital, arriving hot and breathless. She found her family and Tom's boyfriend Kevin huddled in the waiting room more or less where she had left them and could tell from their pale, anguished faces that nothing much had changed while she was away.

'How is he?' she asked her mother, who merely shook her head, too overcome to speak.

'He's not come round from the operation yet,' Annie said. 'The doctor said it had gone as well as could be expected, whatever that means.'

'They've still got two bizzies sitting by his bed, even though he's unconscious,' Kevin said bitterly.

'Did you find out where your da might be?' Bridie asked and tears rolled down her face when Kate shook her head.

'I'm sorry,' she said. 'I managed to track down Mrs Jordan in Formby but she didn't know anything about him. And her husband's still in London, apparently. She didn't even know there'd been an accident at the building site. I went all that way for nothing, really.'

'Didn't your boyfriend take you in his car?' her mother asked. 'He is your boyfriend, isn't he? Though I only had to look at him to see he wasn't the sort of good Catholic you should be going with. Aren't I right?' Kate ignored the angry catechism.

'I've lost track of him,' she admitted. 'I don't know where the devil he is. His car's not where he left it. He said he was going to the police station but they don't seem to know anything about him. He must have gone somewhere else instead.'

'I'm sure he'll turn up,' Annie said, giving her a quick hug. Bridie sat scowling in silence for a long time, glancing endlessly towards the recovery ward where Tom lay and then at Kate, who refused to meet her accusing glances.

'Are you living with him?' she asked eventually.

'I share a flat with Tess,' Kate said, refusing to be drawn further, and watched her mother sink back into what looked like despair.

Eventually Bridie stirred herself again.

'Katie, can you do us all another favour, la?' she said tentatively. 'Can you get hold of Father Reilly for me? I wouldn't want Tom to slip away without the last rites. I know he'll not be in a state of grace but I'm sure Father Reilly will find an answer.' Kevin immediately got to his feet and, obviously biting back his anger, flung himself out of the room. Kate followed him and found him staring out of the window into the car park below. She put a hand on his shoulder.

'It's not what Tom would want,' he said bitterly.

'I know,' Kate said. 'But she's his mother.'

'And as far as the clergy are concerned I'm nothing, less than nothing. I've no right to even exist. Isn't that right?'

'As far as most people are concerned, you and Tom are both less than nothing. I'm sorry,' Kate said. Kevin looked at her with his eyes full of tears.

'I don't think I can live without him,' he said.

'My mother would say pray for him. But you're like me, you don't do that anymore. All we can do is hope, so let's do that.' She gave him a quick hug. 'I want to go back to my hotel and see if Harry has left me a message there,' she said. 'Why don't you come with me? It's not far and the fresh air will do you good.'

'Will you get the priest?' he asked.

'No,' Kate said. 'As you say, it's not what Tom would want.'

'We'll all go to hell together, then,' Kevin said with a crooked smile. They left the hospital together and slowly made their way to Brownlow Hill, buried in their own thoughts. As Kate had expected, the girl on reception handed her a piece of paper as they walked into the hotel. The message was very brief.

'I've been called back to London urgently by the DCI. Don't worry. Harry.' She crumpled the paper into a ball and threw it into a wastepaper basket, feeling totally bereft. At the moment when she needed him most, Barnard seemed to have deserted her.

'Why don't we get a drink?' she said to Kevin, with the world apparently crashing around their ears, and led the way to the nearest pub.

'I won't say "Cheers!",' she said, pulling a face at the kick of the raw spirit as she sipped the Jameson's he brought her. 'It doesn't seem the right thing to say.'

Harry Barnard was sitting in the front passenger seat of his own car as the Liverpool DC, who had not bothered to offer a name beyond Jim, drove quickly out of the city, making him wince every time he misjudged the gears. As they ground their way through heavy traffic to Widnes and over the Mersey to Runcorn, before heading south, he drifted in and out of sleep, pleased to leave a city he devoutly hoped he would never see again but knowing that he had left Kate deeply in the lurch.

They stopped briefly at a service station somewhere in the Midlands, and although DCI Strachan had left off the threatened handcuffs he knew Jim must have had orders not to let him out of his sight as he ostentatiously accompanied him to the gents. He wondered what sort of message had already gone to Jackson, but agonized more over what reason his boss had for summoning him so urgently back to base on a Sunday when they should both have been off duty. Sleep was easier once they joined the newly minted M1 motorway, although his aches and pains had gradually resolved themselves into a generalized discomfort that now seemed to extend from head to toe. The next time he struggled back to consciousness they had slowed down on the approach to Edgware, and Barnard fought to regain some semblance of coherent thought.

By the time they'd driven into the West End and Barnard had guided Jim to a parking space near the nick, his mood had switched from depression to a fierce anger about what had happened in the north. The two men walked into the police station together, and Barnard led the way two steps at a time up the stairs to the DCI's office and knocked. Jackson called them in and they found him at his meticulously tidy desk, as usual, with a distinctly unfriendly expression on his face.

'Sergeant,' he said. 'At last. And this is?'

'DC Jim Bailey,' the younger man said. 'My DCI said he wasn't fit to drive back on his own. He'd had a bit of an accident. But you wanted him back urgently, so here we are.' Jackson looked more closely at Barnard and took in the black eye and visible cuts and bruises. 'You'd better sit down, Sergeant,' he said. 'Thank you, DC Bailey, that was very helpful.' The Liverpool detective shrugged and turned away.

'Euston station is it, to get back home?' he flung over his shoulder as he slammed the door behind him.

Jackson leaned back in his chair for a moment, steepling his hands in front of his face as he surveyed the damage carefully.

'So exactly how did you end up in this state?' he asked at length.

'I'm not sure you're going to believe it, guv,' Barnard said wearily. 'But you got me out of a very nasty situation.'

'A bit of an accident, your colleague said?'

'It wasn't an accident,' Barnard said. 'No way was it that. I went to the nick in Liverpool to ask about my girlfriend's brother who'd been arrested. You remember he was a suspect a couple of years ago in a murder case?'

Jackson looked puzzled for a moment, then nodded.

'Not a case we're likely to forget,' he said. 'So what was he arrested for this time?'

'He's a homosexual, so the usual, I suppose. They dragged

him out of bed, which seemed a bit extreme.' Jackson did not hide his distaste but waved Barnard on.

'When I got there, he was being taken away in an ambulance and it was obvious he'd had a vicious beating. I evidently saw too much for the DCI up there, a bastard called Strachan, and they put me in a cell.'

'He arrested you?' Jackson snapped. 'For what?'

'They didn't bother with legal niceties,' Barnard said. 'Anyway, something I said annoyed them and two of them started in on me. Strachan and a sergeant. I guess they were carrying on where they'd left off with Tom O'Donnell. They obviously both had a taste for it.' He slipped off his jacket awkwardly, wincing, and unbuttoned his shirt to reveal the bruises on his chest and arms. 'And then there were threats to charge me with pretty well anything they could think up. Even to implicate me in O'Donnell's case. It's like the Wild West up there, guv. I couldn't believe what was going on in that nick.'

'Do you want to press charges?' Jackson asked. 'I'm not going to pretend it's a course I would recommend, it could turn into a very unpleasant stand-off between the two police forces.'

'I've got no witnesses to what happened,' Barnard said, grateful that the DCI seemed to believe him implicitly. 'I was in a cell. And I can't imagine anyone would give evidence against DCI Strachan, anyway. He's got that nick in an iron grip.' He managed a weak smile. 'You think you're tough, sir, but he's the hard man, believe me.'

'Tough but fair, I hope, Sergeant,' Jackson said sourly. 'You'd better see the medical officer straight away, because there have been developments here that I need to talk to you about urgently. Arrange to see the doctor first thing in the morning, then report to me. You need to know that the woman you interviewed in Pimlico who called herself Alicia – Alicia Guest as it turns out, a known call girl apparently – has been found dead in her flat. The DCI down there is very anxious to have words with you.'

Barnard drove home at a funeral pace and found his flat stuffy, untidy and tangibly empty after his absence. He flung his holdall into the kitchen, ran a bath, and lay in the faintly pink-tinged water until it was almost cold. Gingerly patting himself dry with a towel – which revealed where his cuts and grazes were still raw – he concluded that, in spite of the way he felt, the beating had inflicted no serious damage. He made himself an omelette, ate it while listening to the Kinks, and struggled to keep himself awake until he reckoned he could contact Kate back at her hotel. She took a long time to come to the phone, and when she did she sounded more forlorn than he could imagine her ever being.

'How's Tom?' he asked quietly, expecting the worst.

'He's through the operation,' Kate said. 'But he's still critical. My mother and sister are staying there tonight. I came back to the hotel partly because I need some sleep if I'm going to do some work tomorrow and partly because I hoped you'd be here. Where are you Harry? You disappeared just when I needed you most. I was going frantic.'

'I'm at home now,' he said. 'I ran into some trouble when I asked about Tom at the nick and then DCI Jackson called me back to London. There are some problems here too.' He heard her sigh heavily.

'I'm so sorry, Kate. Truly I am. They gave me no choice.' That at least was true, but he thought it best not to tell her now what had happened to him at Strachan's hands. It could wait until he saw her, by which time perhaps the damage would look less obvious and her own family problems would have eased.

'I have to go to work tomorrow,' he said. 'Something's come up which according to the DCI is important. But at least you now know where I am, so you can phone me if anything happens. Will you do that?' There was a long silence at the other end before Kate spoke again.

'I'll keep in touch,' she said eventually, and he could detect no enthusiasm in her voice and knew she would stay in Liverpool for as long as her family needed her. Where he figured in her plans he had no way of knowing, and dared not ask.

'I love you, Katie,' he said softly, but suspected she had already hung up. He slept only fitfully in spite of the Scotch he'd knocked back in the hope of oblivion, and by eight o'clock he was driving down Highgate Hill to meet the police doctor at the nick. The medic confirmed his own assessment that although he was black-and-blue he had come to no serious harm, but said he should confine himself to light duties for a few days.

When he opened DCI Jackson's door ten minutes later, he was not surprised to discover that his boss was not alone. A heavily built man in plain clothes was standing by the window gazing out at the heavy Monday morning traffic below easing its way into Regent Street. He spun round with unexpected speed as soon as the DCI called Barnard in.

'Did you see the MO?' Jackson demanded.

'Yes sir,' Barnard said, aware that this time he had not been asked to sit down and that the stranger by the window was weighing him up with unfriendly eyes, as if assessing his visible bruises before deciding to speak.

'Nothing seriously damaged,' Barnard said. 'I'm OK on light duties for a couple of days.'

'Right,' the second man snapped. 'No reason then why you can't explain in detail why you were on my patch messing about with a woman who is now dead. Was it ill-placed duty or pleasure, Sergeant? Or a bit of both? She seems to have been a tart and I'm aware you know plenty of them.'

'Only in the line of duty, sir,' Barnard said quietly. It was obvious this was a man he would be unwise to provoke. And although there had been times in the past when that answer would not have been strictly true, since he met Kate O'Donnell it was.

'This is DCI Tom Buxton from Pimlico,' Jackson interrupted irritably. Barnard merely shrugged and faced down Buxton's scowl.

'As you probably know, I've been working on the Soho Square murder, sir,' he said to Jackson rather than his colleague. 'We'd found out absolutely nothing about the dead woman or where she came from, but the obvious thought was that she was on the game – not necessarily in Soho but dumped there after being killed somewhere else. One of my regular contacts said she knew someone who'd told her there was a network of people offering dubious sex to upmarket clients and she'd got out because she didn't like it. After all the trouble there was last year with John Profumo and Christine Keeler and the rest, I thought I would suss it out quietly to see if it stood up. It seemed like a very long shot to me.'

'And that long shot turned out to be Alicia Guest?' Buxton snapped.

'Yes, sir,' Barnard said.

'What else did she tell you?' Buxton persisted.

'That it was very well paid, that she had little or no idea where she was being taken by car, and it wasn't the usual adults with too much money and kinky tastes. And she said that children were sometimes involved.'

'Did she recognize your sketches of the dead woman?'

'She said not,' Barnard said.

'And you didn't think to come and tell me about your little excursion into Pimlico?' Buxton almost snarled.

'I didn't think she'd told me anything of any significance. She wouldn't name names. In fact she said she didn't know any. And she said if anyone else came round asking questions she would deny the whole lot, say it was all wild rumours.'

'Which happens to be what we believe,' Buxton said. 'I could have told you all that for nothing. Tell me exactly what time you called on Alicia Guest – when you arrived and when you left.'

Barnard thought back to an afternoon when he had been only marginally aware of time.

'I must have got there about three and stayed half an hour or so, not more.'

'Did you see anyone else around Alicia Guest's flat? Anyone going in or out? Or hanging about outside?'

'No, sir,' Barnard said. Buxton glanced across the desk towards an impassive DCI Jackson but made no comment.

'Did you drive straight back to the nick after that?' Barnard struggled to recall what he had done next.

'I sat in the car for a cigarette for a while thinking about what Alicia had told me,' he said slowly. 'I wanted to work out if there was another way of tracking these people down. But nothing much suggested itself, so I drove back to the nick.'

'And decided to tell me or your own DCI nothing about it?'

'It didn't seem worth bothering you if she was going to deny it all anyway,' Barnard said. 'To be honest, I'm still not sure why she told me any of it. I didn't push her particularly hard, she just came out with it. Maybe she felt threatened in some way and wanted someone to know what she knew. And it seems she was right to be afraid. Maybe she knew what was coming and I didn't pick up on it.'

Buxton snorted his disbelief and turned to Jackson again.

'I'd like you to keep this officer under your thumb until we can eliminate him from our inquiries. The medical evidence suggests that Alicia Guest died that afternoon or evening. Anyone who was in the vicinity of the flat has to be regarded as a suspect.'

Barnard suddenly felt very cold. He glanced at Jackson but there was apparently no help available from that quarter.

'You must be joking!' he said, his mouth dry and his heart thumping.

'No Sergeant, I am not,' Buxton said, turning on his heel and flinging open the door behind him. 'I'll see you for a formal interview very soon.'

FOURTEEN

Next morning Kate stood by her brother's hospital bed with a sense of relief, though struggling to overcome the fierce anger that had flared when she saw the battered state of him again. His head was heavily bandaged and as far as she could see every inch not covered by the hospital smock was black-and-blue. But at least he was conscious, his eyes half-open, and he struggled to smile when he saw her, and the uniformed police officers who had been kicking their heels by his bedside seemed to have disappeared, at least for the time being.

'Sorry, sis,' he whispered as he took her hand.

'What on earth was that all about? It's not you who should be sorry.'

'Strachan's a throwback,' he said. 'He hates queers, hates Catholics, hates what he calls Fenians.'

'Surely that was all over years ago?' Kate objected. 'The IRA's long dead and buried.'

'Of course it is, but men like Strachan never forgive and never forget.' Kate ran a hand through her hair in fury. She pulled out her camera and took a couple of flash photographs of the battered figure in the bed.

'I'm taking these in case we ever get the chance to hold Strachan to account. He nearly killed you,' she said.

'There were no witnesses,' Tom said dully. 'They can do what they like in that place. I've known that for a long time. What I don't understand is why me.'

'Kevin said you'd moved out of the city to get away from this sort of thing. He said you kept a low profile, kept out of trouble.' Tom nodded cautiously and Kate could see he was still in pain.

'Kevin was beside himself,' she said. 'I like Kevin, by the way, though mam can hardly bear to look at him.'

'Yes, well, you can't say it's only Strachan who's a

dyed-in-the-wool bigot, can you? It cuts every which way.'
Tom turned his head away and winced again, and Kate could
see he was not nearly as resilient as he was pretending to be.

'Mam wants me to come back to live in Liverpool,' Kate
said. 'There's fat chance of that!' Tom struggled to find another
smile.

'I should stay well away if I were you,' he said. 'If she finds
out you're living with Harry Barnard, she'll set the inquisition
on you.' He looked beyond her and found another smile, and
Kate turned to find her sister Annie and Tom's boyfriend Kevin
making their way into the ward, followed by a slightly flustered-
looking nurse. Kevin glanced around nervously to see who was
watching before giving Tom a hug.

'The bizzies said no visitors,' the nurse said.

'Then the bizzies will have to chase us away – if they dare,'
Kate said and the nurse withdrew looking even more flustered.

'They think he's on the mend, I hear,' Annie said to Kate
and she nodded.

'I bumped into one of the doctors on the way in,' Kate told
her, 'and he said Tom should be fit to go home in a week or
so. But I suppose that will depend on the police. Perhaps they
won't want to take him to court in the state he's in. It wouldn't
look good.'

'Mam wants him to stay with her,' Annie said and Kate
caught the look of horror Tom and Kevin exchanged.

'No way!' Kevin said flatly. 'He's coming home with me.
I'm the one who should look after him.'

'She doesn't really mean it,' Tom said. 'She'd be mortified if what I am and what's happened to me was common
knowledge around the parish. And da couldn't put up with
it for a moment.'

'I wish I knew where da was,' Kate said. 'I've been running
round in circles trying to find him. I'll call in the police station
later to see if he turned up this morning for his interview about
the accident.'

'You need to watch yourself there,' Tom said, his bitterness
suddenly on show.

'I'll come with you,' Annie said, grabbing Kate's arm. 'It
doesn't sound safe for you to go on your own.

'We'll be careful,' Kate said. 'I have to go home tonight too. I've a few more pictures to take this morning and then I must get the train. My boss will be expecting me back.' She looked at the three of them in turn. 'I'm so sorry it turned out like this,' she said. She kissed Tom gently with tears in her eyes before turning away feeling torn in two.

Kate and her sister felt nervous as they went into the police station, but the young constable on the desk didn't appear too intimidating and agreed readily enough to check if Frank O'Donnell was due in to make a statement concerning the death of the young builder and whether he had turned up. But after disappearing into the bowels of the building for a short time he came back looking worried.

'He was due to come in at nine this morning with a solicitor from Macdonald-Jordan Construction, but he hasn't turned up or let anyone know why not,' he said. 'Who did you say you were? His daughters?'

'He's not been home all weekend,' Kate said.

'Is that unusual?' the constable asked.

Annie shrugged.

'He goes on a bender sometimes. He doesn't always tell our mam where he is. But after someone got killed . . . We thought he'd be here.'

'If it's that important, I should think we'll start looking for him. He must be a crucial witness. The coroner will want him traced to give evidence. Give me your details and if we track him down I'll let you know.' Kate and Annie trailed out into the street again.

'I have to get on now,' Kate said. 'I want to be on my way by teatime, but I'll need to collect my luggage from the hotel so you can leave a message there if you need me.'

'I'm sorry this has turned into such a mess, la,' Annie said. 'Mam was really hoping that da had turned over a new leaf with a steadier job, but it looks as if that idea's blown sky high.'

'Keep me in touch,' Kate said. 'You've got the phone numbers in London, haven't you? Both my flat and Harry's? Don't hesitate to call if you need me. Promise?'

'Of course,' Annie said, turning away. Kate watched her walk slowly away towards the buses at the Pier Head, her shoulders slumped, and wondered how her family could have disintegrated so violently and completely in such a short time. She felt very much alone.

She spent the next couple of hours taking pictures of new buildings in fitful sunshine and then, as she was passing the *Liverpool Echo* building, wondered if Liam Minogue was free for a coffee or even a sandwich. She felt like talking to someone who was not part of her private life. He would talk music and city gossip and might provide a welcome antidote for her troubles.

The young man on the reception desk made a phone call and told her that Minogue would be down in five minutes. While she waited, she passed the time reading the first edition of the *Echo*, where Liam was still speculating about the success or otherwise of the Beatles' return home and whether or not they could be expected to come back to Merseyside to live. Local opinion seemed to be divided, with some locals arguing that the Fab Four had already sold out to the south and even to America, while others were keen to see them returning to the roots where they belonged. The perspective was parochial and the tone a bit snarky. Kate would have put a Grand National-size bet on the four of them never coming back.

Liam Minogue caught her smiling over the front page.

'Hello,' he said. 'I thought you had probably gone home by now,' he said. 'Have you finished your assignment?'

'Just about,' she said. 'I'm getting a train at teatime. I have to be in the office tomorrow morning. But I thought we might have a coffee before I go. There's been some stuff going on which you might like to know about here at the *Echo*.'

'Come on then,' Minogue said and led the way to the café across the street that they'd been to before. 'Tea, coffee? A toasted teacake or a sandwich maybe?'

'Just coffee,' Kate said and when it came she gave Minogue a hard look.

'I know you're the Beatles correspondent,' she said cautiously. 'But maybe your crime correspondent would like to know about what happened at the Bridewell over the

weekend. My brother's still in hospital as a result of it.'
Minogue's face darkened and he took a sip of coffee.

'Your brother?' he said when Kate didn't immediately
continue.

'He was arrested on Saturday night and by Sunday morning
he was in hospital after what looks to have been a severe
beating. They had to operate to relieve pressure on his brain.
He could have died, Liam, and we can't get a word of sense
out of the police. My boyfriend is a detective with the Met
and he couldn't get a word of explanation for what happened
from the DCI – what's his name, Strachan?'

'Hang on, hang on!' Minogue said. 'How did he come to
be arrested? Was he in a street fight or what? Liverpool
can be a bit rough on a Saturday night. Especially after all
the excitement there's been with the film premiere.'

'They went to Tom's home and pulled him out of bed,' Kate
said.

'On what charge?'

'Nobody has bothered to tell us that. We assume it's because
he's a homosexual. He was in bed with his boyfriend when
they came calling in the middle of the night.'

Minogue took a deep breath and glanced away, refusing to
meet her eyes for a minute in obvious embarrassment.

'They do that, the bizzies,' he said. 'Sometimes when the
mood takes them, they go out and round up a few queers. Poofs
aren't much liked around here by either the Prods or the
Catholics. Or anyone else for that matter.'

'So it's OK to beat someone half to death when you arrest
them, is it, because you don't like who they're sleeping with?'

'It's still illegal, Kate,' Minogue said defensively. 'And
there're plenty of people who think it should stay that way.
I guess DCI Strachan is one of them. A lot of coppers are.'

'And what about you?' Kate snapped. 'I know only too well
what the Catholic Church thinks. And I dare say you do too. I've
heard all that since I was old enough to understand what was
going on with Tom. But I don't imagine even the Pope thinks
people like Tom should be killed for their sins. And that's what
nearly happened. He was almost killed and I want to know why.
I thought it was a scandal the *Echo* would be glad to expose.'

'It's a stone my editor won't turn over in a million years – neither side of it, and there are two sides, believe me,' Liam said. 'I went to a very respectable Catholic boys' school where the discipline was strict. It wasn't until I'd long left that I understood that the practice of making little boys bare their buttocks to be beaten with a butter pat by the Brothers for various misdemeanours was anything other than acceptable punishment. But attempting to expose that, or DCI Strachan's little games, is a waste of time. My career would be over before it's hardly even started. I'm not that brave, or that stupid.'

Kate looked at the reporter sombrely as he glanced away.

'Attitudes are different in London,' she said. 'A bit different, anyway. I think most people know the law is going to change and they're beginning to act as if it already has.'

'Well, good for them. But this is Liverpool,' Liam said. 'It's not quite Belfast or Glasgow but prejudice lingers in the cracks here, bubbles up when you least expect it, and no one is brave enough to complain. The Churches have fingers in every pie, believe me. We had some sort of a graduate trainee in the newsroom a while ago from some private school and he started going on about it. He was a Quaker or something like that. He didn't last long, and went back down south. I'm sorry, Kate, but I'm not going to be the one to put my head above the parapet. I know it would get blown off.' And with that she had to be content.

Harry Barnard had slept badly and, although he'd resisted the temptation to finish the whisky sitting alluringly in his cocktail cabinet, he felt even more fragile the next morning than when he left Liverpool. And DCI Tom Buxton seemed to go out of his way to make his interview in Pimlico as threatening as it could be.

'Do you want a Federation rep with you? Or a solicitor?' he barked across the interview room table where he was sitting with a DS at his side.

'No sir,' Barnard said. 'I'm happy to tell you anything you want to know. I've nothing to hide. I was following a slightly obscure lead in a murder case, not really strong enough to make a fuss about. I've done nothing wrong except not mentioning it to you in the first place.'

'We'll see about that,' Buxton said. 'So let's start at the beginning. Who gave you Alicia Guest's name and address?'

'A contact in Soho. A tart I've known for years. I mentioned to her that we thought the woman found in Soho Square was on the game and she asked around to see if anyone knew who she might be. They didn't, but she picked up a rumour about Alicia Guest and got me her address.'

'And this tart's name is?' Barnard hesitated, but the two men on the other side of the table waited stony-faced and he knew he would do himself no favours and Evie little harm if he told them.

'Are you sleeping with her, this Evie?' the sergeant asked with a sly grin.

'No,' Barnard said. 'A long time ago occasionally, but not now.'

Buxton nodded. 'This is because you have this girlfriend? The photographer girl? Sounds an odd job for a woman,' he said.

'She's very good at it,' Barnard said.

'So how did Evie find out about Alicia Guest?' Buxton went on.

'She said a friend told her,' Barnard said uneasily, knowing that they would not be satisfied with that as an answer and that he had landed Evie with an unwanted visit from the Pimlico murder team if nothing worse.

'So tell us exactly everything that happened during your visit to Miss Guest – the times, anyone else you saw or spoke to, anyone who might have seen you, and exactly what you talked about. Dot every 'i' and cross every 't', Sergeant. I've already got you marked down for a disciplinary hearing but it could be worse, much worse, if you leave anything out and I find out about it.'

Barnard went over the details of his trip to Pimlico again, slowly and carefully. The sergeant across the desk took notes, but as the interview went on he got the distinct impression that there were specific facts they were interested in which did not necessarily fit with their inquiries into a murder.

'Are you sure that she gave no indication she knew where

she was being taken when she was hired for these trips?'
Buxton pressed.

'She said not,' Barnard said. 'She said it was different places.
But she did say some of them were not far away from where
she was living. A short drive, she said.'

'And she didn't recognize anyone when she got there?'

'It would appear that the men took good care not to be
recognized,' Barnard said. 'But she was being asked to do
things and witness things she didn't like, so she decided to
pack it in. Beyond that she wasn't prepared to go. They were
sufficiently worried about her to pay her off, so she took
the money and left.'

'So there are two possibilities, Sergeant. Either these people
found out that she had talked to you and decided to silence
her, which sounds unlikely. Or she was killed by some random
intruder looking for quick pickings who panicked when she
found him in the flat.'

'How was she killed?' Barnard asked, aware that Buxton
had told him no details about the crime and if he was serious
about counting him as one of his suspects he would be watching
closely to see how much he knew about what had gone on in
Alicia Guest's flat.

'Stabbed,' Buxton said. 'Very messy. A lot of blood. We
may need to take a look at the clothes you were wearing that
afternoon. Purely for purposes of elimination, of course. And
your fingerprints.'

'Oh come on, sir!' Barnard said, finally losing patience. 'You
know that's ridiculous. I'm sorry I trespassed on your territory
and no way could I guess that I might have put this woman in
danger. It was a routine inquiry which I had no great hopes of.
But if you seriously think she was killed to keep her quiet
about the nasty sex conspiracy she got herself involved in,
surely that's where you should be looking for her killer?'

'That's for me to decide, Sergeant, not you. And if I find
you interfering in my investigations again, I'll throw the book
at you. Understood?'

Barnard sighed.

'Understood,' he said.

*   *   *

Kate O'Donnell got back to her hotel about four to collect her
luggage and was surprised to see her mother sitting in an
uncomfortable chair close to the reception desk in what looked
like her best black coat, buttoned up to the neck in spite of
the sticky summer heat. She stood up when Kate came in
and the expression in her eyes was angry.

'Were you going to leave without saying goodbye to me?'
she snapped.

'I'm sorry,' Kate said. 'I thought you would come to the
hospital this morning with Annie. It was important to make
sure Tom was all right before I left. Then I had some work
stuff to do before catching the train.'

'I've just been up there, la,' Bridie said, but her face did
not soften. 'I want him to come home to stay with me when
they let him out. That other young man is a bad influence.'

'Mam, you can't run our lives for us now. We're all grown
up. We make our own decisions.'

'And that's why you've decided not to go to Mass any more,
is it? You're too grown up for all that? Holy Mother of God,
who do you modern children think you are! Do you really
think you're more important than the Church?' Bridie's eyes
narrowed. 'Or is it because you're living in sin with that man
you brought round to my house? Is that what it is? Has he
brought this on? Has London turned you into a little whore?
On top of having Tom the way he is!'

Kate reddened and got to her feet, aware that the receptionist
was casting interested eyes in the direction of their hissed
conversation.

'Come outside,' she snapped at her mother and they went
into the street where their voices were muffled by the traffic
on Brownlow Hill. 'Who told you that anyway?' Kate asked.

'Never you mind,' Bridie said. 'As if I don't have enough
to cope with now your father's missing and Tom's in hospital
and may end up in prison. Couldn't you behave yourself, at
least?'

'I suppose it was Father Reilly, was it? That man thinks he
owns his parishioners and evidently his former parishioners
too. Well, you can tell him to mind his own business. And
you do that as well, mam. I gave up on your precious Church

a long time ago. I had good reason. And I'll make my own friends, come to that. It's nothing to do with you. And now I have to hurry to catch my train. I'm going back to London, and where I live and who I live with is nothing at all to do with you or anyone else up here – especially the priests, who are the biggest hypocrites of all.'

Kate arrived back at the flat she shared with Tess late, tired and hungry. Her friend looked at her in alarm as she dumped her suitcase in her room and slumped down on the sofa and closed her eyes.

'You look shattered,' she said. 'Are you all right?'

'Starving,' Kate said. 'There was no food on the train. Have you got anything in the fridge?' Together they rustled up an omelette and some toast, and as Kate wolfed it down she told Tess roughly what had happened in Liverpool. Tess looked completely stunned by the time she had finished. She put an arm round Kate's shoulders.

'We all know the bizzies used to be complete bastards,' she said quietly. 'But I thought all that was over. I thought all that prejudice had gone away. I thought you went up to get pictures of a shiny new modern city with all that marvellous music going on, a fun place to be . . .'

'Oh, all that's going on all right, la,' Kate said. 'But the old guard is hanging in there when they think they can get away with it. And with Tom the police obviously thought they could get away with it. Tom and his friends are no safer than they ever were. He could have died, Tess.' And for the first time Kate let the tears flow and she sobbed on her friend's shoulder.

'Are you staying here tonight or going back to Harry's place?' Tess asked when Kate eventually calmed down. Kate shrugged dispiritedly.

'I'll stay here, I think,' she said. 'My mother found out about Harry, so that was a bone of contention too. She's furious of course. He came back earlier for some urgent reason, so I'm not even sure where he is today. I'll ring him later maybe and then go to bed.'

She carried her suitcase into her bedroom and sat on the edge of the bed. It was a nondescript room and she started unpacking until she suddenly became aware that nothing in the room looked quite right. It had not been ransacked like her hotel room in Liverpool, but she was quite sure it had been interfered with. Books had been moved, her underwear was not quite as she usually left it in its drawers, her clothes in the wardrobe had been arranged with a mathematical precision on their hangers, and the place somehow failed to feel like home. One incursion into her private space had been enough to upset her, two felt very threatening. The first, at the hotel, could have been a petty thief, a random trawl looking for something to steal, but this was careful and cautious and felt very different, professional almost.

She was so tired that she felt like dropping straight into bed but before she began to undress she heard the doorbell. Hoping that maybe Harry Barnard had called round unexpectedly, she went back into the living room and to her surprise found that Tess had opened the door to a priest in a dark suit and clerical collar, rather than a cassock, who looked more like a wolfish stony-faced business man than a man of the cloth. There was certainly no human kindness in his face that Kate could see, and his eyes were a chilly grey.

'Father Granville came before,' Tess explained. 'He said he would come back to see you.'

'I've only just come back from Liverpool, Father,' Kate said, not disguising her anger. 'I'm about to go to bed.'

'I wanted to catch you, my dear,' Granville said. 'From what your friend Teresa told me, I felt you were in urgent need of help before your life runs completely out of control.' She heard echoes of what her mother had said to her before she left Liverpool and wondered whether Bridie herself, or more likely Father Reilly, was responsible for this evident panic over her immortal soul.

'I am told you no longer go to Mass or confession regularly, my dear. The Church is bound to be concerned about that.'

'You've no need to be concerned about me,' Kate said, feeling a fury building inside her that she did not think she could control for long. 'I no longer regard myself as a Catholic, and haven't done for a very long time.'

'I have a very good colleague at St Aloysius, a colleague

who is a sympathetic adviser to people struggling with doubt,'
Granville persisted. 'I can introduce you to him if you would
like that.'

'I would not like that,' Kate said firmly. 'I would like to be
left alone to live my life in peace. I had enough of the Church
when I was a child. You did my brother no favours.'

Granville changed tack abruptly, his expression harder. 'I
hear that you have been gathering information about the career
of Terry Jordan in Liverpool. Now there is an example of a
man who is a great benefactor to the Church despite a difficult
start in life. He has been more than generous to the cathedral,
and I think we can look forward to a lot more help if his
current negotiations are successful. The Church is very much
involved in a lot of his current plans. We wouldn't like to
think that your own project would in any way hinder his efforts
for such a very important cause.'

'My project is about the rebuilding of Liverpool. And I can't
see any way that would affect Mr Jordan and his plans.'

'Which are at a very crucial stage, both for him and for the
Church. We would not like to think that anything you've been
doing would interfere with that.' There was no overt threat in
what Granville said, but the menace was there in his eyes.

'I have no idea why anything I've been doing should lead
you to think that,' Kate said, turning away from her visitor.
'Now I am very tired and I'm going to bed.'

But she lay in bed for a long time before exhaustion took
over, and she fell into a sleep tormented by dreams.

FIFTEEN

Barnard drove back to Soho feeling alternately frazzled and furious. But instead of parking close to the nick, he turned into the maze of narrow streets where legitimate pubs and restaurants stood shoulder to shoulder with both overt and more secretive haunts of sex workers and petty criminals, extortionists and gangsters, in a teeming den of fun and vice that enticed punters from all over London and far beyond. He knew that eventually he would have to tell DCI Jackson the result of his interview with Buxton but he needed a drink first, and he needed to warn Evie Renton that she should expect a visit from Pimlico detectives sooner rather than later, no doubt with the DCI's blessing. In the circumstances, Barnard reflected, Jackson could hardly refuse without a furious row between the two empires that might well reach the Yard itself.

He knocked on Evie's door for some time before she opened it, obviously just out of bed, in a flimsy dressing gown, her face pale and creased with sleep, and with only the faintest smile of welcome for Barnard.

'What is it now?' she asked, yawning. 'I really need my rest.'

'Don't we all,' Barnard said. 'Can I come in? I need to talk to you.'

She reluctantly held the door open for him and he followed her up the stairs to her room, which was even more untidy and dishevelled than the last time he'd been there. She looked shocked when she took in his battered appearance.

'What the hell happened to you?' she asked, flinging herself back on to her bed and pulling the blankets up. There was no hint of the invitation she had issued last time he'd seen her, and he was thankful for that.

'I met a brick wall,' he said, fingering the bruising around his left eye and cheek. 'You don't want to know.'

'I hope the brick wall came off worst,' Evie said.

'Not so you'd notice.'

'Occupational hazard then, was it? I know all about them.'

'Well, I came to warn you you've got one coming up, sweetie,' Barnard said. 'Some coppers from Pimlico want to know how you tracked down Alicia Guest. I wouldn't have landed you with them but Alicia's dead, murdered, and they're not going to let go until they find out exactly how I came to be talking to her – entirely innocently, I hasten to add – on the day she was killed. I'm sorry.' Evie lay back on her pillows and groaned.

'I had another nugget of information for you too, as it happens,' Evie said, 'but maybe I should keep quiet.'

'What is it?' Barnard said. 'I need to crack this murder case quickly, as it goes, or it's going to hang round me like a bad smell. Tell me and I'll have a sniff around and then pass it on to the Pimlico boys if it looks as if it could be useful. How does that sound?'

'A bit dodgy,' she said.

'Yes, you're probably right,' Barnard said tiredly. 'I'm not thinking straight. You'd best tell them everything you know. But tell me first. I've no idea when they'll get round to questioning you, if they ever do, but you'd better be straight with them. I've got you into enough trouble as it is.'

'One of the girls up West told me that the place to look for kinky goings on is a flat in Dolphin Square – you know, that big posh block in Pimlico. That may be the answer you're looking for.'

'Yes, it well might,' Barnard said. 'I'll bear it in mind, thanks. And now I want to catch my girlfriend if I can and buy her some lunch. I've been messing her around and I'm not sure she's even speaking to me.'

'Good luck,' Evie said and watched him go with tired, sad eyes, wondering why life had not been different.

Closing the street door quietly behind him, Barnard pondered whether Dolphin Square could be the place Alicia said she'd been taken to close to home. It was, he concluded, worth a look if he could manage to keep out of DCI Buxton's way. He walked quickly up Frith Street to the Ken Fellows Agency, where Kate worked. He opened the main door on the first landing cautiously, not sure what her reaction would be, but Kate was sitting facing the door and spotted him at once with a look not of welcome but of shock. She pushed aside the photographs on her desk and stood up with a hand across her mouth.

'What happened to you?' she asked, coming towards him with anxious eyes.

'Can you come out for a coffee?' he asked. 'Maybe with enough caffeine inside me I can tell you about it.' Kate glanced at Ken Fellows' office door and shrugged.

'The boss is out this morning, so I can take an early lunch,' she said and followed Barnard to the door and down the narrow wooden stairs into the street. Outside on the pavement she stopped and turned to face him, putting a finger lightly on the worst of the bruises.

'What happened?' she asked. 'Who the hell did this to you?'

'I got the same treatment as your brother,' he said. 'And from the same bastards who nearly killed him. I went to the nick to see what was going on and saw too much – far too much, in fact. The ambulance had just arrived to take Tom away and I thought for an awful moment he was dead. Of course, when DCI Strachan spotted me he was furious. They stuck me in a cell for a bit, but luckily for me they didn't dare send two bodies to Casualty the same morning so I got away with a beating. But only just.'

'Why on earth did you go to the Bridewell? I told you it was a dangerous place. Going in and inquiring about an Irish queer was asking for trouble, even if you are a copper. And why didn't you phone and tell me what had happened? You just disappeared without a word. I'd no idea.'

'I didn't have any choice,' he said. 'They shipped me back to London in short order. It was that or face some cooked-up charge in Liverpool. And anyway, I thought you had enough to worry about,' he said, turning her around and steering her towards the Blue Lagoon coffee bar, where they had shared many lunches. 'How is Tom?' he asked.

'I rang the hospital first thing,' Kate said. 'They said he'd come round after the operation and had had a good night. Annie's with him.'

'And your father?'

'No news. He seems to have vanished into thin air.' The coffee bar was not busy yet and Barnard chose a table well away from the window, with the worst of his bruises to the wall. Kate looked bleak and, having ordered coffee and sandwiches, Barnard put his hand over hers.

'What's going on?' she said. 'When I got back last night I thought someone had been in my room. It didn't seem to be the way I left it. It wasn't ransacked like at the hotel. It was tidy, but not my sort of tidy. Things had been moved. What's going on, Harry? Is someone watching me?'

'I don't know,' Barnard said. 'There are too many things going on for it all to be coincidence. One thing is for sure. You need to come back to my place tonight, so I can keep an eye on you. I'll sleep on the sofa if you like, if you're still angry with me, but I won't sleep at all if I'm not sure you're safe. I'll pick you up from work at five, then we can collect your stuff from Shepherd's Bush and you can come home with me.'

'And leave Tess on her own? I don't want to do that if someone really has broken into the place.'

'I don't think anyone's interested in Tess. It's you and me who are the targets, though I haven't a clue why. I'm seeing the DCI this afternoon. I'll see if he knows what's going on. OK? Will you do that?'

'Of course I will,' Kate said feeling a slight sense of relief. For once she felt like allowing someone else to take charge of her life, though she guessed it was probably a feeling that would not last long. She reached out for Barnard's hand and covered it with hers.

'Thank you,' she said.

Barnard was strictly on time for his appointment with DCI Jackson and tolerated a searching appraisal of his bruised face before the boss waved him into a chair with some appearance of sympathy.

'I made some inquiries about your DCI Strachan,' he said. 'Apparently he's well-known on Merseyside for his heavy-handed approach to suspects. No one will admit it's anything other than normal or appropriate, though my guess is they're just too scared to tackle him about it. It sounds as if it's a race between his reaching retirement or killing someone before he gets there. He obviously got pretty close to the latter this time, although whether anyone would hold him to account seems very unlikely according to the people I've talked to. Are you feeling better, Sergeant?'

'Better than yesterday,' Barnard said, taken aback by Jackson's unexpectedly sympathetic approach. Then he remembered that Jackson had spent some of his career in Glasgow and wondered if he had seen some of Strachan's prejudices in action there. Perhaps he had even come south to try to escape them, although Barnard reckoned things were not much better in parts of the Met. He might not approve of Strachan's brutality, but there was no doubting that Jackson's attitude to queers was much the same as Strachan's.

'How did you get on with DCI Buxton in Pimlico?' Jackson asked.

'The "Keep Out" sign couldn't have been plainer,' Barnard said. 'I've got no idea whether our murder victim and this new death in Pimlico are connected, but if they are we won't be investigating it from here. He made that very clear. He wants my fingerprints and to pass whatever I was wearing that day to forensics just in case I might have stabbed her myself, but I'm sure that's just another form of intimidation rather than anything more serious. I seem to have carelessly annoyed two senior officers I could very happily have lived without knowing.'

'Well, we've tried all the other avenues, so maybe they'll have better luck,' Jackson said equably. 'The picture of the victim has been circulated widely, even to the provincial forces. Liverpool should have seen it, but no one has come back to us with a missing-person report which might fit. It's going up on all the noticeboards in the Met and it's being released to the Press and television. But so far she is as anonymous as on the night she was found.'

Barnard hesitated for a moment and wondered how far this new, more accommodating, Keith Jackson might go. The fact that he'd been beaten up in Liverpool seemed to have got to the DCI more than he'd expected and, with some trepidation, he decided to play his luck.

'I did go back to the tart who suggested I should talk to Alicia Guest. She's been digging around among her contacts up West and reckons that, if there is anything in this theory of mine that there is some sort of upmarket sex ring operating, one of its venues could be a flat in Dolphin Square.'

'You said this alleged organization was thought to be using children?'

'Yes, sir,' Barnard said – realizing, from Jackson's expression of distaste, what exactly had touched a nerve.

'If I'm seen hanging around there and Buxton finds out, my feet won't touch the ground. But I've thought of a way of sussing it out without annoying him.'

'Do I want to know about this in detail, Sergeant?' Jackson asked.

'It's a bit offbeat,' Barnard said with an attempt at a grin, which hurt. 'But nothing illegal. Just a bit of quiet off-the-radar surveillance.'

'Carry on, Sergeant,' Jackson said. 'Just remember you are on your own if anyone complains.'

Barnard left his car outside the nick and took the underground to Pimlico, then walked down towards the river, coat collar up and trilby pulled low in spite of the heat, until he came out alongside the bulk of Dolphin Square, which must, he reckoned, be one of the largest complexes of pricey flats in London. When he took in the size of it, block after block of anonymous windows looking out on to the street, it seemed so enormous that he could think of no easy way of identifying a single flat among so many. He knew the blocks were built around a central garden, but from the outside the place looked like an impregnable fortress where hundreds of people could conceal themselves and dozens of illicit or illegal activities could flourish undisturbed. Anyone living here with anything to hide had found the perfect place to fade into the anonymity of the eminently respectable crowd. People could come and go here at any time of the day and night, and no one would be any the wiser.

He slowly walked round the entire complex, close to the
river on the southern side and then back up towards Chichester
Street, where what looked like the main entrance faced the
road. As he completed his circuit, he began to despair of
finding any easy way into the bastion that the flats obviously
were. And it would be even harder to trace anyone to a specific
flat without help from the inside and without a single name
of a resident to go on. On the point of giving up and heading
back to the underground station, he froze and turned sharply
away from the entrance and made a performance of lighting
a cigarette against the gusty wind with his head turned away.
When he turned back, the man who had made his stomach
lurch was heading through the doors. He was in no doubt that
it was the man he least wanted to see during his second, and
forbidden, foray into Pimlico.

DCI Tom Buxton had left the doors swinging and Barnard
could still see him as he made his way across the hall to the
lifts. Barnard moved quickly behind him and watched warily
as a lift ascended then stopped at the fourth floor. Almost
without thinking, he hurried into an adjacent lift and pressed
the button for the same floor. When it got there, he held the
door open and glanced carefully out to see which way Buxton
had gone, then followed him at a discreet distance until he
rang a bell and entered a flat. With his heart thumping, Barnard
made a note of the flat number then quickly walked down the
long quiet carpeted corridor and descended to the ground floor
again. He had no idea what Buxton's behaviour implied – but
he could think of a number of embarrassing possibilities as
to what he was up to, which he would take great pleasure in
quietly investigating.

He did not go directly back to his own nick in the West
End. Instead, he sat in the Dolphin Square foyer for half an
hour reading a newspaper until eventually the lift was
summoned to the fourth floor again. Quickly he left the building
to watch from round the corner, under the shade of the trees
in St George's Square, until Buxton had passed down Chichester
Street and he felt safe enough to fall into step at a discreet
distance behind him. When he was sure that the DCI was
heading back to the nick, he turned on his heel and repeated

the journey to Dolphin Square where he returned to the fourth
floor and knocked on the door of the flat Buxton had visited.
The door opened promptly and he found himself face to face
with a tall woman in a loose kimono, her face elaborately
made-up, her lips red, her hair bottle-blonde and her eyes as
cold as chips of ice.

'Yes?' she said.

'Oh, sorry,' Barnard said. 'I was looking for Nigel Crossley.
I thought this was his flat. Or . . .' He hesitated and tried to
looked flustered. 'You're not his wife, are you? His girlfriend,
maybe? Or have I got the wrong number? Number 361?'

'This is 461,' the woman snapped and made to slam the
door shut but not before Barnard glimpsed a flurry of move-
ment behind her and a muffled noise that could have been
laughter or distress.

'Oh, God, I've got out at the wrong floor! I'm so sorry to
have bothered you,' he gabbled before the door slammed in
his face and he turned away, quite sure he had hit the jackpot
though not at all sure it would do him any good with his
superiors if it turned out that DCI Buxton was a regular visitor.
Why that should be, apart from the obvious, he could only
guess. And if this was the flat Alicia Guest had been brought
to, the consequences of his guesswork for his own future could
only be threatening. As he walked back to the lift, he glanced
out of a window and could see that it was a very long way
down to the ground and doubtlessly a very hard landing.

As Kate watched Harry Barnard carry two suitcases filled with
her belongings down the stairs from her shared flat in Shepherd's
Bush, she turned to Tess Farrell and gave her a hug.

'Are you sure you'll be OK?' she asked. 'It's not necessarily
forever. I haven't really made up my mind about that yet. I'm
really not sure. And I'll still pay my share of the rent for now.
But I do think Harry's right. While all this stuff is going on,
we'll both feel better if we're together. And I don't want to
drag you into anything weird that's happening.'

'It wouldn't be the first time,' Tess said. 'But yes, you should
go. You have a genius for getting into these situations and, to
be honest, I'm keener on a quiet life.'

'Is it going well with your new boyfriend, the history man?'

'Yes, I think it is,' Tess said, her eyes sparkling. She glanced at her watch. 'I'm seeing him tonight, as it goes, la.'

Kate followed Barnard downstairs to the car, thinking that Tess might be grateful for unexpectedly having the flat to herself that night. 'See you later . . .' Kate called out to her.

'. . . alligator,' Tess said softly, although there was no one to hear her reply. The phrase felt old-fashioned now – so much had happened since they had arrived in London with so many plans and ambitions, riding on the wave of euphoria that had come south with the Beatles from Liverpool. She had no idea what would happen next, but had a hunch that for herself at least it would be good.

When they got to the flat in Highgate, Barnard dumped Kate's cases in the bedroom and, after a cautious look around the flat, took her in his arms, wincing slightly as his cuts and bruises objected to pretty well everything he had in mind.

'I'm not sure I'm up to cooking,' he said. 'Can I take you out for a meal? Will that help?'

'Let me ring the hospital again to see how Tom is,' she said. When she had been reassured that Tom was still slowly improving, she put her coat back on and they walked up the hill to the new Italian restaurant that had recently opened in the village and took their time over pasta and a bottle of Chianti and an espresso.

'What's going on Harry?' Kate asked as they sipped their coffee. 'Who's doing this to me? Is someone trying to frighten me, or what? And if so, why?'

'I don't know,' Barnard said. 'The only thing that makes real sense is that it's something to do with your family, or just your father maybe. But it could be that your unexpected arrival back in Liverpool after being away so long upset someone. Or maybe there is some other reason, something more than sheer bigotry, which could explain why DCI Strachan decided to go after Tom in the middle of the night. If it was just happening in London, I'd wonder if it was connected to what I'm working on. But that doesn't make sense – I've got no connections to Liverpool and had never been there in my life until this last weekend. I only went there because of you and

I only got thumped because of what I saw by chance in the nick, not anything I was doing down here. Whereas your room was trashed in Liverpool and you think it was searched here in London too. You seem to be the main target, but I can't imagine why.'

'Terry Jordan's down here,' Kate said. 'Maybe it's to do with him and my da.'

'Maybe Jordan has something to do with it, but it hardly sounds likely. Didn't you say he's in top-level meetings, setting up high-powered deals, entertaining ministers—'

He stopped suddenly. 'Did you say his wife told you he'd brought his girlfriend with him?'

'She did,' Kate said. 'Doreen something. I wrote it down somewhere. I can find it for you.'

'I wonder where she is? She can't be attending the high-powered meetings, can she? That wouldn't work. Do you think you could do something for me tomorrow? Ring your Mrs Jordan and ask her if her husband's home yet. And if so, does she know where his girlfriend is? If nothing else, it would rule Doreen out as the victim in Soho Square. Seeing that she was wearing a diamond ring that big, she's either part of a wealthy family or a wealthy man's bit on the side. In the first case someone would have reported her missing, in the second her sugar daddy might have turned very nasty and Terry Jordan might fit the bill perfectly. But I can't very well go to the Liverpool police for help after everything that happened to me up there.'

'Darcy,' Kate said. 'That was her surname. Her name's Doreen Darcy. I'll call Mrs Jordan tomorrow and see what I can find out.'

'And there's another thing you could do for me.' Barnard said cautiously. 'I can't go asking questions in Pimlico because if DCI Buxton found out he would jump on me from a great height. But I wonder if you could come with me to Dolphin Square and discreetly take some snaps of people going in and out? I got the distinct feeling that there was something dodgy going on in the flat DCI Buxton visited. Maybe it's something he's investigating. Or maybe not. I could drive you there and stay in the car while you do some snapping.'

'Your car's a bit noticeable for that sort of undercover operation, isn't it?' Kate objected. 'When I did something similar for Carter Price at the *Globe* he changed his car every time we went out taking pictures, drove something old and anonymous. This sounds just as dangerous as that turned out to be.'

'Well, I'll borrow something more nondescript,' Barnard said. 'But will you come with me? Maybe after work tomorrow? It doesn't get dark till late so the light will be OK, won't it? Obviously we don't want flash bulbs going off, as that might attract attention. But you don't need to worry too much. I'll be with you every step of the way, I promise, and it's a long shot anyway.'

'Just this once then,' Kate said, feeling more relaxed after a good meal.

'So there's only one thing left to settle,' Barnard said, putting his arm round her as they got up to go and giving her a hint of a hopeful smile. 'Are you coming to bed with me, Miss O'Donnell? Or not?'

Kate looked at him for a long time. 'I don't think you are up to it yet,' she said carefully. 'And maybe I'm not either.'

SIXTEEN

Next morning, as soon as she and Barnard had finished breakfast, Kate phoned Carmel Jordan in Formby. A sleepy voice answered and Kate guessed that Mrs Jordan was probably still in bed.

'It's Kate O'Donnell,' she said. 'You remember I came to see you last Sunday, looking for my da?'

'Have you found him yet?' Mrs Jordan asked, sounding more coherent than when they'd met.

'No,' Kate said. 'But that's not why I'm calling. I was wondering if your husband was home yet? I need a quick word with him about some of the photographs I took last week.'

'He's not back yet, la,' Mrs Jordan said. 'He's got more meetings with the housing minister apparently. Or that's what he says. He says it's going very well. But I expect he's staying at the Ritz with that little floozy Doreen Darcy, so maybe *that* is going well too.'

'So she's not back in Liverpool, either?' Kate asked, aware of Barnard listening to her end of the conversation intently. He grabbed Kate's arm to attract her attention and pointed to her ring finger.

'Ask if he would have bought Doreen a diamond ring,' he whispered. When Kate relayed the question it reduced Carmel to silence for a moment.

'He could have done,' she said angrily, as if the words were being forced out of her. 'He likes buying jewellery, doesn't he? He used to buy me lots of diamonds when we first got married and the business started making money, but he doesn't bother now. Maybe he does the same for her. At least I've got most of mine stashed away safely in the bank now, where he can't get his hands on them to pass on to someone else.' Kate was aware that Carmel's voice had become muffled and she realized that she was crying quietly.

'I'm sorry,' Kate said. 'But if Terry's not back, Doreen won't be either?'

'She'll come back with him, I expect. Though I think Terry said he was going down there with someone from the cathedral, so maybe Doreen had to go on the train. You know what the clergy are like. Doreen won't be pleased with that. She likes swanning around with Terry in the Jag, I do know that.'

'The cathedral?' Kate asked, surprised by that unexpected connection although she recalled being told on her own visit to the site that Terry Jordan was a generous benefactor.

'Oh they love our Terry at the cathedral. They think he's some class of saint. He's given them a lot of money for the new building over the years. But this is about some land they own that they don't need which is close to where they're planning this new town.'

'So he's advising them or something?'

'Something like that,' Carmel said. 'He reckons God's smiling on him, the money he's made, and he should pay a bit back. It's just a pity his generosity doesn't extend to me. The last thing he bought me was a feckin' teapot, and that was only because I chucked the one we had at him one night when he was being more bloody-minded than usual.'

'Does he really stay at the Ritz?' Kate asked. 'Could I contact him there?'

'Well, if he's with one of the Monsignors he might be staying somewhere else. They may have special places for special priests. And saints. Who knows? But that might not be such a good idea for Terry if he's got Doreen in tow. It wouldn't do his reputation much good, would it, if they cottoned on to what he gets up to with her? Anyway, dear, you could try the Ritz. If not, the housing ministry should know where he is. Don't they have – what is it they call them? – public relations people? They should know what's going on.' Carmel, Kate thought, was not as clueless as maybe she liked to appear.

'Right, I'll see if I can track him down, one way or another,' Kate said. 'Thanks for your help.' She hung up and turned to Barnard.

'Did you get the gist of that?' she asked.

'He's still in London? Yes, I got that.'

'He's still got meetings to go to at the housing ministry. It sounds as if he's going to build a new town single-handed on some land the Church owns. For a left footer from Scotland Road he's not short of ambition, you have to give him that.'

'And if he's here, Doreen is probably still here too, alive or dead. But no one will have reported her missing up there or down here. She'll not have been missed, will she, except by Terry Jordan. And if he killed her – or is covering up for someone else who did – he won't report her missing in a hurry, if at all. I reckon we could have found our victim, don't you?'

Kate nodded cautiously.

'But how do you identify her?' she asked. 'You won't get any help from the Liverpool police after all that's gone on.'

'I can't even ask them to check out her whereabouts myself. That will have to come from higher up. I'll talk to DCI Jackson later, maybe. And keep you out of the picture. I don't think he'll be too pleased to hear you've been making inquiries on my behalf, so I'll play that down.'

'What, no Robin to your Batman? That can't be right,' she teased.

'Best not. Or not just now, anyway,' he said stealing a quick kiss. She sighed.

'Not just now,' she said.

Kate was in the darkroom at work later that morning, finishing processing the last of the pictures she'd taken in Liverpool, when someone banged on the door.

'There's a phone call for you,' one of her colleagues shouted. The receiver lay unattended on its shelf at the far end of the office, and she had to hurriedly finish what she was doing before she could switch on the light and open the door to the daylight. At first she did not recognize the voice at the other end. The accent sounded so unfamiliar.

'DCI Strachan, in Liverpool,' the man repeated. 'You remember me? It's about your brother.'

'Is he all right?' Kate's stomach lurched uncontrollably.

'As all right as he'll ever be,' Strachan said. 'They've kept him in hospital. Improving, they say. A delicate flower, isn't

he? A pretty pansy maybe?' He laughed, although there was
no humour in the sound.

'What do you want?' Kate asked, her mouth dry.

'I want you to listen to me very carefully,' Strachan said.
'This is not negotiable, so make sure you get it right. If you
don't, you need to remember that I can get your brother locked
up for a very long time. Just depends on what I choose to
charge him with.'

'So what is it you want?' Kate repeated, knowing that
whatever Strachan wanted could not be good.

'I'm not going to spell it out over the phone,' Strachan said,
the man's almost permanent anger seeming to splutter out
from the receiver. 'I want you to meet a colleague of mine.
You're about to take your lunch break, we know that, but I
want you to avoid your boyfriend today. Forget the Blue
Lagoon and go to the Corner House at the Trafalgar Square
end of the Strand, opposite Charing Cross station. Order a
sandwich or beans on toast or something and someone will
join you. Listen very carefully to what he has to say.'

Unnerved by Strachan's knowledge of her usual routine,
Kate glanced around the office and realized that she had the
place to herself. There was no one there either to hear what
she was saying or to help her if she needed help.

'You're trying to blackmail me,' she hissed. Strachan
laughed.

'It's all in a good cause, my dear,' he said. 'But do it, or it
will be the worse for your brother. Someone like him won't
last long in Walton Gaol. You do understand that, don't you?'

Kate's instinct was to give in to her fury and hang up on
Strachan, ignoring the call, but she knew that in Tom he had
a weapon that he would certainly use if it suited him and
which could tear her family apart. The silence lengthened at
her end and Strachan's breathing became more pronounced at
the other.

'I understand,' she whispered at last. She knew she had no
choice.

The man who joined Kate as she picked at a sandwich in the
crowded Corner House was not threatening. Of medium build,

fair and slightly balding, he wore a somewhat crumpled grey suit, a sober striped tie and horn-rimmed glasses. He was not a man to stand out in a crowd in any way. He did not identify himself and, glancing out of the window overlooking the point where Whitehall meets Trafalgar Square and the Strand, she guessed that he had probably emerged from one of the government buildings stretching away towards the Houses of Parliament. He smiled, as if it was an effort on his part, but his eyes remained stone cold. Kate had absolutely no doubt that whatever he promised or threatened would indeed happen, and she and her family and probably Harry Barnard would be steamrollered by the forces he could call into play to get whatever it was he wanted.

'Miss O'Donnell, I'm happy to meet you,' he said, dismissing the hovering waitress with a wave of the hand. 'And I'm very pleased that you have decided to help us. Any other decision could have made life difficult for us all.' He was not as crude as Strachan, she thought, but the threat was still very much there.

'I have no idea what all this is about,' Kate said, her anger bubbling beneath the surface and threatening to erupt.

'You don't need to know my dear,' the man said, his voice cool and quiet. 'We just need your help for a very short time while a small political crisis is defused.'

'What do you expect me to do?' she asked, feeling as if the breath was being sucked out of her.

'This is a crisis that has a Liverpool dimension and a London dimension,' he said, his voice entirely calm. 'The Liverpool dimension is, I am assured, under control. Your role is to keep us in touch with whatever Detective Sergeant Harry Barnard is doing that might impinge on the measures we are taking to resolve the difficulties. I am told he keeps you fully informed. He is what is usually known as a loose cannon. He has an unfortunate habit of taking unilateral actions that his superior officers don't always know about, and we can't afford that in these circumstances. He is a minor player but, in plain words, we need to know exactly what he is up to without alerting the Metropolitan Police as to what measures we are taking to avert a potentially embarrassing situation.'

Kate gazed at the man transfixed. She had been neatly trapped between her brother and Harry and she could see no way of refusing to do what she was being asked to do without putting one or other at serious risk. The man waited and Kate was sure he could see her conflicted emotions ebb and flow like a dangerous tide, calm on the surface but with a powerful current beneath.

'We could, of course, take direct action against Barnard,' he said eventually, still calm, still cold, casting a carefully calibrated chill over the table. 'Given his track record, it would not be too difficult to discipline him and get him out of the force. But from past experience, that would not necessarily stop him doing his own thing or talking out of turn. It would have to be a charge serious enough to put him behind bars. I think you wouldn't want that, would you, Miss O'Donnell?'

'How would I contact you,' Kate whispered, 'if I agree to do what you ask?'

'When you agree,' the man contradicted her. 'Have you moved back into Barnard's flat?'

'Yes, sort of,' Kate said. 'He thought I would be safer there because my stuff was being searched . . .' She hesitated. 'I suppose that was you, or your friends, was it?'

'I couldn't possibly say,' the man said. 'We need you to stay close to Barnard, so stay at the flat, please. Of course we can't contact you there by phone – he would be likely to pick up, or at the least ask who you were talking to. We'll contact you at work. I will ring you every morning when you arrive at nine and you can fill me in about what, if anything, has been going on. We will ask his superior officers to keep an eye on him, too. I'll give you a number where you can contact me or one of my colleagues to update me if anything unexpected happens – but only if what you have to tell us seems serious. Do you understand?'

Kate nodded, feeling utterly numb. The man's gaze intensified for a moment and she realized that she and Barnard must have blundered into territory far more dangerous than they could have guessed when the Vice Squad began investigating the murder of an anonymous woman dumped under the trees in Soho Square. She had no doubt that this man was in some way official and he was evidently ruthless, as ruthless as a government facing a general election within months was likely to be after being blown apart the previous year by a scandal that had run out of control. She and Barnard were very small fish in very deep waters. And she had no idea where to turn to for help.

Kate sat in the front passenger seat of a clapped-out-looking Austin A40 parked about 100 yards from the main entrance to Dolphin Square. Barnard had picked her up from work at about five thirty and they'd made a sedate journey along Oxford Street and down Park Lane then west past the faded Victorian terraces of Pimlico until they reached the fortress-like walls of the square.

'It looks as if it should have a portcullis and a drawbridge,' Kate said, trying to lighten the mood. The atmosphere in the car had been tense on the drive across the West End, as if neither of them dared to raise what really concerned them. That, Kate thought anxiously, was doubly true in her case, but she was sure that Barnard would in part put her uneasy silence down to her uncertainty about their relationship rather than anything even worse.

He parked a little way past the main entrance which, even at a time when residents might be expected to be returning from work, seemed pretty well deserted.

'What do you want me to do?' she asked.

'DCI Buxton went in this door the last time I saw him,' he said. 'So I guess anyone else heading for that flat would do the same. You could have a little stroll around, I suppose, but keep an eye on the doors. I'll recognize the woman I spoke to, if she turns up. I need a photograph of her or we'll never be able to identify her.' He turned towards Kate looking grim, his bruises still pronounced enough to make him look disreputable at least, dangerous at worst.

'I know there was something going on in there that shouldn't have been,' he said. 'Call it a smell, a hunch, anything you like. Maybe it was something I half heard in the background. But there was something wrong. I need to know what it was, and if Buxton was up there he's implicated. Nothing's surer. Believe me.'

'I'm sure you're right,' Kate said, opening the car door, feeling bewildered, uncertain who was straight and who was bent and who was as crooked as a corkscrew. 'Keep an eye out for me,' she said as she closed the car door and began to walk slowly back towards the main entrance to the square, where a couple of men with briefcases were hurrying indoors, looking suitably hot and bothered after their underground journey from the city. She used her camera cautiously, keeping it largely hidden behind her handbag and a folded copy of the *Evening News*, which she had chosen because it had bigger pages than the *Standard*. As far as she was aware no one noticed what she was doing, and there was nothing at all to indicate that anyone she took a picture of was anything other than a legitimate resident on the way home.

But the comings and goings subtly altered as the evening wore on. Increasingly people came out of the building, smartly dressed and clearly heading for an evening's entertainment, and the trickle of people going into the building began to dry up.

'The light's getting tricky,' Kate said as she returned to the car, which was filling with cigarette smoke as Barnard struggled to fill the time, his fingers drumming intermittently on the steering wheel as he fought to contain his impatience. 'I'll give it another twenty minutes. After that we won't be able to make anyone out in the gloom. The pictures will be pretty useless.' She changed the film in her camera and set off again. Barnard watched her in the rear-view mirror, his eyes following her walk down the street, and marvelled at her apparently endless patience.

But although Kate had taken pictures of people returning home to the flats and going out to meals and theatres and films, either alone or in pairs or groups, there was no one who looked even remotely suspicious on the street or going in through the doors to Dolphin Square, which appeared to be the epitome of middle-class respectability. But just as she was about to give up she saw a woman smartly dressed for an evening out – in stilettos and a short tight skirt underneath a fun-fur jacket, her hair not unlike Cilla Black's, though dark not red – coming out of the foyer unusually cautiously, scanning the street carefully before setting off in the direction of Barnard's car. As she passed by, Kate quickly took a photograph of her, keeping the camera low in case it was seen. The woman overtook the parked A40 without glancing at it or at Barnard. Kate followed close behind and opened the passenger door quietly.

'She looked a bit different,' she said softly.

'She was the woman from the flat,' Barnard said, starting the engine. 'Get in, we'll follow but I don't want her scared off. Let's see where she goes.' He drove down the quiet street a hundred yards or so behind their quarry. Eventually she stopped at one of the few shops in the neighbourhood, went inside and came out smoking, with the packet of cigarettes still in her hand.

'I'd stop her, in spite of DCI Buxton's threats,' Barnard said quietly. 'But judging by the way she's dolled up there must be something going on there tonight. It might be better to hang about and see what happens, and then report back to DCI Jackson with a bit more hard evidence.'

He held the car back until the woman disappeared inside the mansion block, and then accelerated past and did a complete circuit of the square before approaching the main doors again. As they did so, an opulent-looking black car pulled up outside the entrance and a heavy-looking man who had been driving leapt out and held the doors open for the occupants, three men in dinner jackets and black ties – not out of the ordinary, Barnard knew, for Dolphin Square, but these men kept their heads down low and glanced around nervously before scuttling inside, unaware that Kate had her camera following their every move in spite of the gathering dusk.

'The kindest interpretation would be an illegal gambling joint of some kind,' Barnard said. 'But I strongly suspect it's much worse than that. Did you recognize any of them? Do you know what Terry Jordan looks like?'

'Only from photographs,' Kate whispered. 'I know he's not very tall. But the very tall man I do know. He's called Monsignor Dominic Johnson. I met him at the cathedral in

Liverpool, he's in charge of the building work there.' She
pushed open the car door quietly. 'I'll go and see what floor
they go to,' she said. 'That should indicate whether they're
heading for the same flat you went to. I won't go inside until
they're in the lift. They won't see me.' Barnard grabbed her
arm but she slipped free.

'We need to know,' she said and pushed the car door firmly
closed behind her, leaving Barnard breathing hard in sheer
frustration. By the time she had crossed the foyer the lift had
gone. She watched until it stopped at the fourth floor. What she
had not realized was that there were three lifts in a row, and on
an impulse she got into the next one when its doors opened and
cautiously slipped out when they opened again at the fourth
floor. There was no one in sight in the stuffy empty corridor,
nor was there any noise apart from the quiet hum of the heating.
But when she stood outside the door of flat 461 she could hear
men's voices raised in greeting and the sound of a champagne
cork popping. It sounded like any other social occasion and
there was no sign that anyone behind the closed door felt in
any way at risk – it could have been a family party or a celebration of a business deal concluded successfully. But then, as she
turned away, cutting faintly through the jollity, came the sound
of a child crying, cut short almost immediately by the
sound of a slap. Breathless with anger, Kate made her way back
to the lift, punched the down button furiously, and ran out of
the building to the car, where she slumped into the passenger
seat beside Barnard, fighting back tears, her fists clenched tight.

'What is it, Kate?' Barnard asked. 'What's going on?'

'There's a child in there,' she said. 'There were a lot of
men's voices and just for a moment a child crying, then a
slap.' She looked at Barnard and she was unnerved by the
despair in his eyes.

'I can't do anything on my own,' he said. 'I have to report
back. And if one of those men is your priest and one of them
Terry Jordan, who's the third man in the car? I half recognized
him. Jordan's supposed to be down here to talk to a minister.
Surely a minister wouldn't be so bloody stupid as to come to
some sort of illegal joint, would he? Especially after what we
think probably happened there.'

Kate shrugged, overwhelmed by what she dared not tell Barnard. There had to be a very good reason for the massive effort that was being made to protect somebody's back. If the men in flat 461 felt safe from intrusive questions, they wouldn't need to curb their appetite for whatever was happening there.

'One thing's certain,' Barnard said. 'If there is a minister involved, then there's no way we are going to get anywhere at all. We are stuffed.'

Kate said nothing although she had even more reason than Harry to think he was right.

SEVENTEEN

Harry Barnard dropped Kate off at the Ken Fellows Agency just before nine the next morning. They had spent the previous evening talking round and round the problem of what he should do next and in the end decided he had no choice but to tell DCI Jackson everything he'd learned about the flat in Dolphin Square, without admitting that he had sat outside it for a large part of the previous evening. For her part, Kate had said nothing about the threats she'd received from Strachan and his friends. Nor had she any intention of telling anyone, least of all the mysterious man from Whitehall, where she had been the previous night. They had been at home, they had decided to say if anyone asked, with the TV turned up loud and a clutch of empty bottles dumped in the dustbin at breakfast time. Barnard had no reason to be uneasy about their cover story, although he could see that Kate was worried despite the fact that throughout the evening his car had been parked outside the flats.

'No one saw us,' he said as they set off for her office. 'You don't need to worry about me.'

'Right,' she said, with what she hoped was the right amount of confidence, and spent the rest of the journey through the rush hour chatting about the relative merits of the Beatles and the Rolling Stones.

But when the phone call came, dead on time, at just a minute past nine, it set her heart racing and her hands shaking. It was not that this man made threats. He was, by the standards she had grown up with around Scotland Road, physically unthreatening and impeccably polite. But he gave the impression of being totally intractable.

'So what have you got to report, Miss O'Donnell?' the voice asked. The tone was the same, quiet but menacing, and it left little space for prevarication.

'Nothing,' Kate said. Her mouth was bone dry. She picked

up a coffee cup on her desk and found it empty. 'Absolutely nothing. Harry Barnard picked me up from work and we had a quiet evening watching TV.'

'Did he tell you anything about what he had been doing during the day?'

'Nothing,' Kate said. 'I told you, he doesn't talk much about his work. He's on a murder case as far as I know. Some woman found dead in Soho, a prostitute they think. That's all. It's not exactly what I want to talk to him about when we're together.'

'Well we very much hope that you can nevertheless encourage him to keep you up to date on his activities,' the voice said. 'We'd like to hear his take on that murder case. Remember, your brother is dependent on you, Miss O'Donnell. DCI Strachan is itching to make an example of him. So we will talk again tomorrow morning, at the same time.' And he hung up without saying goodbye.

Kate went to the cloakroom feeling as if her legs did not belong to her and had a long drink of cold water. She looked at herself in the mirror before splashing her face, realizing that however bad she felt she had not changed much apart from an increasingly haunted look in her eyes. But however she considered her predicament, she could not work out a way to escape it and eventually she went back into the photographers' room, resumed her seat and got her head down, spending the rest of the morning putting the finishing touches to her Liverpool project and, together with her boss, preparing it for delivery to the magazine that had commissioned it.

'Well done,' Ken said when he was finally satisfied with the portfolio. 'You've done a really good job with this assignment. And as you worked over the weekend, you can take the rest of the day off if you like. Go and buy yourself a mini-skirt or two. You know how much the boys like them.'

'Thanks,' Kate said, glad of the free time, but decided almost immediately that she could spend it in an entirely different way. Harry might be constrained by the labyrinthine politics of Westminster and the Yard, and she would not encourage him to take any risks, but she wasn't subject to any such constraints. Although she might be forced to tell the grey man from Whitehall what Barnard was doing she had not agreed to provide details of anything she undertook herself, and she was if anything even more driven than Barnard by the need to find out what was happening to the child apparently being confined in the flat in Dolphin Square.

She spent an hour in a darkroom processing the photographs she had taken from the car the previous night then, having locked them in one of the drawers of her desk for safekeeping, went out and headed for the Tube at Tottenham Court Road. She had only the vaguest idea of what she could do if she went back to Dolphin Square, but she was determined to give it a try.

The streets around the square were quiet at lunchtime and she ate a sandwich in the gardens close to the river before doing a complete circuit of the flats that told her nothing she did not know already. The only chance of finding the woman they had seen the previous evening, she reckoned, was to venture inside and see whether or not there was anyone at home in Flat 461. As she watched the entrance to the flats, a group of people made their way in that direction and she followed them inside into the hallway and towards the lifts. She watched as they travelled to the fifth floor, where the lift stopped, before taking the next lift herself to the fourth floor and making her way along the thick carpets of the corridor to the innocent-looking door of 461.

She hesitated before ringing the bell, but decided that as she had come this far she wouldn't back off now, knowing that there was a child involved in whatever went on behind this innocuously respectable façade. She waited impatiently but got no response to the bell. The only sound was the almost imperceptible hum of the heating system in the corridor. After five minutes of fruitless hanging about, finding it harder and harder to breathe easily in the oppressive heat, she reluctantly headed back downstairs. It was not until she stepped back into the street that she unexpectedly found herself face to face with the woman she and Barnard had followed the previous evening. Slightly scruffy in dark slacks and a waterproof jacket, she was not so smartly dressed this afternoon, but she was smoking as avidly as when she walked along the road to buy cigarettes the night before.

'Were you able to sort your little boy out last night?' Kate asked casually, hoping she did not look as shocked as she felt at the unexpected encounter.

The women stared at her with something close to panic in her eyes and her hand over her mouth. 'What?' she said. 'What do you mean?'

'Oh, I heard him crying when I was walking past your door last night. My sister's got a young family and I know how hard it is to get kids to bed sometimes.' She was, she thought, becoming rather good at lying but told herself it was in a good cause. At least no one would be expecting her to go to confession and say a few Hail Marys as penance.

'Yes . . .' the woman started to say, then 'No. No, he's not mine. You must have heard someone from another flat. Someone else's child.' She had a faint foreign accent, though not one Kate could identify.

'No,' Kate said. 'It was your flat, without a doubt.' The woman stared at her in confusion, and then instead of heading for the front door she spun on her heel and sprinted away down the street in the direction of the Tube station. Taken by surprise, Kate lost a couple of seconds before giving chase but, being younger and fitter, by the time they'd come level with the gardens of St George's Square she was gaining on her quarry. The woman flung a despairing look behind her, then turned into the gates to the gardens and gave up almost as suddenly as she had run away. She hurled herself down on a bench crying uncontrollably, her head between her knees and her shoulders shaking convulsively.

'He's not my child,' she said, her eyes desperate. 'I can't stop them doing what they do, but he's not my child.'

'You'd better tell me about it,' Kate said quietly. 'It sounds as if you need to talk to somebody. Maybe the police.'

'No, no, no police,' the woman said and would have run off again if Kate had not hung on to her arm and kept her firmly in her seat.

'Will you tell me your name?' she ventured when the woman had calmed down slightly. She shook her head fiercely.

'No, no names,' she said. 'I must get away from here. No names.'

'Then tell me what is going on. What's been happening at that flat?'

'Terrible things,' she said, and lit another cigarette and lapsed into trembling silence. Kate rooted in her handbag and pulled out the drawing of the woman found dead in Soho Square.

'Do you know this woman?' she asked. It was obvious from the horrified reaction, tears pouring down her face again, that she did. 'She came with three men,' she said. 'She talked like you do, and one of the men, the small one, was the same. A funny accent. I couldn't understand everything they said. The woman said her name was Doreen. She seemed all right, all dressed up for a night out, nice dress, high heels, lots of make-up. She was quite happy and excited, though I couldn't work out what she was expecting. We don't get women there very often. The other two men were tall, very tall. They seemed to be in charge. Wanted champagne, then a bottle of Scotch. And a private room. Two private rooms, in fact. They more or less took the place over. There was no one else there.'

'Do you know who they were?'

'They never tell me any names,' she said. 'Sometimes I hear names, but not that time.'

'So did you see what happened? Anything at all?' Kate asked, afraid of the answer.

'No,' she said. 'I don't see what happens behind the closed doors. My job is to keep the drink flowing, provide everything they want and take the money when they have finished.'

'Finished what?' Kate asked, although she did not really want to know the answer and the woman did not want to tell her. The silence lengthened and in the end the woman shrugged helplessly.

'Will you help the children?' she asked.

'If I can,' Kate said, although she had no idea whether she, or even the police, would be able to do that or not.

'So . . . I tell you what happened,' the woman said very quietly. 'One of the men, one of the tall men, took the boy into a room and the boy never stopped crying afterwards. The other two took the woman into the other room and it didn't sound good. They told me to stay in the kitchen and just bring them what they ordered. I am a sort of waitress. I don't know what they do in there. I don't want to know. They took things from me at the door. I never went inside, though I could hear the woman crying. And then screams, eventually there were lots of screams. But then they stopped and there was silence, an awful silence.' Kate looked at the woman for a long time before she felt able to speak at all. She took a deep shuddering breath.

'And the boy? Where is he now?' she asked.

'A couple of men I'd never seen before took him away this morning. Said they would take him back where he came from.'

'Do you know where that is?'

'Usually they come from homes, orphanages. That sort of place. Not places where there are mothers and fathers to look after them. It's not unusual for men to want boys, is it? It happens. Mr Buxton finds them for us.'

'Mr Buxton?' Kate asked, with a sick feeling in her stomach.

'He has contacts,' she said with a weary shrug.

'I expect he does. He's a detective. Did you know that?' Kate asked. The woman shook her head and began to cry again.

'I need to get away,' she said through her tears. 'I need to get away. I thought this was an easy way to make a living.'

'Tell me what happened to Doreen,' Kate said, very much aware that the woman had not given her own name and that the more she went on the more unlikely it was she would do so. If she disappeared now, it would probably be impossible to ever find her again. The woman looked at her in despair, in such anguish that Kate was afraid that if she decided to run again she would not even be able to catch up with her. But in the end the woman sat still and seemed to be trying to decide whether to tell Kate all she knew, though whether she would ever be willing to give her name or repeat her story to anyone official Kate very much doubted.

'One of the men came out, the tall thin man. Not the man with the accent, one of the other two, and he told me to stay in the kitchen while he made some phone calls. So I waited. Then they brought the boy to wait with me, out of the way, and they put the radio on so we couldn't hear. To try to make the boy happy, I gave him some ice cream, but that didn't really work. I did hear the doorbell in spite of the radio, and then there were more voices in the hall and some banging about. When the two tall men came back in, they paid me what they owed me – and some more, quite a lot more extra – and then they all disappeared. I saw them go, the two tall men on each side of the small man, propping him up almost. There was no sign of the woman then. If she is the woman who was found in Soho Square she must have been dead by then, mustn't she? One of them must have killed her, and the others took her away and tried to cover it up.'

'Someone else is dead too,' Kate said. 'A woman called Alicia. Do you know her?' The woman looked at her in horror, in tears again.

'She used to come to work with me sometimes,' she said. 'But when some of the men started wanting boys she left. She said she did not like that sort of thing. She decided to work on her own.'

'Mr Buxton is investigating her death,' Kate said. 'Perhaps it's not a good idea for you to see him, but will you talk to the detectives trying to find Doreen's killer? Meet me in Soho. You don't need to go back to the flat and you don't have to tell me your name, but you need to tell the police what happened. Not Buxton, someone who really wants to find out the truth. Please. Meet me later and talk to my boyfriend, who's one of the detectives investigating Doreen's death. Meet me anywhere you like. She deserves that much, she just got caught up in all this somehow.'

The woman looked at her for a long time.

'I'll meet you in the French pub in Soho at six,' she said slowly. 'I have a friend who lives close. But if anyone else is there, I won't stop. It's too dangerous. This is a nightmare. I've got my passport and I am going to go home.'

Kate went back to the office shaken by what she had been told. She developed her hastily taken photograph of the woman from Dolphin Square, then printed more copies of the photos taken in the street the night before and made up two sets in plain brown envelopes. She felt uncertain and insecure, and decided to place one set in the office files for safekeeping and put the other in her bag to pass on to Barnard. Then she went back downstairs into Frith Street to wait for him to pick her up. When he pulled up alongside her, she slipped into the passenger seat quickly and turned to face him, not far from tears.

'What is it?' he asked and listened to her in silence, his face like stone as she recounted every detail she could remember of her encounter with the woman from Dolphin Square. But when she told him about her arrangement to meet the woman at the French pub, he looked at her in amazement for a moment and smiled, though there was not much more than cynicism in his expression.

'I don't suppose for a moment she'll turn up,' he said. 'Couldn't you get a name out of her? We'll never track her down without it.'

'There was no way she was going to tell me her name,' Kate said. 'But I did manage to get another picture of her. I called her back as she walked away and took a quick snap. It's a bit blurred because I took it very hurriedly and she was furious when she saw what I was doing, but with the ones I took the previous evening it gives us a rough idea of what she looks like. See?' She pulled the picture out of her bag and showed him.

'Where are the rest of your pictures?' he asked.

'I left them locked up in the office while I went to Pimlico, but I thought I'd better go back for them and make copies,' Kate said. 'They'll be safe at home, I think, though none of them are very clear. The light wasn't good.' She handed him the complete set of prints she'd made for him and he sat studying them for a long time in silence.

'Well, I suppose we might recognize her if she turns up,' Barnard said, focusing on the shots of the woman. 'Though I don't reckon that's the least bit likely. Couldn't you have called me once you tackled her?' But before Kate could reply he shook his head.

'No of course not,' he said quickly. 'Sorry, silly question. It's just that we've got so close and it could all still slip through our fingers, especially with DCI Buxton involved.'

'There was no way she was going to stand there and let me

make a phone call,' Kate said. 'And I couldn't call the local police, anyway, could I, after what she said about Buxton? He sounds as if he's up to his eyes in it all. And you were too far away to be much use.'

'She definitely told you that our victim was someone called Doreen?'

'She said that was her name and she had a Liverpool accent, and so did the man she thought was with her. You should be able to identify her from that, shouldn't you?'

'Not me personally,' Barnard said with feeling. 'The DCI can ask for help from the Liverpool police. It's his job after all. That's what he gets paid for, and I want nothing more to do with that bastard Strachan. But let's stroll down there on the off-chance that she does what she said she'd do and turns up at the pub. We might be lucky.'

'If she comes, you'll arrest her?' Kate asked.

'If she comes, I'll have to interview her one way or another,' Barnard said. 'You know that, Katie.'

'She won't come, will she?' Kate said miserably. 'It stands to reason she won't come.'

Barnard parked his car and they cut through to Dean Street and found the French pub crowded with after-work drinkers. Barnard took a long time to work his way through the crowd round the bar to order and made a hazardous push back through the crowd to deliver their drinks.

'If she's here, we'll be hard pressed to see her,' he said.

'I've had a good look round, but she doesn't seem to have come,' Kate said. 'I thought she might run. She was obviously scared out of her wits. But there was no way I could stop her.'

'We'll wait half an hour and see if she turns up,' Barnard said. 'If not, I'll have to go back to the nick and see if I can contact DCI Jackson. I can't let this go until the morning. We've been trying to get an ID for the murder victim for days without success, and you waltz off to Pimlico and come up with one in half an hour. He won't be best pleased if I don't tell him straight away.'

'I haven't done anything illegal have I?' Kate asked.

'If you've identified our victim, you've done something we've completely failed to do so far,' Barnard laughed. 'He should give you a medal. Wait for me in the Blue Lagoon while I'll fill him in. He needs to know about this as soon as possible or I'll be in trouble up to my neck.'

DCI Keith Jackson was still in his office when Barnard returned to the nick and knocked on his door.

'Do you have a minute, guv?' he asked. 'It's important. I think we've nailed the ID of our murder victim at last, with a bit of help from my girlfriend.'

Jackson waved him in, looking startled. 'Your girlfriend? How did she become involved?'

'I told you I would do some off-the-radar surveillance around Dolphin Square . . . You agreed to that.' Jackson nodded, though he didn't look happy to be reminded of his reluctant acquiescence.

'That was a long shot and I really don't want to know about it given the second murder in Pimlico, unless you've turned up something crucial,' Jackson said quickly.

'Well, I think we have, guv,' Barnard said quickly. 'I went down there by car – not my own car as it's a bit conspicuous – and took Kate with me as I reckoned it would look less suspicious if there were two of us. I wasn't planning to do more than have a quiet recce to see who was going in and out, if anyone. And we were lucky. We saw a woman come out, all dolled up. She bought some cigarettes and then went back in. A bit later a chauffeur-driven car dropped three men off. Kate followed them in, at a safe distance, and saw them go into the suspect flat. She took photographs of everything she safely could, and we've got those for you.'

'Did you identify any of the men?'

'Not then,' Barnard said. 'What I didn't reckon on was that Kate would decide to go back again this afternoon, off her own bat, because she was worried about a child being involved. Anyway, she struck lucky again and bumped into the woman we'd seen the night before. This time she was on the street and seemed very upset, in tears in fact, and when Kate showed her the drawing of the victim in Soho Square she IDed her, said she was called Doreen and had a strong Liverpool accent. Just like Kate's in fact. Doreen Darcy, if that's who she is, is

Tony Jordan's bit on the side. His wife told Kate about her when Kate was doing research in Liverpool for some photographs she was taking for work. And Mrs Jordan reckons both of them came down to London, where Jordan's been negotiating some building contract or other. The woman from Dolphin Square got the distinct impression something bad happened in Flat 461 the night the body was dumped, though she didn't see what exactly it was. She was told to keep out of the way. She had decided to bail out completely but bumped into Kate first, and Kate managed to get the whole story out of her.'

'Name? Does this informant have a name?' Barnard shrugged slightly, knowing this was the weak link in the story.

'The woman refused to give it,' he said. 'She was obviously scared to death. She promised to meet Kate again tonight and talk to me as well . . .'

'But of course she didn't turn up?' Jackson said sharply.

'She didn't turn up,' Barnard agreed. 'We've lost her.' Jackson did not explode, as Barnard thought he might. He looked thoughtful for a moment, his hands steepled in front of his face.

'Another problem is that Doreen Darcy's sugar daddy, Terry Jordan, is some sort of big cheese in Liverpool,' Barnard continued cautiously. 'In the building trade, and not in a small way. He's doing some housing deal with the government for a new town up north.'

Jackson looked grim.

'Well, we all know people in high places can get up to no good,' he said. 'We saw plenty of that last year. People with all the privileges who should have known better. But I need to talk to the Yard. I need to find out just how likely this tale of yours is. I need to liaise with them and with the Liverpool police. It shouldn't be too difficult to trace this woman and find her family or friends in Liverpool, if that is in fact where she comes from. And this man Terry Jordan can be tracked down easily enough if we need to talk to him, once we know definitely who the woman is.' Barnard hesitated, then decided it would be very unwise to hold anything back.

'You know my girlfriend is a photographer, guv. While we

were driving round, keeping our heads down, just sussing the place out, she took some photographs, people going in and out of Dolphin Square. As I said, I've got copies of all of them for you. But today she got a second picture of the woman who worked in the flat, a bit blurred but better than the one she took the night before in poor light. I've got copies of everything for you to look at.'

'In due course, Sergeant,' Jackson said. 'In due course. Let's put a name to our victim first – find out if she really is this woman from Liverpool – and then take it from there. I need to talk to Liverpool and the Yard. This could turn out to be a can of worms that no one will be very pleased about.'

EIGHTEEN

When they got back to Barnard's flat, Kate flung herself on to the sofa close to tears. 'Are there any honest cops anywhere?' she asked bitterly. Barnard winced slightly as he fingered the barely fading bruises on his face, and shrugged. He was not, he thought ruefully, the person she should ask just now. 'It would certainly be good not to have to fight both sides against the middle,' he said circumspectly. 'Anyway, it's out of our hands now. The DCI's taken over.' Kate wondered if the fact that DCI Jackson had taken over would make any difference to the grey man who was trying to prise information from her, and indirectly from Barnard, for purposes she could only guess at. But whatever Jackson was trying to organize officially, she didn't think it would be safe to tell anyone about the threats she'd received over a seemingly innocuous lunch at the Corner House, which she had barely been able to eat because she had been so close to the edge of panic. Until she was absolutely sure the threats had been lifted she didn't dare do anything that might put either Tom or Harry at risk.

'Can I ring the hospital to see how Tom is?' she asked.

'Of course you can,' he said. 'You need to keep in touch with him, or that bastard Strachan will take as many liberties as he likes.' Kate nodded and picked up the phone. When she got through to the hospital, she was put through to a harassed-sounding ward sister who demanded to know who she was and offered no more than a formulaic 'as well as can be expected' once satisfied that she was in fact Tom's sister.

'Are any of my family with him?' Kate asked sharply. 'Or his friend Kevin?'

'Just a policeman,' the nurse said sourly and hung up. If anything, the information imparted by the sister made Kate feel worse rather than better.

'I know it's not much comfort, but he's probably better off

in a hospital bed than he would be in a cell at the mercy of DCI Strachan,' Barnard said. 'Do you know if he's got a solicitor?'

'I've no idea,' Kate said. 'Probably not. Tom was never the most organized person.'

'You should ring his boyfriend and make sure he gets some legal advice. He'll be entitled to legal aid. He shouldn't talk to Strachan again without a lawyer present.'

'Let's have something to eat, then I'll call Kevin,' Kate said. 'He may be visiting at the hospital this evening, though I'm sure the police will do their best to keep him away.'

'They'll take a pleasure in it,' Barnard said, looking grim.

They ate in a subdued mood, then slumped on the sofa to watch *Z Cars* on TV because Barnard said it made him smile.

'It's popular in Liverpool,' Kate said. 'A lot of little lads want to be Fancy Smith. But I suppose not that many of them have come across bastards like Strachan face to face. Inspector Barlow isn't quite in his league, is he?'

'He's not far off, I reckon,' Barnard said, putting his arm round Kate. 'But maybe it's just the accent that amuses us down here. And the tune's jolly.'

'Everton are talking about making it their team song,' Kate said as the doorbell rang.

'Who the hell's that?' Barnard said irritably and got reluctantly to his feet. Kate could hear him talking to someone in the hall and then he came back into the living room followed by a tall blond man, who was looking concerned.

'Kate, this is my next-door neighbour, Steve Keighley. He says someone came round looking for you today, a man dressed as a priest. He thought it was odd as he didn't realize you were staying here, so he thought it best to play a bit dumb. I know you've already talked to one priest, so tell Steve what your man looks like and we'll get an idea if it's the same one.'

Kate's stomach clenched slightly. She had hoped no one from the Church would be able to find her at Barnard's flat, but it looked like that was overoptimistic.

'I've already had a conversation I didn't want with a Father Granville,' she said quietly. 'I've no idea how he could find out I'm staying here, and I certainly don't want to talk to him again. Nor anyone else from the Catholic Church. I gave all that up years ago.'

'I didn't like the look of him,' Keighley said. 'He was wearing a clerical collar, but I wouldn't have trusted him further than I could throw him. He looked more like someone out of an American gangster film to me.'

'Some of them do,' Kate said, with a wry smile.

'Anyway, I didn't know you were here so I denied all knowledge of Harry's friends. It looks as if I did the right thing. They can be very persistent some of these Church people, can't they?'

'They can,' Kate said. 'Very persistent.'

'Thanks for that, Steve,' Barnard said. 'If you're a cop, you need neighbours who can be a bit discreet. I'm grateful.'

When Keighley had gone, Barnard sat down again by Kate and turned the television off.

'What's going on Kate?' he asked. 'Is this the same man who went to your flat in Shepherd's Bush?'

'It sounds like it,' Kate said. 'But how did he find out I'd come here? I can't imagine Tess told him.'

'You asked her to be careful?'

'Of course,' Kate said and saw the anxiety in Barnard's eyes at the thought of his own privacy being invaded.

'This can't just be about you missing Mass, can it?' he asked. 'You're one person among millions going – or not going – to church every week. They can't make this sort of fuss about everyone who backslides.'

'Of course they can't,' Kate said. 'It's years since I gave up on them. It can only be connected with my trip to Liverpool. Something I did or said – maybe some questions I asked, maybe some pictures I took – must have worried them. But I haven't a clue what it might be.'

'Or might it be connected to what happened to Tom when he was a kid with the priest who pestered you both? What was he called? Father Gerard?'

'Father Jerome,' Kate said. 'I can't imagine how anyone could find out about that. We never told anyone. Not even our mam and da. More fool us, maybe, but we were very young and our parents would have gone completely crazy – they'd probably have accused us of making up vicious lies. The Church and the priests were untouchable back then. And from what I saw in Liverpool, it's not much different now.'

'Maybe Father Jerome's still at it, though,' Barnard suggested. 'Someone else might have complained more recently.'

Kate hesitated for a moment.

'Father Reilly knew,' she said. 'I'd forgotten. I told him in confession. And he told me never to talk about it – ever. He told me Tom was telling lies and I was never to mention it again. He told me that Father Jerome was a holy man and God and Our Lady would never forgive me.' She hesitated and looked away. 'So I didn't, to my shame. I was terrified and Father Jerome disappeared, moved away. We never heard anything of him again. But as I got older, I knew we should have told someone. He could have gone on doing the same thing to other boys somewhere else.'

'You were only a child, Katie,' Barnard said. 'You couldn't take them all on by yourself. Neither you nor Tom.'

'But if that's connected with what's happening now, what I don't understand is why DCI Strachan would get involved. He's a Northern Irish Proddie. He'd be more likely to be over the moon to see the Church embarrassed, but instead he seems to have embarked on a crusade to shut Tom up. It makes no sense at all.'

'They say Catholics are good at guilt,' Barnard said quietly. 'But I don't think you have anything to feel guilty about. It all happened a long time ago. You said you went to confession, so the Church knew about it and it was up to them to take action.'

'But if they didn't believe me? Or if they did believe me and just moved Father Jerome on somewhere else? It's not good enough, is it? Hearing that little boy in the flat at Dolphin Square brought it all back to me . . .'

Barnard put his arm around her but she pulled away quickly and took a deep breath, aware that there was far more for her to feel guilty about than what had happened to Tom all those years ago. She was much more concerned about how she could keep Tom and Barnard safe from the threatening man in the grey suit, who would no doubt be ringing her again in the morning. By now, she thought, he would almost certainly have learned that Harry had pinned an identity on the dead woman that linked her to Liverpool and to Terry Jordan and his much publicized negotiations in London.

'The problem's in Liverpool,' she said flatly. 'I think you should mind your own back and stay out of it. Let them sort it out up there.'

'But Terry Jordan's girlfriend was dumped in my manor, even if she was killed somewhere else. My nick's involved one way or another. We don't pick and choose our cases, and this one is ours.'

'Leave it to your DCI,' Kate said. 'You said he's taken charge. Leave it to him if there are important people up to their necks in this, not to mention DCI Buxton and the bizzies in Liverpool. It's not down to you any more, is it? It's too big and too serious, and you're the one who will come off worst if it all blows up in your face because you will insist on doing your own thing.'

'There's only one thing wrong with that as a strategy and it's the thing you should remember better than anyone,' Barnard said, angry now. 'It wasn't just Doreen Darcy who got hurt that night. Somewhere in the middle of that nasty little business going on at Dolphin Square was a child. He was frightened and hurt to gratify some evil bastards. If DCI Jackson tells me there's going to be a serious investigation into what's going on at this end as well as in Liverpool, then I'll opt out if I'm told to. But if not, if there's a cover-up because this involves important people who believe they can do as they like, even get away with murder, then I won't back off. One way or another, I'll nail them.'

'I think you're taking a dreadful risk if you try to do that without your boss behind you,' Kate said, feeling hollow inside.

Barnard sighed, then pulled her towards him and gave her a tentative kiss. To which she responded hungrily, in spite of her fears.

'Forget all this and come to bed,' he whispered. 'It's been too long.' And clinging to each other like shipwrecked mariners struggling to shore, they went into the bedroom and pulled the blinds closed, shutting out the threatening sky.

*   *   *

Next morning Barnard dropped Kate off at the Ken Fellows Agency just before nine, just in time to take the call she expected from the man in the grey suit. She answered him with more confidence this time. Harry, she told him, had been talking to DCI Jackson the night before but she had no idea what about.

'You might as well pack this in,' she said. 'I've told you, he doesn't discuss work with me and I don't ask him. If you want to know what he's working on, why don't you ask his boss?'

'Thank you, Miss O'Donnell,' the voice said, 'We'll let you know when we no longer need you. Just keep focused on your brother's situation as well as Sergeant Barnard's.'

He hung up before she could respond, and she had to disguise her fury when Ken Fellows emerged from his office with a rare smile and headed in her direction.

'I've just had a call from Derek Matthews,' he said, putting a hand on her shoulder. 'He's very pleased with your portfolio and is already getting it set up for the next edition. He just has a couple of questions about the captions.' He handed her a piece of paper with a few scribbled notes on it. 'If you check these queries out and get back to him by the end of the day, then we're all systems go. Well done, Kate. I'm really pleased.'

Kate was suddenly aware that she was being watched by the three male colleagues who were preparing to go out on assignment and that their expressions were uniformly hostile. She flashed a beaming smile at them before turning back to Ken.

'Lady photographers aren't such a waste of space as you feared, then?'

'Not in your case, anyway,' her boss said. And she knew she would have to be content with that.

She was soon alone in the office and began to answer the magazine's queries, most of which were easy enough to deal with. But when it came to a request for more details about Terry Jordan's involvement in the regeneration of the city she picked up the phone and called the *Liverpool Echo* in search of some information from her helpful contact there.

Liam Minogue picked up the phone quickly. 'Hello Kate,' he said, sounding slightly surprised, but pleased to hear her voice. 'I was only thinking about you this morning and wondering how your project is going.'

'That's nice,' Kate said. 'Why was that?'

'Well, the city's alive with rumours about Terry Jordan. Apparently he's landed some massive contract in London to build a new town near Runcorn. You remember Billy Jones, our municipal man? I was talking to him this morning and he says Macdonald-Jordan Construction have got a press conference laid on at the end of the week. Jordan will apparently be back by then and will be announcing all the details. At this rate he'll be even more of a local hero than he was during the war. You might want to put something in your captions so they'll be right up to date. It sounds as if the Catholic Church stands to benefit too – more money for Paddy's Wigwam, perhaps. Apparently, they own some land that will be needed.'

So that's why Jordan was travelling with Father Dominic to meetings in Whitehall, Kate thought. If Jordan was already a benefactor, no doubt hoping to bank credit in heaven as well as on Merseyside, she could imagine how interested the Catholic hierarchy would be in his sudden good fortune, which would affect them too.

'Funding for another strut for the crown, maybe?'

'I didn't realize you were that bitter,' Minogue said, sounding shocked.

'You have no idea, Liam,' Kate said quietly, surprised at how deeply she had been affected by the last few days and the memories of Father Jerome that had been stirred up by the small boy in Dolphin Square. But that was not something she intended to share with the *Liverpool Echo,* even if she thought for a moment they would print it. 'Could you give me a call when you know exactly when the press conference is going to be? I'll tell *Topic* magazine what's going on at your end. I'm sure they'll want to include a mention in the captions to bring them up to date. I might even get another trip out of it.'

'As a matter of fact, there is something else that may interest you,' Minogue said. 'There're always lots of rumours floating about, but the latest one Billy Jones whispered in my ear was a bit of a surprise. He told me Terry Jordan was likely to be arrested because someone has dug out proof he's been lining the pockets of planners to get contracts. I'm sure your friend DCI Strachan would love to haul him down the Bridewell to talk about that. I'm not absolutely sure that Billy himself may not have done some of the digging now control of the Corporation has changed. He wouldn't have wanted to embarrass his Tory mates, but he'd be keen to do down both the new lot and Jordan if he could. These things are difficult to prove and the editor won't want a libel writ flying through the door, so the story would have to be cast-iron to get into the paper. In any case, if it's true that Jordan's the flavour of the month with the planners in Whitehall, then perhaps the idea has sunk without trace. Surely Whitehall would know about it if Jordan has a dodgy past! Anyway, Kate, good to hear from you again and I'll let you know if and when the press conference is supposed to be.'

Barnard belted down the stairs and out of the main door of the nick, hands clenched, face pale, and his whole body rigid with anger. He hurried across Regent Street and through the narrower alleys of Soho, with his jacket over his shoulder and sweat staining the back of his shirt, at a pace that alarmed the shoppers and tourists packing the pavements, seeking souvenirs or lunch or just a grandstand view of the alleged dens of vice that were the area's trademark, even though they were mainly locked up and barred at this time of day. When he had dodged his way through the startled crowds and reached the photo agency in Frith Street where Kate worked, he lurched into the dark lobby, took the stairs two at a time, and flung open the main door without ceremony.

'Is Kate O'Donnell in?' he asked loudly, putting his head round the door to the photographers' room, but he could see immediately that her desk was deserted.

'She's gone with Ken to *Topic* magazine,' one of the two men who were at their desks said. 'I think they are having lunch there. She gets all the treats. All we need to know is what she gives in return.' For a moment Barnard was severely tempted to hit the man, but retained enough self-control to realize that would not be a very good idea.

'Damn!' Barnard muttered, knowing he should have phoned first. He took a deep breath and brushed the sweat out of his eyes as he tried to decide where to go next to calm the demons that had flung themselves at him across DCI Jackson's desk ten minutes earlier. The DCI had sent for him halfway through the morning and not asked him to sit down when he came in, which Barnard knew was an ominous sign.

'I've consulted the Yard,' Jackson said, his face impassive. 'They have decided to take over the investigation into the death of the woman in Soho Square. As they rightly say, she was not killed there, Soho was just a convenient place to dump her. So, as the inquiry will be Londonwide, they will appoint a senior officer at the Yard to handle it. They also pointed out in no uncertain terms that your inquiries in Pimlico were outside our jurisdiction and must stop immediately. And don't imagine that you can use your energetic girlfriend as any sort of proxy down there, either. They will hold you responsible for any interference she is involved in, and you will risk being suspended or worse. Is that understood, Sergeant? You – we – are to leave it well alone.'

Barnard's mouth had gone so dry that he was almost unable to respond, but as he fought for breath he managed a strangled sound which could have passed for assent.

'You can pass any evidence you have collected to me and I will pass it on,' Jackson said, avoiding Barnard's eye. 'And give me a full report by lunchtime on every aspect of the case, or cases, that you have in statement form.'

'Sir,' Barnard said, finding his voice at last but unable to hide the outrage he felt. 'Does this mean the victim wasn't who we think she was? Or is someone doing a massive cover-up?'

'I think you should get back to work, Sergeant, before you say something you will really regret.' After looking at his boss for a second for some sign of emotion, and finding none, Barnard turned on his heel and left. He picked up his jacket from the CID room, wanting to talk to Kate urgently, only too able to predict her anger at this unexpected turn of events and wondering how far he would be able to deter her from following her heart rather than her head. If he wanted to keep his job, he had no choice. But Kate was a different matter, and he was not at all sure how she would react.

Still rooted to the spot outside the Fellows agency, he was surprised to see Evie Renton weaving her way down the street towards him, slightly unsteady on her feet. She looked startled when she saw Barnard, and there was no welcome in her smile as she stopped beside him.

'Well, your mates from Pimlico came to see me at crack of dawn,' she said angrily. 'Bloody charming they were. Almost broke the door down when I didn't answer fast enough.'

'I'm sorry, I did try to warn you,' Barnard said. 'What did they ask you?'

'All sorts of stuff about you, about me, whether I paid you to leave me alone. They were digging for dirt. And then, how did I know Alicia? And what did I know about where she used to work? I told them I thought it was Dolphin Square but I wasn't sure. And did I know who the dead woman in Soho Square was? And why did I think she wasn't on the game? They went on and on, Harry, and I had to answer them. They said they'd put me in Holloway for years if I didn't cooperate.'

Barnard put an arm awkwardly around Evie's thin shoulders and could feel her shaking as he turned her back in the direction of her flat.

'Come on, we'll go back to your place,' he said. 'It's all over now. Scotland Yard have taken over the case, no doubt working with the Pimlico detectives, and I'm not on the case anymore. I'm sorry I got you involved.' She led him up the stairs to her room and flung herself into the only comfortable chair, beside the unmade bed. For the first time in all the years he'd known her she allowed herself to cry.

'Did DCI Buxton turn up personally?' he asked. 'That man is a bully and probably bent as a corkscrew, though I've no way of proving it now.'

'Oh yes, it was him and a sergeant, detectives both of them,' she said.

'They've already interviewed me as a suspect because
I talked to Alicia the day she was killed, so I know just what
thugs they are. Can I get you a drink of something? Coffee?
Something stronger?'

'There's a bottle of Scotch under the sink by the bleach,'
Evie said with a half-smile. 'Might cheer us both up.'

'Sounds like an excellent idea,' Barnard said. 'Then I
suppose I'll have to go back to the nick, and hand over all the
evidence to the Yard and toe the line. I don't seem to have
much choice.'

NINETEEN

Kate O'Donnell woke up in pitch darkness with a splitting headache that felt as if it had taken over her whole consciousness. She could hardly think coherently but knew she was not anywhere she recognized: the air felt cold and damp and had a musty smell, like in a long-closed cellar. She lay for what felt like a long time with her eyes shut, then reached out tentative hands to see what she could feel around her. She seemed to be half-covered with a rough and scratchy blanket and to be lying on a hard surface, with a wall to her left and a drop on the other side. She could be on a bed or even a table, but with no indication of how high she was above the floor she didn't dare risk moving far; and when she rolled over slightly the blanket slithered away and, although she reached over the edge as far as she dared, she found no way of retrieving it. She carefully inched into a foetal position and wrapped her arms around herself in a not very effective attempt to keep warm, but soon began to shiver.

After keeping her eyes closed for a while, the headache slowly began to recede and she began to focus on other discomforts. Her mouth was very dry and in a moment of blind panic she wondered if she had been left to die of thirst. She took deep breaths and told herself that she would soon be missed, and Harry Barnard would move mountains to find her. But in the inky darkness she even had trouble persuading herself of that.

She tried to think back to what she could remember before the darkness descended. It had seemed a normal enough day, even a good day. She recalled Ken Fellows taking her to meet the staff at *Topic* magazine, where the work she had done for them was welcomed enthusiastically and she watched the page proofs for the feature being put together. She remembered filling them in on what Liam Minogue had told her about Terry Jordan's latest success in the building trade, and she remembered having lunch with some of the staff in a little Italian restaurant, close to their offices off Kingsway, and the talk turning to the possibility of other commissions in the future. In an expansive mood, Ken had hailed a taxi to take them back to Soho and she remembered following him up the stairs to the office, feeling slightly muzzy after an unaccustomed three glasses of wine over lunch.

But after that her memory was hazy. She would normally have waited for Harry to pick her up around five, but she had no idea whether or not that had happened. Sometime towards the end of the afternoon this blackness had descended, but she had no idea when or how she had come to this place of terrifying cold and silence and pitch dark.

As usual, Barnard drove back to Frith Street at about five thirty and parked half on the pavement opposite the Fellows agency to wait for Kate, leaving just enough space for black cabs to slide through the gap and earning a few curses from their drivers as he sat there smoking patiently.

By about a quarter to six, when Kate had not come flying down the stairs at the end of the day as she usually did, he got impatient and, leaving the car badly parked, made his way for the second time that day up the stairs to her office, where he met Ken Fellows coming out.

'Is Kate still busy?' he asked her boss, not disguising the impatience in his voice.

'Didn't she let you know she was going home?' Fellows said. 'We had a slightly boozy lunch and she didn't look too good, so I told her to get a cab about four o'clock. She was lucky, she picked one up right outside. I happened to be looking out of the window just after she left and actually saw her get into it.'

A worm of anxiety infiltrated Barnard's brain as he turned on his heel with a curt thanks to Fellows and headed down the stairs and into his car. There was no need to worry, he told himself, Kate had felt unwell so it was not really surprising that she hadn't called him. No doubt he would find her in bed at the flat, sleeping off the overindulgent celebration she'd shared with her boss. Or maybe not, he thought as he accelerated into Oxford Street and headed north through the rush-hour traffic, attracting hoots and fist-waving from other drivers as he took chances at every junction and set of lights he came to.

He parked carelessly outside his block of flats and hurried indoors with his anxiety now at fever pitch. As soon as he opened his front door he could tell, from the silence, that the flat was empty. Clinging to the hope that perhaps she had gone back to her own flat in Shepherd's Bush for some reason, he rang that number and the phone was quickly answered by Tess.

'Has Kate come back to your place?' he asked peremptorily.

'No,' she said. 'Were you expecting her to?' He could hear the surprise in Tess's voice and it confirmed his worst fears.

'Not really,' Barnard said, his voice strained. 'I'll track her down. But if she does turn up, ask her to give me a ring, would you?'

'Harry . . .' He heard Tess speak but had hung up too quickly to hear what she had begun to say. He poured himself a generous Scotch, downed it in one, and called the nick to report Kate missing. Panic stricken, he wondered if he would ever see her alive again. And if a hair of her head was hurt, how he would ever forgive himself.

The scalding white light came on without warning, illuminating what turned out to be a windowless room with stone walls and a stone floor, the only furniture the narrow bed on which Kate discovered she had been lying. She turned her head away from the dazzle, which was making her thumping headache worse, and put a hand over her eyes, barely able to see the two men standing over her. When one of them spoke, she instantly recognized the voice of the man in the grey suit who had bullied her into a promise to spy on Harry Barnard, a promise she had not strictly kept.

'You're awake, my dear,' the man said almost solicitously, although she recognized the touch of steel behind the concern. 'I'm sorry we could not issue a more conventional invitation to our chat, but the situation had become urgent. We needed you here quickly and there was not time for any objections on your part.'

'Who are you?' Kate asked angrily, turning away from the wall and putting her feet tentatively on the floor, though lacking the confidence to actually stand yet. The man was still wearing the same crumpled suit and glasses; if she had passed him casually in the street she would barely have noticed him, so insignificant did he appear. His companion looked more threatening: broad-shouldered and long-armed, with a bull-like neck and the same stone-cold eyes. He was obviously his inferior in some way – just muscle, she thought, although why his boss needed it she didn't dare imagine. With her thumping headache and still disoriented senses, she would scarcely have presented a threat to a reasonably healthy five-year-old.

'You don't really need to know our identity,' the man said. 'I told you when we met in London that we faced a potentially embarrassing crisis and needed your help for a short time. You agreed . . .'

'I was blackmailed,' Kate hissed. 'I was put under pressure by DCI Strachan, as I'm sure you know. He threatened my brother.'

'You agreed,' the man continued, as if she had not spoken. 'But you decided not to stick to our agreement and, as I understand it, not only did you not tell me what Barnard was doing, you actually decided to help him on your own account. That was very, very foolish. Why on earth did you decide to interfere? What on earth made you think you could get away with it?'

Kate looked at the two men and felt the fury she had tried to control ever since she and Harry discovered what was going on in the flat in Dolphin Square well up again. Suddenly her brain became quite clear and she could think of no reason why she should curb her feelings.

'Two women are dead,' she said. 'And somewhere in London there is a little boy who has been abused, probably raped. These are crimes, serious, horrible crimes, and they are all connected to that flat in Dolphin Square. Harry Barnard's job is to investigate crime, and he has apparently been hindered at every turn. I don't care how important the men are who were using that flat. If they are murderers, rapists and abusers of children, they should get what's coming to them.'

'Your sentiments do you credit, Miss O'Donnell, but
unfortunately there are other considerations. I think for the
moment we will have to detain you here while we finalize
the situation.'

'You can't do that,' Kate objected. 'You can't go round
London kidnapping people and locking them up. Does Harry
Barnard know where I am? He'll be going frantic.'

'You'll come to no harm, Miss O'Donnell,' the man said.
'Sergeant Barnard will be reassured on that point if we think
it is helpful but your absence will keep him in line, as I'm
sure you will appreciate. We'll go over what you saw, or think
you saw, later but there is one point I'd like cleared up now.
Barnard has told his DCI that you saw three men arriving at
the flat. Did you recognize any of them?'

Kate hesitated for a second and decided that there was not
much point in lying, as Harry had already passed on the
information they'd gathered to DCI Jackson, who would
undoubtedly pass the information on to Scotland Yard and
anyone else they felt needed to know.

'I'd met Father Dominic in Liverpool when I was working
there recently, and I recognized him although he wasn't
wearing his collar. Apparently he's an important fund-raiser
for the new cathedral. And we guessed the smaller man was
Terry Jordan. That's why Harry decided the dead woman in
Soho must be his girlfriend.'

'And you were able to confirm that through photographs?'

'Yes,' Kate said defiantly. 'She didn't deserve what happened
to her, did she? Is she what this is all about? Are you actually
trying to cover up a murder?' The man in grey didn't answer
but simply turned to the other man, who had made no contribution at all to the conversation, and nodded.

'Put her in with her father,' he said. 'I'm sure they'll find
a lot to talk about.' Kate looked at him in astonishment.

'My father?' she said. 'He's here? What's he got to do with
all this?'

'As you've worked out that Terry Jordan is involved in this
affair, you'll know your father has known him for a long time.
He has become a very useful source of information for us, my
dear. You can compare notes, if you like, and try to work out

how to extricate your family from the difficulties your ill-advised crusade has caused it.'

Kate took a sharp breath but decided that it was safer not to respond and let the silent man escort her up the stairs, with a firm grip on her arm, into fading daylight and what appeared to be the ground floor of a modest house. He unlocked a door and, still saying absolutely nothing, pushed her inside and locked the door behind her. The windows of the room were shuttered, so she had no idea how late it was. Her watch, she noticed, had been taken away. The room was dimly lit by a single bulb hanging from the ceiling and at first she could not see anyone else. But eventually she saw her father slumped in an armchair close to the fireplace, his eyes tightly shut, evidently asleep or perhaps drugged, as she guessed she had been. She shook his shoulder and he slowly opened his eyes, which were red-rimmed and rheumy.

'Holy Mother of God!' he croaked. 'How did you get involved in this, Kathleen?'

'I wish I knew exactly what it is I'm involved in, da,' she said. 'All I thought I was doing was helping my boyfriend by taking some pictures, but it's turned out to be a lot more complicated than that.' He sat up in his armchair and began to cough.

'I'm in desperate need of a drink, pet,' he said. Kate glanced around the room and saw a water jug on a table with two glasses. He followed her eyes.

'Something a bit stronger than that,' he said, with a whine in his voice that told her he had been seeking what he craved without success for some time.

'You'll be lucky,' she said, with no sympathy at all. 'I haven't the faintest idea who these people are. Or where I am or why I'm here. Perhaps you can tell me?'

Frank groaned dramatically.

'It all goes back a long way, to the war,' he muttered, not looking her in the eye.

'And to Terry Jordan?' Kate asked sharply.

'To him too, maybe,' he said.

'Come on, da,' Kate said. 'The whole family's involved in this now. Do you want to see Tom in jail for years because

of something that happened years ago which had nothing to
do with him – or, for that matter, with me?'

'Father Reilly says he's in a state of mortal sin,' Frank said.
Kate clenched her fists to stop herself saying something she
knew she would regret.

'And all you could find to do to help was to vanish into
thin air when Tom was arrested,' she said. 'Where the hell did
you run to? And how did you end up here?'

'I went to Dublin,' Frank admitted. 'I stowed away on a
ferry. I know those boats like the back of my hand, don't I?'

'And then you came back?'

'That was a mistake,' he glanced away again, not meeting
her eye, which was a sure sign that he was lying. He shuffled
in his chair for a moment, as if making a desperately difficult
decision, and then sighed.

'All right, all right, I talked to some old friends of Terry's
in Ireland and they said that I'd get him into bother if I didn't
turn up to talk to the bizzies about the accident that happened
last week. They didn't want any more fuss or any inconvenient
questions just now.'

'Because he's been negotiating a big contract in London?
Was that what they were worried about? According to the
Echo, they're supposed to be making an announcement about
it this week. But why would his friends in Dublin be worried
about that?'

'They go back a long way,' Frank whispered.

'How long?' Kate asked, feeling a sudden shiver of
apprehension.

'Before the war, maybe, before you were born,' Frank said.
'There was an IRA bombing campaign before the war . . .'

'What are you telling me, da? Was Terry Jordan involved
in that? Was he an IRA man? I thought he was a big hero
during the war, pulling people out of the bomb sites, risking
his life.'

'He was, he did, I was with him some of the time,' Frank
said quickly. 'All that was real and he built his business on
the strength of it afterwards.'

'But?' Kate said. 'There's obviously a "but"? What else
was he doing?'

'You don't understand what was going on in Ireland back then, when war was declared,' Frank said with a flash of anger. 'I think the Brits hoped Ireland would support them. But De Valera declared a state of emergency so he could stay neutral, and the Irish people were divided. Thousands went off to fight with the British, and some got punished for it when they came back. And there were others who still hated England with a passion and saw the war as a chance to get back at the old enemy. Some thought that if Germany won, there might be a chance of getting a united Ireland at last. Some in the IRA especially. One of the leaders even went off to Berlin to try to get arms, but he died on the way back. And after that, De Valera cracked down and a lot of Republicans were interned and some were hanged for treason.'

'And Terry Jordan was part of all that?'

'On the fringes, at least,' Frank said. 'We were very young, hot-headed. There was a lot of talk in the Catholic docks in Liverpool. But that's all it was for most people, just talk.'

'And you?' Kate asked. 'Was it more than just talk for you, as well as your friend Terry?'

'No, not me,' Frank said. 'You were on the way by then, Kathleen, and me and your mam had other things on our minds. But I knew what was going on.'

'And now?' Kate persisted.

'The IRA's dead now, everyone says so,' Frank said. 'Dead and buried.'

'Is that what they told you in Dublin? You see what I can't get my head round is why we are here. If Terry Jordan killed his girlfriend, why don't they just arrest him and put him on trial? But it can't be as simple as that or they'd have done it by now. They are either covering something else up or trying to find out what else he's been up to. Otherwise you wouldn't have been dragged into this, and nor would Tom and now me. Something more complicated has to be going on.'

'Terry Jordan's always been dodgy,' Frank said. 'He played around with the IRA before the war, and he was up to his eyes in the black market during it. And he built his business by greasing palms wherever he could. So if he's ended up killing his girlfriend I wouldn't be at all surprised. He's got a mad streak. The only thing I don't understand is why you and Tom have been dragged into it.'

'Terry Jordan sounds like a monster,' Kate said, not hiding her bitterness. 'I don't understand why you stuck with him all these years.' Her father shrugged.

'When you crawl about for hours underneath tons of rubble you don't forget the man who helped you get out safely,' Frank said. 'Not once or twice, but over and over again. Terry Jordan was the bravest man I've ever met as well as the most reckless. Maybe the two things go together. And now they want me to help them put him in gaol. Well, I've told them I won't do it. They can put me in gaol before I'll give evidence against him, and they probably will. That's just the way it is, Kathleen. There's no changing it.'

After finding his flat deserted, Harry Barnard had driven back into London at a more sober pace. He knocked on DCI Jackson's door without much expectation that he would still be in his office, but a voice called him in and he found his boss sitting at his desk with a glass of Scotch in his hand – something which, in spite of Jackson's Scottish heritage, Barnard had never seen him do before. He took it as a sign that something exceptionally serious was going on.

'Ah, Sergeant Barnard,' he said. 'I had a feeling you might turn up.'

'Were you told that my girlfriend has gone missing, guv?'

'I was,' Jackson said. 'And I was also told that you should not be concerned for her safety.'

'What?' For a moment Barnard felt the ground was shifting beneath his feet.

'I am not at liberty to tell you any more than that until an important ongoing operation is complete.' Jackson drained his glass and waved an irritated hand in Barnard's direction. 'Sit down, Sergeant, before you fall down. You must have realized that you and Miss O'Donnell had blundered into matters that were no concern of yours – or mine, for that matter. Miss O'Donnell will be returned safely when she has helped some of our more esoteric colleagues with their inquiries.'

'You mean Special Branch?'

'You know I can't confirm that,' Jackson said, refilling his glass. 'And you know as well as I do that the security services come in many shapes and sizes and are pretty much a law unto themselves. Didn't a member of one of the security services recently boast of burgling his way round London?'

'But what's so special? If Jordan killed his girlfriend, which looks highly probable, why aren't we charging him and sending him down?'

'There seem to be reasons for that, though I can't guess what they are. My task, it seems, is to tell you that as far as we are concerned the case is closed and you are to go home and stay there until further notice. Miss O'Donnell will return when the case is concluded. She is, I suppose, a hostage for your good behaviour. But make no mistake, Sergeant, if you were foolish enough to intervene again they will throw the book at you. Do you understand?'

'Sir,' Barnard said bitterly, and turned towards the door, knowing when he was beaten.

It was, Harry Barnard thought as he watched the grey light of an early midsummer dawn creep through the curtains, the worst night of his life. He had neither undressed nor found any way of sleeping, though after an initial glass of whisky he had put the bottle firmly back into his cocktail cabinet and found sufficient self-control to leave it there. As a result when, just before five, a powerful car with darkened windows pulled into one of the parking spaces beneath his window he was stone-cold sober and clear-headed enough to get to his front door and open it before the occupants of the car made it through the main door of the block. He saw Kate immediately, and immediately took on board how pale and tired she looked and how the taller of the two men with her seemed to be propping her up.

'What the hell happened?' he asked, his own voice sounding as if it was coming from the bottom of a deep well. Kate looked at him briefly, but her eyes were blank and her expression impassive.

'Please go inside, Sergeant Barnard,' the shorter of the two men instructed, more sharply than Barnard expected. Balding and unimpressive, in a crumpled grey suit, it was obvious he was in charge. 'Miss O'Donnell is fine, but we need to talk before we can leave her with you. And there are some papers that you need to sign.' Trying to conceal his fury, Barnard took Kate's arm and steered her towards the sofa, where she sank down against the cushions and gave him a wan smile.

'Sorry,' she whispered. 'It all went a bit pear-shaped, la.'

'So are you going to tell me what the hell is going on?' he asked the man who had taken control of the situation.

'Sit down, Sergeant,' the man responded icily. 'My name is Marchmain and I work for the government. That is all you need to know about me. What seems to have happened, although we did our best to avoid it, is that you and Miss O'Donnell have ventured into a situation which you were clearly and repeatedly warned to avoid.'

'I was under the impression that I was just doing my job,' Barnard said.

'And I am now doing mine,' Marchmain said. 'And that takes precedence. Before we go any further, I have to ask you both to sign the Official Secrets Act. What you and Miss O'Donnell have stumbled into – although I am sure it was much more deliberate on your part, Barnard, than stumbling implies – concerns the security of this country and you are required not to discuss it with anyone on pain of prosecution and probable imprisonment. Do you both understand what I am saying?' Kate looked aghast and although Barnard's mind was full of questions he simply nodded, feeling almost as stunned as he had been by DCI Strachan's physical assault in Liverpool. He glanced at Kate briefly and could see that she was as aware as he was that Marchmain was allowing them no space for argument. He opened the briefcase that he was carrying and placed papers on the table, then unscrewed a fountain pen.

'You first, Sergeant,' he said and Barnard took the pen, read quickly through the legalese and signed his name. He helped Kate to her feet and she did the same. When they had finished they both sat down again, watching in disbelief as Marchmain picked up his documents and shuffled them back into order.

'Thank you,' Marchmain said. 'And make no mistake that

we will hold you to the letter of the law. There may possibly be developments you learn about which you may think are concerned with the cases you have been aware of, or should I say interfered with, recently. Such events will also be covered by this ban. It is as if the events of the last week or so never happened. Do you fully understand?'

'I think we understand perfectly,' Barnard said, his voice little more than a whisper.

'Miss O'Donnell?'

'Yes,' Kate said, her voice dull with fatigue and shock, although there was still a touch of anger there too. Marchmain put the signed papers away in his briefcase and nodded to his silent companion, who moved towards the front door.

'We will leave you then,' he said. 'And thank you for your earlier cooperation, Miss O'Donnell, although it wasn't as whole-hearted as I might have wished or you promised. Good day.' They heard the main door shut sharply, and Barnard brushed Kate's cheek with a kiss and got to his feet.

'I'll make some coffee,' he said. 'And something to eat?' Kate shook her head.

'Just coffee,' she said. 'Then a shower and I'll try to tell you all about it.'

Barnard listened in silence when Kate eventually curled into a corner of the sofa, her hair wet and her eyes full of pain, and described what had happened to her the previous evening and overnight when she had found herself so unexpectedly closeted with her father. When she had finished, he kissed her again.

'So what happens to your father now?' he asked.

'I don't know,' Kate said. 'He was still there when they brought me away. But he was determined not to give evidence against Terry Jordan. Can they force him?'

'They can try,' Barnard said. 'And if he refuses, they can lock him up for contempt of court. But it sounds to me as if they could charge Jordan with any number of things corruption, involvement in the IRA, and the murder of Doreen Darcy. That must be the easiest to prove, so I don't understand why they're not going for it. They could do that without evidence from your father.

Kate shrugged.

'Maybe Jordan didn't do it,' she suggested. 'Maybe it was one of the other men who were at the flat.'

'A minister maybe? At least he must have been a witness.' Barnard said. 'A minister they've been asked to protect from another sex scandal before we get to another general election? The government must be terrified of another scandal erupting. That could be why the security services are involved. From what I hear, they specialize in covering things up.

'Including the abuse of children?' Kate said bitterly. 'Nothing's changed, then, since Father Jerome was conveniently spirited away when Tom and me were kids.'

'I'm sorry,' Barnard said. Kate sat silently for a moment, running through everything they had uncovered which would now be buried again.

'If Jordan was working for the IRA before the war that could explain why DCI Strachan was so incensed,' she said. 'He would have hated to think he might get away with what he did. And according to my friend at the *Echo*, the paper had been digging up evidence of his dodgy business practices. One way or another, Terry Jordan was in deep trouble. But these people seem to be prepared to let him get away with it all.'

Barnard drained his coffee cup and looked at Kate speculatively.

'Why did your man thank you for your cooperation?' he asked quietly. 'Was he joking?' Kate looked away from the inevitable question she had been dreading, knowing that the poison had been deliberately planted and no less deliberately used against her by a man whose prejudices were icy cold and very deliberate.

'He locked me up with my da for a while, and he explained a lot of the background to what has been going on. But what they told the two of us afterwards was that they had recorded everything we said. I suppose they might count that as cooperation. It never entered my head that they would have a microphone somewhere in the room, and it wouldn't have crossed my father's mind either.' She pushed her damp hair out of her eyes, knowing that if she and Barnard were to have any sort of a future together she had to tell him everything.

'But that wasn't the whole of it,' she whispered. 'First of all they contacted me at work and tried to make me tell them what you were investigating at Dolphin Square. They threatened to make sure Tom got a long sentence if I didn't help them keep tabs on you. I'm sorry, Harry. I didn't have any choice.' Tears streamed down Kate's face as Barnard took a deep breath.

'I'm sorry too,' he said and took her in his arms. 'They used you, blackmailed you, and now they've very effectively shut us both down. We'll have to live with that.'

He cooked them both breakfast and after they had eaten he turned on the radio for the early news. A short item towards the end warned of traffic disruption on the M1 motorway out of London following a fatal overnight accident on the northbound carriageway involving a Jaguar. One of the two casualties was believed to be a senior cleric from Liverpool's Roman Catholic Cathedral, the other a businessman who had been in London discussing the building of a new town in the north-west of England with government ministers. Both men in the car had died instantly. Police and fire officers were investigating the cause of the incident, in which no other vehicles were involved. The church authorities in Liverpool regretted the untimely loss of a valued colleague. There was no mention of who might be grieving for Terry Jordan.

'How very convenient,' Barnard said quietly.

'You think it wasn't an accident?' Kate asked.

'I think it was a problem solved,' he said. 'The bastards!'